TERROR AUSTRALIS

The Western Front

by

Nathan Seidel

DEDICATION

To my incredible wife, Karly – your love, support, and unwavering belief in me made this journey possible.
Also, to my parents for their valuable input and to my close friends, whose inspiration and encouragement have fueled my creativity—thank you for always being there.

"To the brave souls who venture into the unknown, facing their fears and overcoming the darkness within. Your courage and resilience inspire us all. This book is for you, the true heroes of our time."

CONTENTS

EXPOSITION

Chapter 1 — The Infection Spreads Like Wildfire

Chapter 2 — Ribbons of War

Chapter 3 — Leap of Faith

Chapter 4 — Summertime Shenanigans

Chapter 5 — It Can't See Us

Chapter 6 — Home Away from Home

Chapter 7 — Old Friend

Chapter 8 — Medication Mission

Chapter 9 — High Above the Horde

Chapter 10 — Hook, Line and Sinker

Chapter 11 — What Lurks in the Shadows

Chapter 12 — A Home Among the Gumtrees

Chapter 13 — Star Struck

Chapter 14 — Run Baby, Run

Chapter 15 — Chalet 153

Chapter 16 — Our Island Safe Haven

Chapter 17 — Smoke and Mirrors

Chapter 18 — Let Darkness Come

Chapter 19 — Hope

FOREWORD

Welcome to "Terror Australis," where the wild beauty and unforgiving landscape of Australia serve as the perfect setting for a tale of suspense and survival. This book will take you on an unforgettable journey into the heart of darkness, where the only certainty is the unexpected.

In "Terror Australis," Nathan Seidel invites you to explore a world where the lines between myth and reality blur, and the human spirit is tested against nature's most formidable challenges. The Australian wilderness, with its vast deserts, dense forests, and treacherous coasts, is more than just a backdrop – it is a living, breathing character in this gripping narrative loaded with zombies.

As you delve into this story, you'll meet characters who embody resilience, courage, and the relentless will to survive. Each page will pull you deeper into their struggles, fears, and triumphs, making you feel every heartbeat, every breath, and every moment of tension. Prepare yourself for a rollercoaster ride of emotions as you navigate the twists and turns of this thrilling adventure. Nathan Seidel's storytelling will keep you on the edge of your seat, with every chapter leaving you hungry for more.

So, brace yourself, turn the page, and step into the world of "Terror Australis." The adventure awaits, and it promises to be a journey you'll never forget. Can Nathan and his friends survive the apocalypse?

If you enjoy Terror Australis, I'd love to hear your thoughts! Your ratings and reviews not only support my work but also help other readers discover this thrilling journey into the heart of horror. Thank you for being part of this Australian adventure!

EXPOSITION

In 2024, a deadly virus swept through the world, leaving billions of casualties in its wake. The virus was highly contagious and aggressive, causing chaos and destruction in nearly every corner of the earth. Infection was spread through a bite, fluid and particle transmission. Once a person was infected, the virus rapidly attacked the central nervous system, leading to severe neurological damage. The initial symptoms included high fever, chills, severe headaches, and muscle pain. Within hours, the infected individual would experience uncontrollable aggression and a compulsion to bite others, spreading the virus further.

As the virus progressed, it caused the body to enter a state of necrosis while keeping the brain partially active. This led to a grotesque transformation: the skin would become discoloured and decayed, muscles and tissues would deteriorate, and bodily functions would cease. Despite the extensive physical damage, the virus managed to keep the host mobile and capable of basic motor functions, driven by an insatiable hunger for human flesh. World governments mentioned a few of the types of zombies, apart from the slow ones –

Glazzer: Normal zombie, slow, majority of zombies are these

Shreiker: Zombies with a high-pitched, ear-piercing scream that drew other zombies in and very fast.

Zoggo: Man's best friend, zombie style.

Absorber: Equipped with whip-like appendages ending in arrowheads, they can heal themselves by absorbing the life force from other zombies.

Crawler: Resembling large cockroaches, their bite causes rapid, irreversible infection leading to cardiac arrest and reanimation.

Oozer: Slow-moving and highly infectious, they release spores into the air, spreading the infection through particle transmission.

The scientific community worked tirelessly to find a cure, but their efforts were initially in vain as the virus mutated and evolved, making it even more deadly. As the death toll continued to rise, a small team of researchers discovered that the spread of the virus slowed in hot, dry conditions which made the Australian outback seem like a perfect choice.

The Australian government made a controversial decision to build a facility, named the Infected Persons Research Centre (IPRC) to house the infected and study the virus in hopes to find a permanent cure. IPRC was a huge military complex with medical centres, living quarters, and everything necessary to keep the infected contained and monitored. Its perimeter was said to be as vast as Alice Springs to the east, the Nullarbor Desert and Little Sandy Desert to the west. The infected were free to roam within its walls when not being studied. The government believed they would eventually find a cure and end the global pandemic. The Hostile Organism and Pathogen Eradication Unit (HOPE) was formed with experts from around the globe, military special operatives, and numerous other support departments.

The Australian community was outraged by this decision. Many believed that it was wrong to bring the infected into our country and that the government was putting our citizens at risk. Despite large and fierce protests and petitions, the government pressed ahead. Soon, IPRC was filled with the infected from all over the world. As time passed, the infected in the IPRC were studied, and progress was made in understanding the virus.

Most Australians left the country to live in the United Kingdom, which had initiated border control to prevent infection almost immediately after the virus broke out. The choice was simple: stay and go about daily life in Australia or leave for the UK. Essential workers were paid well to remain in Australia and maintain essential infrastructure. Stores and businesses were left abandoned.

This story follows the journey of a group of young Australians fighting to survive the apocalypse.

THE INFECTION SPREADS LIKE WILDFIRE

It was a typical day, as typical as it could be post-evacuation. I sat up in bed and glanced at Karly beside me. She was stunning with her wavy, shoulder-length brown hair, dreamy green eyes, and infectious laugh. She had a great body, too.

I looked at myself in the full-length mirror, noticing the beginnings of a beer belly. Maybe it was my slowing metabolism or lack of exercise, I thought. I had short brown hair and blue eyes. Karly thought I was cute, so I took that as a win. Yawning, I inadvertently woke Karly. 'Urghhhh, what time is it?' she moaned, rolling towards me.

'It's just after seven. What time do you have to be at work?' I replied. 'I have to get up and go to Osborne Park for an investigation, probably around 8:30 a.m.,' she said, her tired eyes looking up at me as she placed her head on my chest. She enjoyed her job as an Occupational Health and Safety Advisor, but it was exhausting. 'Can I just tell them to piss off and quit?' she asked. 'Yes, you can, but I'm pretty sure you would miss the pay,' I said. 'Mmmm, yeah... I suppose. I'll text them,' she replied.

I chuckled at the comment as I picked up my phone. The usual international news is that there are more zombie outbreaks in Europe. Civil war in Zimbabwe. 'Anything interesting this morning, Nath?' Karly asked. Just as I was about to say no, something caught my eye and Channel 9's Facebook page. The headline read Truck Rollover - Three Dead. 'Holy shit, babe, have a listen to this incident out east this morning,' I said. The article read, "A road train was involved in a significant accident early this morning.

This morning, an unmarked truck rolled over on the Great Eastern Highway near Darlington around 01:38 a.m. Initial reports from WA Police state that three persons were fatally injured and that the road will remain closed indefinitely while investigations are conducted. Early reports suggest an unconfirmed witness who pulled over to assist saw a small group of zombies jumping from the back of the truck. Western Australia Police are searching the immediate area. There has been no comment from military sources as yet. Additional details will follow as this incident progresses. HOPE or the IPRC has released no information."

The news noticeably shook Karly. Fear in her eyes as she looked up at me, 'I'm taking a day off, Nath. I can't go in; the thought of something like that happening around Osborne Park scares me,' she said. 'Where's Darlington, babe?' Karly asked, now sitting upright, looking at me intently. 'It's about thirty minutes' drive east of here, a bit close to home if it is zombies.' 'I doubt it's zombies; there's no way they'd make it all the way here. Plus, surely there would be communication about an outbreak,' I mumbled as I looked up the WA Police website and saw no mention of it there at all.

Similarly, as expected, there was also no information from military sources. 'IPRC is a fortress with huge walls. There's no way they could have gotten out,' I said sharply. 'This would be a bloody killer excuse not to go to work, ha-ha, get it! Did you see what I did there? Maybe it's started,' Karly laughed, obviously impressed at her dad joke. We always thought there could be an outbreak, but surely not so soon.

I rolled over and looked through the blinds; it was a rainy day today. Black clouds gathered as far as I could see beyond the neighbour's red tile roof across the street. The palm trees rocked back and forth while deep, rumbling thunder reverberated in the distance. Raindrops began to hit hard against the windowpane, creating a rhythmic sound that mirrored my racing thoughts. Karly was watching me for signs of worry.

She turned her back to me and ran her hands through her hair.

I continued staring out the window as the rain fell heavily from the skies, lost in my thoughts. This wouldn't happen. That place is a fortress. Then I wondered… what would it be like to survive an outbreak? The uncertainty gnawed at me, a mix of fear and curiosity about the unknown future. I snapped out of my head, 'You want a coffee?' I asked. Karly grinned, 'Yes, please! You know me too well; now that I'm not going to work, I can stay in bed for longer,' Karly said as she snuggled back down under the doona.

I swung out of bed and felt the cold floorboards creak under my feet as I got up. The house was an old-fashioned two-bedroom and one-bathroom 1930s model in Rivervale, with high ceilings, white walls, and brown wooden floorboards. The house's charm always made it feel like home despite its age. The house was excellent for what we needed as a couple but was damn cold in the mornings, especially during winter. The bin had a fly hanging around it in the kitchen, so I took it out, waiting for the kettle to boil.

The door creaked as it opened to the fresh and wet morning. The chill in the air was biting, and the overcast sky didn't help my mood. What a shit day, I thought to myself as I pondered the thought of the earlier news article. Could it be possible that an outbreak had occurred? Of course, it would happen during winter without the heat to slow them down, and it's typical of the government to try and cover it up if it was the truth, I thought. I sighed and headed to the living room to draw the curtain. The sound of rain against the windowpane only added to my unease as I realized that we might need to brace ourselves for whatever was to come.

Our strategy for an outbreak had been decided between us and a small group of friends who had chosen to stay. We would wait for our mate Dan at our place here in Rivervale, then make our way to Sophie's apartment complex near the Swan River. From there, we drove south to Donnybrook, where Karly's mum lived. The plan was simple but required precise execution to avoid being unprepared.

Dan was thirty-two, tall and lanky, with short brown hair. I've been friends with him for about thirteen years, and his knowledge and preparedness made us confident that he would have good plans to survive with us for as long as possible. Sophie was short, athletic, and soft-spoken, with curly black hair and dark skin. Despite their different backgrounds and personalities, Dan and Sophie had an undeniable chemistry that made them an ideal match. They had only been dating for a few months, but it already felt like they had known each other for years, and Sophie was a welcome new member to our group of friends.

My phone rang as I walked back inside and began pouring the coffee. It was Dan. I answered quickly. 'Hey man, things are going a bit crazy up here. Did you hear about that truck accident this morning? Well, all I've heard this morning is constant sirens, and people are starting to panic,' he responded. As he said this, Karly came out, looking like she'd seen a ghost. I lowered the phone against my face, gesturing a 'what' look at her. 'Nathan, there's been an explosion in Perth, and there are videos of zombies running rampant,' Karly said.

I quickly raised the phone and said, 'Dan, I think there has been an outbreak in Perth. Do you want to grab your stuff and head down here so we can get to Sophie's?' I replied. 'Karly, are you sure!' I almost yelled, starting to panic. 'Yes! Why would I joke about that!' she yelled back from the room. Dan laughed 'Man, the amount we used to joke around about zombies, anyways, I'll be there within the hour. Peace, love, and zombie attacks,' he said. 'Man, do you need me to whip up and give you a hand getting back?' I asked Dan. 'Nah, I'll be right. If what Karly has seen is happening now, staying off the streets is better. 'Ok, drive safe and hurry up,' I replied, hanging up the phone.

Of all the joking around we did as teenagers, we never considered it would be our reality. A sense of fear washed over me. Maybe we would have to face the harsh world of the undead. I had heard stories about the zombies, but I never thought they would get here to Perth after Australia had survived for so long.

'Karly, I think we should start securing the house. I'm going to go and load supplies into the back of the Ute,' I said as I walked out the back door. We'd already put extra deadbolts on the doors and installed steel blinds that pulled across the large windows a few months prior, just in case. Dan and I both had 4WDs with plenty of room for supplies. I had a Holden Colorado Z71, and he had a Ford Ranger. The vehicles were kitted out with plenty of luggage, equipment, food space, and custom-fitted scene lights on the roof racks.

I lowered the tailgate and quickly went to the back of the shed to collect all our stuff. I grabbed my Paramedic kit, hammer, crowbar, collapsible water jerrycan, solar panels, and USB battery pack and returned to the Ute. The benefits of being a Paramedic include lots of medical equipment that I hopefully won't have to use anytime soon. Most of the equipment was ready to go and stored at specific locations down south, both at Karly's mum Sharon's house and at a campsite prepared months earlier. Our contingency plans gave us a vital sense of security.

Karly appeared at the back door, 'Nath, I've messaged Sophie to tell her we're coming soon and to get ready. She said that she could see the carnage from her balcony.' No shit, I thought, this is it. Dan and I always talked of living in a zombie world, but now I was starting to feel scared. 'Karly, can you go turn the TV on and see if there are any updates? Information is key right now,' I called as she vanished back inside. I let out a chuckle. I sounded like a fool saying it, but it was true. Helicopter blades whirred in the distance. I was drawn to its noise, so I poked my head around the side of the shed.

A strong voice boomed over the loudspeaker from the black helicopter: 'All residents. Remain in your homes and secure your property. This is a lawful directive.' I slammed the tailgate shut and locked the Ute as I walked back inside, closing the house door and locking it behind me. 'There's an emergency tone on the TV on every channel,' Karly said. 'Okay, well, let's close up those last few windows, but leave the back door unlocked for Dan. He'll be here soon. I hope,' I said.

We were ready to leave once Dan arrived. One rule we always

followed was to never leave friends behind. The city was going to be a dangerous place, and it was becoming clear that time was a key consideration. Police sirens wailed in the distance, and the increasing number of sirens began to cause further dread in my mind. I went into the office and turned the computer on.

I called to Karly, 'How long do you think the power will last?' 'Your guess is as good as mine,' she yelled back. I pulled up the house's security camera system on the computer so we could see what was happening outside. The footage flicked to life, showing empty streets that felt eerily calm. I knew the cameras wouldn't guarantee our safety, especially in the face of a zombie outbreak. But they would at least give us some peace of mind and a fighting chance.

Before drawing the steel plate across, I walked into our bedroom, checking that the window latches were secure. I checked the front door deadbolts and went through my mental checklist. Each lock clicked into place with a solid, comforting thunk sound. The front bedroom window is secured, the bathroom window is locked, the bedroom window is locked, and all the internal doors are locked. The inside kitchen door closed, the outside door closed, and all the blinds were pulled closed. Our house was secure. All we needed now was for Dan to arrive, but he knew the drill and had done it with us before. I'm not sure if it was for fun practising it, but I'm happy we did.

'Have you packed our toothbrushes, Nath?' Karly yelled from the lounge room. 'Yes,' I said back. Karly was prepared for all angles, including dental hygiene, which many people would easily overlook. Without a dentist or doctor, even that had the potential to kill us. In a world where infection is constantly threatened, even minor details matter.

The rain had temporarily eased as new, dark clouds slowly rolled in. Karly's phone rang. It was Sophie again. 'I'm not sure what's happened, but dead people are walking around!' Sophie said, crying. 'How has it spread so fast?!' I could hear the panic in her voice from the phone ten meters away. 'Just lock the door, and we will get to you soon. Don't worry; even when the phones switch off, we will be there; breath, and Sophie, I don't care what you hear; don't open the door to anyone but us,' Karly said.

I messaged Dan, 'Where are you!?'. 'Karly, can you ring your mum and let her know it's kicking off and to remember the plan, secure her house, and don't answer the door to anyone she doesn't know,' I said as I walked into the dining room. Karly spoke briefly to Sharon on the phone. 'It's ok. Just follow the plan we discussed, and you'll be fine,' Karly said. 'We'll see you in a day or two; don't stress; I love you,' Karly said as she hung up the phone.

'She's terrified and told us to be safe and that she loves us and will see us soon.' I paused for a second and watched Karly take a deep breath, stand taller, and give an almost imperceptible nod. I took a deep breath, knowing what this was—not fear or panic, but determination.

For twenty minutes, sirens, distant screams, wailing, and the odd gunshot filled the air. It was terrible and nearly impossible to control the rising panic. A car alarm sounded, maybe three streets away. The increasing anxiety and not fully knowing what was happening were killing me. Where was Dan? My head was spinning, and thoughts about what was going on out there ran over and over in my head. Has Dan been caught up in it? An explosion sounded somewhere in the distance, and I jumped. Were we safe here? Where was it safe, though? I asked myself. 'Wonder what that was!' Karly yelled from the toilet.

I went back to the security camera vision on the computer. We didn't have many neighbours left on our street; most left when they got the chance. I could now see people running frantically in the streets towards the intersection, some carrying bags and backpacks, others dragging children behind them. It was clear they were trying to escape the chaos unfolding around us. Some had weapons, a sign that they would defend themselves against whatever threat.

I heard a brief screeching of tyres as a Ford Ranger swung into our driveway. 'Here we go!' I said loudly. I ran to the back door as Dan frantically ran from the driver's seat, slamming the car door shut. His face was pale, and his eyes were wide with fear. 'Get inside the house,' he yelled, rushing around the back of his car. 'Jesus, man, calm down, get in,' I said, holding the door for him.

Dan was anxious as he shoved past me. 'Holy shit! It's crazy out there. I'm pretty sure I hit a zombie on the way here. There's chaos on the freeways. I tried taking backstreets, but they were hardly any better, although in some suburbs, you wouldn't even know anything out of the ordinary was happening,' he said. You could see the adrenaline coursing through his body, as seen by how visibly he composed himself and his breathlessness. 'Can confirm that zombies have made it here!' Dan said.

Karly was still in the toilet. 'Hey Dan!' she yelled through the door. I followed him into our bedroom, and we double rechecked everything, not only for Dan's peace of mind but also because, as a Paramedic I know the effects of adrenaline and how easy it is to miss things. I rechecked the security cameras, making sure that there were no signs of movement or activity. 'Looks clear,' I said, relieved that we were still safe for the time being. For now, at least, we had a moment to breathe.

'Well, you're here now. Let's wait until it sounds like it's calmed down outside and then make our way to Sophie's,' I said. Dan shoved his hands in his pockets. 'Unbelievable. I can't believe it's happening; we don't want zombies,' he said. 'Neither man. Have either of you messaged Sophie? Let her know we'll wait for it to calm a bit?' I said. Dan pulled his phone out and began tapping the screen, 'Yeah, I forgot. I was a bit distracted from the drive here,' he said.

A shiny knife hung from his belt. We all had belt knives. It was another rule from day one that if anything were to unfold, minimum protection must be a knife on us at all times, no exceptions, even beside you whilst sleeping. The house creaked as rain began to fall heavily again, muffling the sounds of the commotion in our local neighbourhood. The rain provided a welcome and somewhat calming sound. Dan picked his backpack up off the floor and began riffling through it, mumbling as he went. 'As soon as my head can calm down, we will get to Sophie's. She's terrified,' Dan said, glancing at me.

The thumping rain outside became louder and heavier over the next few hours. As welcome as this was, it created a problem for us: not being able to hear any unwanted guests. The downpour relentlessly hammered against the roof, a constant drumming that drowned out all other sounds. The gutters and downpipes struggled to keep up with the torrential flow. I was becoming hyper-aware of my surroundings. I flinched as I heard the squeak of the clothesline in the backyard, snapping me back to reality. The three of us huddled around a small table in the dining room, straining to hear any sign of danger. The dim light of a single lamp cast long shadows, making the room feel smaller and more confined. We took turns scanning the streets outside, wary of any movement or disturbance that could threaten our safety.

'Who wants a coffee?' Karly said. 'Yeah, that's a great idea, thanks' Dan said. Dan appeared to be in another world, wide-eyed and pale, fixated on what was happening outside. He was right to be. 'It's still storming; we can't go yet, maybe give it another ten?' Dan said. 'I suppose so. Let's finish our coffees and have a quick smoke, and then we can hit the road,' I said. 'Guess I will have one too,' Karly said. We sat in silence for a little longer. After what felt like forever, the rain finally began to ease—the day had turned to evening. 'I think we make a move soon and use the cover of the darkness to get around,' I said. They both agreed.

Dan's phone vibrated a few minutes later, breaking the silence. 'Sophie, hey, how are you holding up?' Dan spoke into the phone, his voice carrying a mixture of concern and relief. I couldn't hear the rest of the conversation, so I wandered into the master bedroom and peered through the tiny steel crack past the curtains. The few streetlights outside eventually flickered out, and the area became dark. An eerie mood settled. All three of us were finally waiting for the power to go out, but none of us wanted to mention it.

In preparation, we had all charged every piece of equipment we thought might be handy, including phones and charging docks. It was a gloomy thought, cast into darkness each night with no reliable light source besides camping equipment. Karly entered the room silently, on her tiptoes. 'How long until you want to leave, do you think?' she asked. I shrugged, 'Give it another twenty to thirty minutes, and we can go. Let things possibly calm down a bit outside, hey? Want to ask Dan what he thinks? I'm not sure if we should go now or wait!' I walked back into the dining room with Karly.

Dan looked stressed, still from the faint glimmer of light illuminating his face from his phone. The tension was etched into his features, making him look older and more worn. 'Dan, let's go soon, hey?' Karly whispered to him. 'Yes, hell yes! No offence, but I'm sick of this place. It's eerie here, and the thought of Sophie being alone,' he replied. Karly and I looked at each other as I walked around and put my hand on Dan's shoulder. The world suddenly no longer seemed as friendly. I sighed. 'Yeah, let's go.'

Dan grabbed his backpack as we crept through the house to the back door, removing the reinforcements against the door and flinching at every sound. Each creak and groan of the door seemed unnaturally loud in the quiet stillness. I slowly opened it and paused, surveying the outside conditions, blinking as my eyes adjusted to a dark city. Since the streetlights had long gone out, everything was plunged into an unsettling darkness. We stepped out into the cool night. Dan walked out and closed the door behind Karly.

Dan opened his car door and jumped in as we crept past him to my Colorado. 'Shit, the handgun is in the ute tray, Karly. I need to grab it,' I whispered as I opened the tailgate as quietly as possible. Karly had grown up on outback farms, so she could probably shoot better than any one of us. I pulled the 9mm Beretta out of the black case.

Safety first, I know. I walked to the passenger door and opened it, passing her the firearm. I walked back to the tray and closed the gun case, pausing to grab my small medicine bag filled with essentials, prepared for what was to come, and gently closed the tray behind me. The night was silent except for the faint rustle of leaves and our cautious movements.

As I turned, I heard soft, rapid footsteps approach. My heart skipped a beat as I felt a chill run down my spine. The creature slammed into me with such force that I was winded. I felt like I had been hit by a truck. The impact forced me into the closed tray at the back of the ute, medicine flying everywhere, leaving me breathless and in pain. The creature's forearms had torn strands of flesh hanging from them, making a sickening, squelching noise with each movement. The flesh looked ragged and decomposed, with maggots writhing within the open wounds.

The stench of rotting flesh and decay was overwhelming, causing me to gag and struggle to catch my breath. Its tongue was hanging out of its mouth slightly. Even in the dark, it was clear that its teeth were blood-stained. The broken teeth were jagged and chipped, with remnants of flesh clinging to them. The grotesque sight made my stomach churn. Its eyes were like pools of darkness, cold and empty, yet full of malice. As it gasped and continued to claw at my clothes, I felt a sense of dread wash over me, overwhelmed and trapped. I knew that I was in serious trouble.

Two loud rounds were discharged from behind me in the direction of the shed as bullets flew from the Berretta. The sharp crack of gunfire shattered the eerie silence. Karly heard the commotion and ran around the side of the car. She emerged from the shadows, her face pale and sweat-drenched. The zombie hit the ground with a sickening thud, its limp body rolling over with a slight thwacking sound.

The smell of gunpowder and the stench of decay created a nauseating blend. 'You, okay?' she gasped, her voice trembling with fear. 'Yeah, I'll live; damn, that was close,' I replied, my heart still racing. 'Now get in before more come,' she said urgently, grasping my arm and pulling me towards the car. Karly grabbed the medicine bag as I scrambled inside the vehicle. I couldn't help but wonder what other horrors awaited us in the darkness. Thank God I gave her the gun; she was a great shot.

Dan reversed down the driveway, straight over the zombie's limp, dead body. Crack and splat sounds were heard beneath his tyres. It was sickening. We only had a short distance to travel to Sophie's. Dan led the way, with us following closely behind. 'Are you sure you're ok, babe?' Karly asked with an unsteady voice. 'Yes, thank you so much for just saving my ass back there,' I replied, but before I could go on, Karly yelled,

'Oh shit! It's a police car, and, oh my god, look at the street!'.

Actual carnage lay before us: abandoned vehicles, burning cars, and, worst of all, bodies strewn around on the cold, wet road. This road was once a busy thoroughfare but is now a scene from a horror movie. The acrid smell of smoke and gasoline filled the air, making my eyes water and my throat burn. 'Stop!' Karly yelled. 'I need to look quickly in that police car; there might be weapons, babe!'. I flashed the headlights, and Dan's car stopped and began to reverse backwards. She jumped out and made her way to the driver's side door, gun drawn ready. Blood could be seen on the top and outside of the door. I'd hate to think about what happened to those officers.

Dan's car pulled up beside mine. 'What's she doing, and are you okay, man?' he asked. 'Looking for weapons. It might be the only police cruiser we come across for a while, so let's just watch her back, and yeah, I'm ok!'. Karly came back to the passenger door two minutes later with an assault rifle, including a 9mm Glock Handgun and a map. 'Look at this! What a jackpot! Zombie idiots won't know what hit them!' she said joyfully.

She walked over to Dan's car, holding out the Glock. 'Dan, this one's for you; it's a 9mm Glock, so this is a pretty sweet weapon, but inaccurate sometimes,' she said. 'Awesome, let's get out of here. I have a bad feeling being out in the open, so show me how this works later,' Dan said, putting the weapon in the side of the door. His hands were shaking slightly as he secured the gun. Karly jogged back to my car and got in.

We left the scene and continued along the Great Eastern Highway. It was a tragic scene, with bodies strewn everywhere, illuminated by the burning cars that were casting long shadows over the streets. There is not a living soul to be seen. The smell of burning rubber and flesh lingered in the air, making breathing hard. I wondered where all the zombies had gone.

RIBBONS OF WAR

We pulled off the Great Eastern Highway onto Brighton Road and stopped against the large black security gate. The gate was stuck shut. Of course, no power. I hadn't thought of that; I was shaking my head. We left the vehicles outside on the street. It wasn't ideal, but we had no choice. We took our weapons and a backpack containing essentials with us. 'Got to take the stairs; power's out,' Dan said.

The thought of navigating in complete darkness made me uneasy. Stairs, dammit, my arch nemesis. I wasn't the fittest, but I didn't mind a workout here and there. 'I call shotgun on leading!' Karly whispered insistently, holding the rifle closely—eight flights of stairs. We took our time as it was unknown territory—slow and steady. We didn't see any signs of life the whole way up. It was spookily quiet, I thought, and I could feel goosebumps rising on my arms.

Sweat trickled down my back in the cool air, combining physical exertion and anxiety. We got to the 8th floor, pausing to look around as we opened the door, letting the torch guide our way as we tiptoed to room 82, which was right next to the fire escape. Dan knocked on the door, saying, 'It's me,' and it slowly opened, a slit revealing one of Sophie's eyes. She was so happy we had made it as I watched her breathe out as if she had been holding her breath for hours. She was pleased to see Karly hugging her as if she were scared to let go. At least we would all be together for the night to decide the best time to leave tomorrow.

A few small burning candles slightly illuminated the apartment. The walls were dark cream with modern downlights and flooring, well made and decorated for those born with money. Our eyes were immediately drawn to the two large glass panels that overlooked the breathtaking view of the Swan River and the Maylands district to the north. The glass was so clear it almost felt like we could enter the night sky. The door to the apartment was thick and heavy, with a sturdy deadlock providing an added sense of security.

However, the thought crossed my mind that we could be trapped here if the tower were overrun. You could see the Perth skyline dominating the mid-west for miles out on the balcony. Usually, the night was filled with beautiful city lights, the smell of tempting food from all the busy local restaurants, and music dancing through the air. The usual vibrancy of the city now seems like a distant memory. From what we could see now, Perth appeared to have a bright orange glow, with smoke billowing from towers and the casino. Sophie showed us where we could sleep. I looked at the two other beds in the room.

I was jumping for joy when I saw the bedding and comforter. The beds were extravagant and plush, covered in silky soft satin, and had more pillows than anyone needed. I was tired. 'I'm so glad you're all here; I've been terrified. I thought I was going to die here waiting alone all day,' Sophie said. 'Sorry, my girl, we're here now. Have you heard anyone else on this floor since the power went out?' Dan asked. 'No, I don't think so. Not since this morning. I have seen a few people leaving in a hurry. I think the weird guy at the end of the hall is still there with his dog. I heard some noises earlier,' Sophie said. 'I'm not keen to hang around here for too long tomorrow. I vote we get out early and head south to Donnybrook, ' I said.

We pulled up chairs around the small wooden table, its surface cluttered with maps and notes. We began discussing our route options using the map Karly had found in the police car. Some routes seemed promising, offering potential safety and shelter, while others seemed like a one-way ticket to disaster. 'We need to avoid the main roads,' Dan suggested, tracing a path with his finger. 'Too much of a risk.' We decided it would be a good idea to take a break and have something to eat.

Karly put the food she had brought from the house in Rivervale on the counter—possibly one of the last proper decent meals we may ever eat, I thought. I unrolled the towel and washed my hands. 'I don't feel very hungry after that crap back at the house. Did you see the way it went for me?' I said. 'Yeah, man, beast of a thing. It was disgusting. We're just glad you didn't die or get bitten.' I forced the food down—a delicious though cold Thai green curry.

After a further hour of debate and discussion, we decided to leave at midday tomorrow, when the sun was highest and hopefully warmest. With any luck, no one or anything had messed with our cars. Initially, we considered going the direct route south via the Forrest Highway, but we all agreed that would be too dangerous, and there was probably a higher likelihood that we may not make it through. Taking the back roads was the final decision. 'OK, so do you think it would be a good idea for someone to take sentry duty, no matter where we go, if we can stay awake?' Dan said. 'Yep, wicked idea, just like in the movies. I'll go first so you can get some rest,' I offered.

I doubted that I would be able to get much sleep after my encounter. Karly turned her mouth downwards in protest. I laughed and kissed her on the forehead. 'It's for everyone's safety, my love. We're in the worst type of shelter at the moment. If something goes down, there aren't many ways out if the tower is overrun, so we must keep an eye on things'. She nodded and walked towards a room. 'Dan, I'll come to wake you up in five or six hours so I can get some sleep before the drive tomorrow if that's cool,' I said to Dan, who was already yawning and looking towards the bedroom.

'No worries, I'm so tired I'll probably be gone within five minutes anyway. Looking forward to a decent, comfortable mattress,' he yawned. The following five hours were tense as I sat on the balcony, lost in my thoughts. What a mess. I wondered how my parents were going, I thought to myself.

I missed them dearly. They gave me a great childhood and raised my brother and me well. Kim and Sid both worked in the mining industry before the world stopped. They were bright and left a year ago, but Karly and I had decided to stay. I rubbed my eyes, thinking about the last time I saw them at the airport. They had begged us to reconsider, but we thought we would be safe. The memory of their worried faces haunted me. Karly's mother, Sharon, remained in Donnybrook, a tactical area to retreat to if anything went wrong. I looked to the west.

The South 32 tower continued to billow smoke. Other buildings emitted an orange, burning glow that lit up the Perth skyline. No electric lights are to be seen anywhere. The odd vehicle could be seen driving around, military jeeps speeding past, and intermittent gunfire on the streets below. It was going to be a war—a war between those of us still alive and those who had been infected. We would have to do whatever it meant to survive, but at least we'd had time to prepare.

I was deep in thought when roused by some commotion in the direction of the city. Not long after, a convoy of military vehicles sped along the road with a police cruiser behind them. I couldn't tell what the other cars were, apart from the jeeps in front. It sounded like there were a lot of them, though. The convoy slowed and stopped, pulling up in the line it had initially travelled in while one vehicle pulled up alongside the convoy. It was a more significant military vehicle. It hadn't been long since I'd heard the gunshots in the city. The jeep troops jumped out and started running towards the front of the convoy, taking cover in a defensive formation behind cars abandoned on the road. In one fell swoop, it appeared all of the soldiers opened fire beyond what I could see. Automatic gunfire rang out, bouncing off the steel and glass jungle.

The larger vehicle's top section appeared to rotate towards what the soldiers were firing at. At that point, I realised what it was: a tank. The unit erupted in a series of deafening booms, belching out thick clouds of smoke as six sleek rockets shot out of it. Smoke trails snaked like writhing serpents, hurtling towards the city. The explosions were intense, with a brilliant orange glow lighting the night sky.

One missile darted out from behind a building, resembling ribbons in the air. It zigzagged through the air before slamming into the corner of another building. The impact was enormous, causing a massive explosion that shook the ground and sent debris flying in all directions. I felt the apartment building shake beneath my feet, and a shiver ran down my spine. A quick glimpse from the balcony showed hundreds of figures in the streets. I wasn't sure whether they were living people or zombies. I was in shock and disbelief at the scene I was watching unfold.

Everyone appeared at the glass door to the balcony, looking as scared as I felt. As I went to open the sliding door, a low-flying jet screamed over our tower towards the city. 'Get inside, Nathan,' Karly cried out. She grabbed my arm and pulled me in, slamming the door shut. I rubbed my arm where she grabbed me, looking on in shock. It was like watching something in a movie as the jet tore towards the city, straightening itself, with a single missile deployed from its base. It veered rapidly to the left and out of sight.

The missile continued towards the city, impacting behind a building about two hundred metres before the military convoy. We watched on in silence as there was a massive explosion and felt the shudder as the fireball wrapped around and hugged structures, glass violently exploding from the buildings surrounding the point of impact. We stood there in total disbelief at what was unfolding right before our eyes. Military personnel appeared to be running back towards their vehicles as fast as possible.

The larger unit was abandoned, and the jeeps and police cruiser sped from the bridge much faster than they had arrived. The scream of the jet was heard once more, about a kilometre to our left, destined for the city once again. Another missile soared towards the back of the city and exploded beyond what we could see. Sophie let out a small cry and looked up at Dan. 'Do you think there were still people there?' Dan opened his mouth to say something but decided against it and hugged Sophie. I walked over to Karly and held her hand as we watched in horror.

As we stared on in disbelief, not a word was said. Far out on the horizon, what must have been miles out to sea, I noticed five very faint flashes of light. Only very briefly. 'Did anyone see that off the coast?' I asked the group. No one seemed to have seen the flashes. We felt the next boom, though we couldn't see it. As I went to say something, a missile collided with the Riverside Drive causeway, destroying it instantly and sending debris and metal flying. Two seconds later, to our right, the Garratt Road Bridge and Tonkin Highway bridges exploded after being hit quickly by missiles.

Karly raised a hand to her mouth, and a tear ran down her face as the causeway collapsed into the water. I put my arm around her and held her close. Karly was strong and didn't like to break down, but I was her safe space; she held me tight, shaking. 'We're going to be okay,' I said. 'Those flashes you said you saw before must have been the Navy, maybe?' Dan said. I nodded and stared blankly at the devastation presented before us, obviously brutal but done to slow the spread.

We sat inside for twenty minutes in stunned silence in the relative darkness as Sophie's candles flickered, casting an ominous glow. I studied the faces of my closest friends. Sophie's face was mainly in shadow as she looked out the window. Dan looked down at his hands, deep in thought, occasionally shaking his head. Karly was looking on high alert between the door and windows, ready for our escape. I sighed. 'Get some sleep, guys,' and everyone except me retreated back to bed.

At around 05:30 am, I heard the sound of footsteps inside the apartment. I immediately gripped the Berretta. 'Whoa, bro, it's just me,' Dan said. Geez, that got my heart racing. 'Sorry, man, you startled me,' I said. 'How's it been out here?' Dan asked as his eyes stared transfixed in the direction of the city. 'Well, we're alive and kicking, but there's been a little action in the streets—nowhere near here. Did you get much sleep?' 'Couldn't sleep; I kept tossing and turning, too worried about all this going on,' he grumbled. His face was drawn and tired, reflecting his sleepless night. We sat there in silence. 'How's your shoulder? You hit your shoulder pretty hard on the back of your car when that zombie attacked you earlier,' Dan asked.

I winced slightly as I touched my shoulder, the memory of the zombie attack still fresh in my mind. The pain flared up, a stark reminder of how close it had been. I calmly shrugged it off and said, 'Yeah, it got me good, but I'm ok. I can't believe we've had a close shave so soon. We need to be more careful.' Dan nodded as he walked to the bench and grabbed a bottle of water for each of us. The smoke from the different fires began to disperse, heralding the first light of the day on the horizon. We had survived the first night.

LEAP OF FAITH

There was a chill as the morning air hit us, and the sun began to creep over the horizon. In the middle of September, the days should start to warm up again soon. The only sounds to be heard were the sporadic gunshots around the corner to the west. 'I'm going to grab a jacket, man. Can you grab the Glock, and I'll give you a rundown on how it works, safety, and that?' I said. I quietly entered the room not to wake Karly, but she rolled over immediately. 'You okay, Nath? Everything alright?' she asked, propping herself up on her elbows to look at me.

I nodded, raised the jumper, and headed back past the bed. As I passed her, I kissed her on the cheek. 'Get some more rest. We're going to need all of our energy. I'll be in soon,' I said quietly. I closed the door and walked to the balcony, again admiring the clear lines of Sophie's modern apartment. It is so clean and elegant; I sure would miss the Rivervale house, though.

Dan was holding the Glock when I went back to the balcony. 'Ok, man, Karly always taught me that you must always be careful with Glocks because the safety mechanism is on the trigger, directly in the centre. This assists with unwanted discharge. The most important rule with any gun is to treat it as if it were loaded constantly. Even if you believe there's no bullet, you don't aim it where you aren't willing to shoot.

Never aim it at yourself or anything that you don't want dead. When you fire, exhale to steady yourself, and then squeeze the trigger.' I took the sidearm from him and slid the casing open to check for a bullet in case one was in the chamber, even though the mag had been removed. 'This is important to check, Dan.

A bullet in here without the mag will still shoot a round,' I said as I raised the gun, found my target across the river, and aimed, exhaled, and squeezed the trigger. The gun clicked. 'Look, best advice; just don't shoot yourself, ok,' I laughed. He grinned at me. 'Ok, man, so aim, exhale, squeeze.' 'Yep, exactly. Give them the lead poison and send them back to where they belong,' I said.

As we were laughing about cleansing the streets, Sophie emerged from the glass door leading to the balcony. 'You guys look like you're having fun? Huh? Hey Dan, did Nathan finally show you how to handle a weapon?' she laughed. He rolled his eyes. 'No,' was sarcastically blurted out of his mouth. 'Ok, well, can I interrupt?' she said as she approached the balcony. 'Sure, are you going to join us? You can't sleep either?' asked Dan. 'Nope, it has been a restless night. Nothing short of fucked if you ask me.' A look of sorrow and fatigue swept across her face. 'Actually, I'm going back inside; I can't stand the sight of the city,' she said as she turned to walk back inside.

She left, but not before I heard the door shut behind her. The door suddenly flung back open. 'I forgot what I came out here for, boys—the old dude, the creepy guy a few doors up. Do you think we should check on him?' Sophie asked. 'Ah, probably not at the moment. Let's wait until later,' I gestured to them both.

The door shut again as Sophie left us unsatisfied with my answer. Dan leant into me, his eyes meeting mine. 'You remember how we always said we'd keep count during the apocalypse? Well, Karly is one nil already.' He just heard the world's best joke as he laughed and slouched back in his chair. 'Bring it on,' I replied, staring at the door.

'Right, bro, I'm going to sleep. Are you happy to keep watch for a bit? It should calm down during the day since the zombies apparently don't enjoy the sun as much,' I said. 'Go to bed, you tired unit. I got this,' he laughed. I jumped up and opened the door as quietly as I could. The haze of the night was still clinging to the atmosphere as the sun pierced the horizon. Karly was fast asleep again.

I placed my Beretta on the glass coffee table, slid my boots off, and slowly lowered myself into the plush bed, giving her the biggest hug I could manage. It was a magical feeling to lay my head on the pillow. I sank into it almost immediately, like that feeling you're floating. The last twenty-four hours had been utterly crazy—a barrage of activity and a close call—but still, the peacefulness of the bed was overwhelming, and within minutes, I was snoring.

I was suddenly woken by the bedroom door flinging open. The abruptness jolted me upright. It felt like five minutes, but I could tell it had been hours by the way the sun poured in through the windows. Karly quickly ran to the bed. 'Babe, we have a situation,' she said, panting. Her eyes were wide with urgency. I immediately sprung out of bed. 'What? What's happened!?' I exclaimed.

Karly pointed towards the door to the living room. 'Just go out there and see.' I could hear Dan yelling. I wonder what has happened now, I thought to myself. I'm not good in the early morning, let alone being awakened by commotion. I quickly leapt into my pants on the floor and ran to the living room. Sophie was in the corner, curled up in a ball and sobbing into her knees. Dan stood about ten metres away with the Glock aimed at the door. 'What the hell is going on?' I yelled.

'Someone decided not to tell anyone and went to check on the idiot down the hallway. Guess what she brought back—a dog!! Not a normal dog, Nathan, a zombie dog. No person, just a dog now patrolling a single hallway—a hallway trapping us in here!'. Now, we were actually in a sticky situation. A dog, I thought to myself, no way. Cross-species viruses that survive in animals as well as humans are very rare. We had heard reports about it, but it rarely survived in animals. How, on day two, had we already come across this? I thought. This was instantly lousy news. 'How aggressive is it, Sophie?' I whispered in a panicked state, shooting a look at her.

Just as I asked the question, a loud bark and scratching at the door followed—violent, terrifying, and an immediate answer to my question. I stepped past Sophie as the bone-chilling whimpers and wailing slowly inched away from the door. At that point, I was very happy with the sturdiness of the door. I instantly moved to ensure it was appropriately locked and checked the deadbolt. I slowly turned around and slid down the door. 'Did you get bitten, Sophie?' I asked.

A sense of dread instantly filled the room as everyone turned from the door to look at a crying Sophie. 'No, well, I at least don't think I did. Karly, can you check my back, please?' she sobbed. I replied calmly, soothingly, trying to contain my true feelings. 'We're going to be okay, Karly. Please check Sophie over to make sure that the dog didn't bite her. If there is the faintest sign of a scratch, tell me.'

Dan walked over and hugged Sophie as Karly gave her a look. 'I think she's good,' Karly said. 'Good, good, good,' I repeated whilst pacing the room. 'Ok, it is still early. Please try to stay calm, everyone, and listen for any other dog noises. We may either need to distract it or wait for it to return to its apartment and break to the stairwell,' I suggested. That was a risky move for four of us and one dog.

We'd have to be sure it was back in its room. I approached the door quietly and peered through the peephole. No dog was to be seen in the empty hallway. 'Sophie, how far away is the neighbour's room, do you think, like ten metres or twenty meters?' I asked. 'It's right down the other end of the hallway, so a decent distance, maybe forty metres?' she replied. That may give us sufficient time to escape. I sat down, thinking of alternatives. After a short while, I stood up. 'Ok, where's Dan?' I asked. 'He's just outside on the balcony. Not sure what he's doing,' Sophie said.

Around 11:00 a.m., we heard the dog back at the door again, whimpering and licking at the small clearance at the bottom of the door. The pitiful sounds were chilling. 'Man, I don't like the noise it's making. What if it has attracted more zombies into the stairwell?' I said to Dan. 'Yeah, that would not be great. Is there any other way? Man! There's a pool! We can make that jump,' he said. 'Nah, not a chance, man, we're on the 8th floor! We'll have to stay here, wait for it to return to its room, and then make a break for it,' I replied. 'But that needs to be soon. We have ammo, but the noise might attract more zombies, and if the dog gets us, well, we know what happens then. We're 8 floors up and may be trapped by zombies at the bottom.' 'I agree; it's not a bad idea if we get lucky and it walks into its room. It will have to be a very quick move for all four of us to squeeze from that door to the stairwell,' Dan said. I didn't have a plan, but it was too risky to do anything different. I grabbed my Beretta and slid it into my trousers. I approached the door and pressed my ear against it, listening for a few minutes.

I couldn't hear anything. 'Maybe it's eating its owner,' I said to Karly, standing closely behind me. 'Yuck, Nathan, really?' she replied, screwing her face up. 'Well, I don't know! What do Zoggos eat?' I replied. Another ten minutes passed without any sign of the dog. 'Right, is everyone ready to run when it's time?' I asked the group. We all nodded in agreement.

Karly spoke up. 'Right team, we open the door, Nathan out first, then Dan, then Sophie, and I'll go last. I've got the police rifle, so I'll shoot it if it gets too close.' We looked around the circle and nodded in agreement. 'Are you sure you're happy going last?' I asked Karly. 'Yeah, I'll be fine. I like adrenaline.' she said with a wink. 'We should be able to get past it fast enough, but I'll be ready to take a shot if needed,' she said. We slung our backpacks on, making sure the guns were loaded and that we were all ready. What could prepare any average person for what we were about to do, I thought?

I peered through the peephole. I couldn't hear or see anything. 'Ok, everyone ready?' I whispered. I quietly unlatched the deadbolt. My fingers trembled slightly as I released the lock. I felt as though I was breathless, and I paused, taking a long, deep breath as I pressed my forehead against the door. In one smooth motion, I rotated the doorknob and pulled it open. I stepped into the hallway and took three rapid steps to the stairwell door.

I swung it open, which resulted in a large creak. Before I had time to register, 'Urghhhh,' Sophie screamed. I turned around in horror; the zombie dog was right upon us. It jumped and latched onto the backpack

Sophie was wearing, digging its teeth firmly into it. Dan lurched forward and kicked it in the stomach, freeing the dog's teeth from the bag. As the dog hit the floor, Karly shot a round at it from her rifle, striking it in the back. Blood sprayed up the wall, and it howled louder than ever. 'Nathan, run!' Karly yelled.

She was too far away from the stairwell to make it. 'Karly!' I yelled as Dan slammed the stairwell door shut and grabbed me. We raced down the stairs, no longer caring for the noise we were making. Our footsteps thundered in the narrow stairwell, echoing our desperation. We just knew we had to get out. My heart sank when I saw the look of terror on Karly's face as she turned away and ran back to the apartment. We sprinted down the stairwell toward the ground level. The momentum and adrenaline raced through my body as my heart pounded. Before I knew it, we had reached ground level. Dan reefed the door open. My legs felt like jelly.

Karly slammed the door and locked it. 'Bloody thing!' she yelled out loud, frantically looking around the apartment. The adrenaline coursed through her veins, making her hands shake. The thought of being trapped suddenly made her stomach turn. She raced over to the balcony and peered over the edge. The height was dizzying. 'Ok, it's a decent height, but come on, you've got this. Just pretend it's Blackwall Reach cliffs and jump,' she said to herself. The clearance of the jump wasn't the issue; just the height was confronting and certainly higher than anything she was used to.

As soon as we were outside, we saw Karly looking over the balcony. Sophie clasped her hand to her mouth in shock as we all realized her plan. 'Throw your stuff over first, Karly!' Dan yelled from below. Karly threw her backpack over first and then the rifle, landing with a plash into the pool, each item disappearing momentarily beneath the surface. She steadied herself and stepped up onto the railing with the help of the chair, arms shaking with nerves.

Even from ground level, we could hear the zombie dog going berserk at the door, barking and gnashing. We watched as Karly closed her eyes and took a deep breath, then counted to three before pinching her nose closed and jumping. The intensity of the fall became too much, and she let out a short scream before hitting the water. Pain shot through her feet as the cold water engulfed her. Instantly soaked and deep underwater but alive, she pushed off the bottom and surfaced as the rest of us came crashing through the pool fence.

'Jesus! You okay, babe?' I said as we watched Karly swim towards us, breathless. 'Yes, I'm good. Jesus, that was an epic height to jump from,' she said as she laughed. 'We saw you hit the water. That was pretty cool', Dan said with a smile, holding his hand out to help Karly out of the water. 'We need to move now!' Dan said.

Karly waved off Dan's hand and took a breath before diving down to collect the rifle while Sophie fished the backpack out. I helped her out of the pool and hugged her wringing, wet body. 'I'm so glad you're okay. That was terrifying! The thought of losing you, but yeah, that jump was wicked,' I said with a smirk.

Karly's body was still trembling from her jump and the cold water, and I could feel her cling to me as we walked towards the vehicles. I didn't mind it; after all, the fear she had experienced was real, and she needed my comfort. She was fearless, though she didn't have a choice. I'm glad she was okay. 'Ok, guys, here's our objective. Ignore the zombies scattered on the road. They're in no way significant while we're in the cars. We're heading straight to Donnybrook,' Dan said firmly.

A zombie that no one had seen rose from the front of my vehicle. Sophie squealed. Dan removed his knife from his waist belt and drove it deep into the zombie's skull. It dropped to the ground in a heap. As we approached the fallen zombie, we realised that it was a young lady with a single bite mark on her neck. Her appearance was so human-like that we would not have known she was a zombie without the apparent bite mark. 'She looks fresh,' I joked.

The girls threw their stuff in the cars, and Karly quickly changed into dry clothes. The sun was warm on us now. It was a nice distraction for a moment before having to drive all the way to Donnybrook. I prayed that we didn't run into any drama along the way. 'Nath, do you want me to drive because you've had next to no sleep?' Karly asked. 'Aren't you on edge after that jump?' I replied. 'Ha-ha, Nah, I'm wide awake now, so it's not a problem at all. I'll just follow Dan,' she said.

I smiled and agreed while we did a quick walk around the cars to ensure no hidden damage would disrupt the trip. 'I wonder how far south the outbreak has spread,' I said to Dan. 'Who knows, man? I'm not even sure how any of this has kicked off. I wonder what's going on at the IPRC. Did you see anything on the TV before the power went out?' he asked. 'Karly said something about the Hostile Pathogens Unit about to release a statement, though I think it cut out before she heard much more,' I replied. We started the cars, and our trip south and out of the city was underway. I fell asleep almost instantly.

SUMMERTIME SHENANIGANS

I drifted off into my dreamy thoughts of the good old days. I dreamt about when most people left Australia about two months ago. We had a massive party at the beach. It was beyond awesome. Hot days, kegs, good friends, and jet skis. 'Hey man, what time do you want to go for a fish or check for some crayfish?' Dan asked as I just finished pouring myself another beer from the keg. 'Whenever, mate, it's midday, so let's go soon, hey?' I replied. What a picturesque moment this was. I looked to the left, where Karly and Sophie were playing 1-on-1 volleyball, and a small group of friends were drinking and talking about what they would do when the world returned to normal. Times like these were perfect.

The sand was golden white, and the water was crystal clear with a blue tinge. The sun's rays danced off the water, creating a shimmering effect on the surface. I dropped my fishing gear on the jet ski and deeply breathed. I downed a long drink of my beer and watched the sun glisten off the water. The air was salty, and seagulls were drifting effortlessly through it. Little schools of baitfish and even some herring swam close to the shore. It felt like you could pick them right up out of the water.

I noticed a stingray gliding on the ocean floor, not too far out, as I watched the tiny waves trickle against the shoreline. Thousands of tiny seashells scattered the coast with the odd bit of seaweed and driftwood. The sand felt silky and warm as I buried my toes into it. I was in a dreamy haze, and it was all so beautiful. I watched as a small wave crested by, bringing with it a swirl of sand, sea life, and foamy water as it dispersed. This was so satisfying and relaxing that I never wanted the day to end.

I turned around and looked back at the cars. The utes were parked up near the dunes, facing down towards the water. A side roof rack canopy provided sunshade for a few who were sitting under it, and beside them, to the right, a large gazebo stood proudly. Tables of food and large ice buckets with kegs were positioned under it. Another group was laying on the sand, sunbathing. Others were lying close to them, laughing and talking. In the background, a few guys debated how many years it would be before life returned to normal and everyone returned home.

Our friend Chance was there also. At 32 years old, he loved a good debate. He was an intelligent, very well-read man who knew a great deal about various things. He often shared his knowledge in conversations, whether he knew the topic or not. He had worked in sales before the world went to shit. I wondered what he did these days because we hadn't seen him for a while. Our tents were to the left of the vehicles. They'd been set up for camping that night. That's the magic of Australia: being able to drive your car onto a beach, set up camp, get on the beers, and have a fantastic time.

Karly and I had a large double swag in the back of the ute. I reached into my pocket, pulled out a cigarette, and lit it. Karly and Sophie came bounding over to me breathlessly. 'We are going for a fish soon; get those crayfish?' Karly asked. 'Absolutely, I'll finish my smoke and let's head out,' I replied. Sophie laughed. 'I'll change into my swimmers,' she said. 'Ha-ha, yeah, that's a good idea,' Karly said, spraying her with water. 'Oi,' Sophie said in response and ran off laughing. Karly looked at me with a grin. 'Ok, let me change, eh,' she said. She turned around and ran back to the Ute. Dan came walking out to me. 'You ready, mate?' I asked him. 'I was born ready, mate.'

The jet skis were tied off about five metres from the shoreline and were bobbing gently with the rhythm of the waves. Their sleek designs glistened in the afternoon sun. We had three skis between us. The funny thing about the new world rules was finders' keepers with pretty much anything within reason. Dan and Sophie on one, Karly on another, and one for me. Karly turned to me and held her beer between her lips as she put a six-pack in the Eski on the back of the jet ski.

'You ready to get dinner?' she asked. I chuckled. 'Well, seeing as though I'm the only one who can catch a decent fish, I am most definitely. Are you guys?'. Dan burst into laughter. 'Bro, remember that time we went fishing, and I caught three huge tailors one after another? Because I do, what'd you catch, huh, huh?'. Everyone laughed, including me. 'Ha-ha, screw you, man. It's hard to forget when you always remind me you twit.' I said. Dan twisted the accelerator with one hand and stuck the middle finger with the other as his jet ski roared to life and took off from the shoreline. I gave a cheer to Karly, and we knocked beers.

I rotated the accelerator, and the engine rumbled loudly. The fresh air was almost instantly whipping against my face as the machine skimmed effortlessly through the ocean water. Spray from the water misted around me, adding to the thrill of the ride. It felt as though it was floating across the surface. We had set up the jet skis with navigation systems, a fish finder, fishing rod holders, and skis.

The engine hummed away as the machine sped along the water. It was so flat and smooth that it looked like glass. We were out between the small islands in no time, heading to the fishing spot we had found last time we were here; it was only about 25 metres deep.

The view was incredible as we cruised along. I could see the horizon, and the crystal-clear water was like a mirror. Dan and Sophie's jet ski was slowing down, so I backed off the accelerator and pulled up alongside them, closely followed by Karly, who swiftly turned to wet us all with the water spray from the jet ski.

Baited lines were thrown over the sides of the jet skis, bobbing on the ocean floor as we sat on the surface, laughing and talking. 'Cheers, guys, I love this shit! It's great hanging out with you two and Dan, of course,' Sophie said. 'Cheers!' we all said as we raised a beer.

The portable speaker on my jet ski was pumping out the beats. Suddenly, Dan's line got hit, and the rod bent over. He launched himself towards it and began reeling. 'Ha-ha, suck it, Nathan, 1-0, the fish love me,' he laughed. A beautiful silver trevally made its way to the surface as it battled to escape back to the depths. It was a decent size and a good start for dinner. Simultaneously, both Karly and my rods bent over. We grabbed them and reeled quickly but smoothly.

Karly's fish seemed larger than mine, which was evident by how her rod was bent down towards the water. As my fish surfaced after a short battle, I could see that it was a tailor and a great size. 'Woo-hoo!' Dan and Sophie cheered. I threw it straight into the eski. I looked over just as Karly surfaced her fish. I couldn't believe it. A bloody pink snapper is a trophy fish. Karly grabbed the gaff hook and pulled it aboard her jet ski. She was smiling from ear to ear. I don't blame her because it was a nice fish that barely fit in the eski.

'That's a nice one. Good work, mate,' Dan said. She smiled widely and pointed. 'Look over there,' she said. Out of nowhere, a giant manta ray swam past, almost seeming to be peaking at us in curiosity. It was an incredible sight. We fished for a little longer before deciding it was time for a swim and to look for crayfish hiding under rock and coral formations on the ocean floor. The idea of diving into the clear water was too tempting to resist. We started our jet skis and were off again, heading closer to shore, where the water wasn't as deep. We did have a crayfish pot on the ocean floor we'd left there last time, and it was baited as soon as we arrived at the beach this morning.

It was about 100 metres from the shoreline, besides a rock shelf and a coral formation about 50 metres long. 'Let's check the pot first and swim around the coral,' I said, diving into the water. It was refreshing but not too cold. I opened my eyes and looked at the crayfish pot, which was easy to see in such clear water. Four crayfish appeared to be inside the pot. You beauty, I thought as I surfaced. 'Yewwwww, there's at least four in there, guys!!' I exclaimed with a huge smile. Everyone was ecstatic. We took turns swimming down to pick them out one at a time, leaving the pot there so we could go out again tomorrow morning as we collected the sweet haul to the surface and into the eski's.

When crayfish are attacked, they rub the hard cartilage against their antenna, making a dull but piercing eek-like noise underwater. It's a defence mechanism to ward off predators. Unfortunately, this can also attract sharks, so with this in mind, we knew this would be a short swim. No one cared, though, because we were having crayfish for dinner! We continued to swim around the reef, looking for more crays and enjoying the vivid coral and small fish surrounding us.

The underwater world was a kaleidoscope of colours and movement. Karly dove down and swam through a small cave and out the other side, near the reef's edge. Fish swam through the formation, not knowing we were there. I swam down for one more look, one more attempt to find a crayfish, but with no luck.

As I pushed off the sandy ocean floor, I noticed a reef shark cruising about twenty metres away along the bottom. It was only about 1 metre long, though. Still, I thought it was probably a good sign to head in before we came across any of his buddies.

Our group headed back to shore and tied off the jet skis, taking the fish and crayfish to the shaded area after they were scaled and gutted. Chance wandered over to us. 'So, who's up for a beer, and did you catch anything?' I held up some of the crayfish in celebration. It was around 4:40 p.m., but the sun seemed to be still high in the sky. We grabbed a beer from Chance and took a sip. 'Who wants to help me dig the fire pit out?' I asked.

For the next twenty minutes, three of us shovelled out a hole about one metre deep and five metres around. We grabbed all the logs and sticks collected earlier and constructed them into a tepee shape in the fire pit. Dan and Karly went off into the dunes to gather more kindling while Chance and I stood around the tepee admiring our handiwork. 'Cheers for the hand, mate. Let's see if we can't light it first in about thirty minutes, I reckon,' I said.

We grabbed another beer and found a place to sit and enjoy the relaxing sounds of the ocean as Karly and Dan added their gatherings to the fire pit. Dark clouds had been building up far off the coast.

We saw them on the way home from fishing earlier—possibly a coastal lightning show tonight as we partied. I took the next swig of beer and placed the empty beer can in the plastic bin. 'What do you think, Chance? Do you think the weather will hold out tonight; stay offshore?' I asked. 'Yeah, I think it will stay away and hopefully produce a nice light show for us if anything.' I nodded as I peered out to sea. 'What have you been doing since everyone left, man?' I questioned myself as I looked at Chance.

'Oh, you know, not much, just chilling out, reflecting on stuff, gathering supplies, and securing the house in case anything happens. We are lucky to be in Australia; what happened overseas doesn't seem real. At least we are safe here,' he continued as he wiped some sand from his wrist. 'You're a good friend, Nathan. I appreciate everything you do, buddy,' he smiled as he gestured a hand towards me.

Chance, Dan, and Karly came over and sat with us. Dan handed us a shot of tequila each. 'Love it, man. Thanks all for a wicked day, so let's back it up with an amazing night,' I said as we raised our glasses. 'Peace, love, and zombie attacks,' Dan said through a laugh. The shots were downed, causing Karly and Chance to cough. 'Dan, why did you get the cheap shit?' Chance said, holding up the bottle to examine it.

Dan grinned, 'Hey, it's not about the price; it's about the company! And besides, cheap booze adds character to the night, don't you think?'. Smiling at Chance's comment, Dan looked around. 'Where's Sophie?' Karly replied, 'I think she said she wanted to change and lay down for an hour.' We shared a few tequila oranges as the setting sun met the ocean. 'One of my favourite drinks,' added Chance.

The sun was slowly fading behind the horizon between darkening clouds. We all jumped when lightning flashed in the distance. 'Does anyone want to go for a last quick swim before it's too dark?' Karly asked. 'Sure,' replied Chance. 'You two are crazy. Won't it be too cold now? Dan and I will start the fire so you can warm up when you get out,' I said, grinning at Dan. Chance and Karly walked to the water and dove in. 'Bugger that, shark bait,' Dan laughed as he turned towards the fire pit.

We threw a couple of firelighters at the base and lit them with a match. Within a minute, the fire was going, the flames licking the edges of the wood and up through the middle, heating everything as it crackled and popped. We remained content, sitting around the fire, drinking beer, and listening to the calming sounds of the ocean tide washing up on the sand and the waves breaking. I turned the portable speaker on.

Karly and Chance joined us at the fire after ten minutes. Sophie emerged from her tent and headed over. 'Feeling better, Sophie?' I asked. 'Yeah, much better, thanks. That nap was exactly what I needed,' she said with a smile. Karly and Sophie decided they would sort dinner out; no arguments came from anyone's mouth.

'Are you sure you don't want a hand, babe?' I said to Karly as she stood up. 'No, no, it's all good. You know I love cooking seafood anyways,' she replied. Dan said, 'We'll ensure the fire is perfect for cooking. Just let us know when you're ready.' Karly nodded. 'Thanks, guys. We'll get started right away. Sophie, let's get the ingredients ready.' Sophie smiled. 'On it. Let's make this a feast to remember.'

As they walked toward the makeshift kitchen area, I turned to Dan. 'Think we have enough wood to keep this fire going all night?' Dan shrugged, 'Might need to gather some more just in case. I don't want to run out before the food is done.' 'I'll grab another round of beers while we're at it,' I said, getting up and dusting the sand from myself. 'Can't have a bonfire without a cold drink in hand.'

Dan and I removed some thick bits of wood from the primary fire and made a more minor fire to cook on. Karly and Sophie prepared the food and brought it over to place on the fire, rejoining the party. Garlic-butter crayfish had to be my favourite meal by a long shot. We were spoiled for choice with the feast prepared. Zesty prawns from the freezer at home, crayfish, whole snapper, tailor, and trevally had a yummy spicy sauce on them and were cooked perfectly close to the flame.

The smell was amazing—fresh seafood, cold beers, a bonfire, and excellent company. What else could a person ask for? All the world's cares seemed to vanish, leaving behind only a serene and untroubled calm. We sat around the fire, sharing stories. Dinner was a huge success; the seafood was juicy and deliciously tasty. We feasted in silence and threw the scraps into the fire.

Off the coast, a perfect summer storm brewed. Flashes and bolts of lightning rumbled in the distance and illuminated heavy clouds. An angry, rapid bolt flashed from the tips of the clouds to the ocean in one solid strike, followed by a loud bang of thunder. I loved it when there was storm activity in the sky. Chance went off to get supplies to make more cocktails he had designed and named after himself. He was always up for trying something new, whether mixing alcohol or flavours; he always had some idea. We all continued to laugh and chat, watching the fire and lightning.

He returned a few moments later. 'This one is my creation. I call it Chance's taste of Australia.' We all took a swig of the rocket fuel; it was harsh on the throat but warmed me inside. It was pretty good, though; it had to be one of the most potent drinks I had ever tasted. 'Way to try to kill us, man? Fire and booze in one hand, zombies in the other. If I die, at least I die in Australia,' Dan said. We felt safe in Western Australia, or so we thought.

The music blasted on the portable speaker as we danced around the fire while the flames licked the night sky. We sang, danced, and talked for a while as it became apparent the alcohol was taking hold. The conversation went from random topics, from cars to even death, to what we'd do if we were rich. I told Dan war stories about my time as a Paramedic in mining, which he loved hearing. Chance climbed to the top of a dune nearby and waved a fresh beer around in his hand, dancing wildly.

We watched him as the beer slopped out of his cup. 'Which of you legends wants a game of beer pong!?' he yelled. We quickly cleared the table under the sunshade. It had an LED light strip, perfect for lighting up the area immediately under it. We agreed to let the girls play first. Chance and I would join them in the next game. 'Don't go too hard on me, Karly,' said Sophie with a smile.

Dan and Chance laughed, 'Yeah, Karly, please be gentle with my miso, but we're going to watch,' Dan said, making all of us roar with laughter. Karly explained the rules to Sophie, and we added anything Karly missed. 'I think I will just learn as I go; it isn't rocket science, guys.' Karly won as usual, so they changed the rules to make it better for Sophie, and we all had a great time. Sophie and Karly were total opposites and complimented each other well. Sophie is shy and quiet, clumsy as anything, and Karly is outgoing and full of life.

We played for hours, and the beach was filled with laughter and excitement, boos and cheers. Around the tenth game of beer pong, Dan tried to catch a ball, tripped over his feet, and faceplanted. 'Hahaha, useless prick,' I managed to get out through uncontrollable laughter. We helped him and returned to the raging fire to catch our breath.

The girls were over the other side of the fire talking about us, I thought, as I could see them looking over at us. I handed Dan and Chance a cigarette, and we lit them. 'Damn, I'm drunk. Why do I suck so much at beer pong?' Dan asked. Chance smirked at me and replied, 'Well, we've been trying to figure that out for years; maybe it's because you're so tall?'.

Flickering light and laughter floated through the air, and we didn't want to let it go. 'So, Dan, if you're too drunk, you don't want any more tequila?' Chance asked. 'Nah, man, I'm going to chill for a bit,' he replied.

The tequila oranges were dropped into my and Chance's stomachs individually. 'Cheers to the last of the great tequila oranges,' I slurred to Chance as I raised my glass to the sky. 'You can say that again! There's none left, you piss-wreck of a person,' he laughed as he finished his glass.

The girls joined us around the dying fire as the wind picked up. Dan snored loudly and passed out in his chair as Sophie cuddled into him. Karly hugged me tightly and kissed me.

IT CAN'T SEE US

I was about to get out of my chair when a whole-body jolt occurred, waking me suddenly and startling Karly. The sun beamed through the windscreen as the ute cruised the road. 'You have a bad dream?' she asked. I shook my head. 'No, I was just dreaming about when we had that party on the beach a while back. I'm pretty sure we were about to have some hanky-panky, but I woke up' I replied. 'Ha-ha, hanky-panky!? Boy, the sayings you come up with,' she replied with a smile, touching my leg. 'Where are we?' I asked as I looked out the windows through tired eyes. 'We're still on the Southwestern Highway, just heading past Keysbrook, ' said Karly.

The landscape outside was a blur of green fields and distant hills, starkly contrasting the city chaos we had just fled. We'd decided travelling down the main highway would be too dangerous and congested, so we agreed to go as far inland as possible. The route was longer, though, and the roads seemed far less crowded. The plan was to head down the Southwestern Highway through North Dandalup, Pinjarra, Waroona, and Waterloo.

From there, travel east through Dardanup, Ferguson, and Lowden and finally circle back to Donnybrook. That way, we kept well east of urban, more populated areas. We would have to stay on the highway most of the way, but the journey would be pleasant enough. At least it was a scenic route with green fields surrounding the empty road and small townships. The roads were in good condition, and even the odd zombie appeared. 'That's probably not a good sign,' I said, looking at Karly.

'Can you pull over soon?' I asked. 'Hmmm, no,' she replied. 'What do you mean?' I said, fighting a giant yawn. 'I need to piss badly; can you pull up in a safe spot for me to go, please?' I argued. 'Ok, but be careful and quick about it,' she added. 'You know me, Karly; my middle name is Safety,' I replied sarcastically, leaning over to kiss her cheek before she argued the point. We approached North Dandalup, and a Caltex petrol station and roadhouse stood prominently along the highway. Its sizeable red roof, especially with the attached Australia Post Office sign, could not be missed. The tall fuel price sign was dark, as there was no power here either. It looked deserted, with no one in sight except a Winnebago and an elderly couple standing beside it.

Karly parked the car about fifty metres away from the fuel bowsers, and I got out. Dan and Sophie pulled up in their vehicle and jumped out. I yelled out to the older couple, 'You two, ok? We need to use the toilet inside. Do you know if it's safe in there?' The lady replied, 'We haven't been in yet. We come in peace also!' Karly jumped out of the car and walked towards the roadhouse with her rifle slung around her back, alongside us.

'Hey, I'm Rob, and this is Marilyn,' the man said. 'Karly and Nathan, Dan and Sophie,' I replied. 'Did you come from Perth? We've just come from Leederville and gone through the city. The other couple we were travelling with never left the city. Those vicious bastards didn't let them stand a chance,' Rob said, sadly shaking his head. 'That's terrible, we were just in the city. It was carnage,' Karly said.

At that moment, we became aware that we all had one major thing in common: we were all running from the dead. 'How bad is it in the northern suburbs?' I asked Rob. 'Mate, it is ghastly, absolute chaos. There are zombies everywhere and fires burning out of control. Not to mention the city. They've lost control. There are thousands of zombies in the central area of Perth now,' he said miserably. I dreaded to think of the people who were trapped in those buildings, zombies slowly taking over levels due to desperation and hunger for people. I'm so glad we left when we did.' 'Yes, yes, let's build a big box in the middle of Australia and house them there, they said sure that would work,' Rob said, rolling his eyes and shaking his head.

The roadhouse was empty, and the large glass doors were firmly closed. I peered through the glass and could see behind the till—no one in sight. I walked over to the browser and grabbed a bucket, tipping out the water. I went back to the large doors. Karly stood with her rifle aimed towards the entrance. I forced one of the sliding doors open about a metre and lobbed the bucket toward the middle of the store. I stood back as Karly changed spots with me at the entrance, gun poised and ready to fire.

She slowly scanned from side to side, searching for any sign of danger. The tension in the air was notable as we waited for the all-clear. 'Right, all is clear; please don't let your guard down here. Rob and Marilyn, if you'd like to come in with us, please do. I think there is some safety in numbers. I'll stay out here, just inside the door, to guard the vehicles and be on the lookout,' Karly said. That rifle she found sure had advantages and would hopefully deter unwanted visitors. I felt as though her knowledge of firearms made us all feel much safer.

Dan carefully forced the glass door open and briefly peered in before entering with the rest of us behind him. The interior was silent, with dust motes floating in the shafts of sunlight streaming through the windows. Magazines still lined the shelves, and drinks filled the fridges. The counter lay unattended. The till and cigarette lockers had been cleaned out. Marilyn and Sophie headed to the ladies' toilets while Dan, Rob, and I headed to the men's. 'What'd you do before this all broke out?' I asked Rob as we stood at the troughs. 'I was a doctor, general practice. I used to work in a little surgery clinic in the city. Then, I was assigned as the general doctor's contact in the northern suburbs. That is, until this all kicked off. What about you?' I laughed and replied, 'I wanted to do medicine but never thought I'd have the brains to be a doctor, so I settled for paramedic. I did it in mining, mostly as a Medical Emergency Services Officer. Both fire rescue and medical. It was an interesting career, to say the least.'

Rob looked my way and said, "Good on you; a challenging career indeed.' Rob was a fascinating character. I guess he was pushing sixty. He had salt-and-pepper hair and a well-groomed moustache. He was a good-looking man. He was tall and wore a comfy pair of jeans and a high-quality plaid shirt. A respectable gentleman, one you'd expect to look after you as a doctor, and very well-spoken.

'What about you, young man?' Rob gestured towards Dan. 'Nothing like you two. I've worked in hospitality for much of my life, managing bottle shops and pubs. It's been a pretty nice career for me. I can't complain,' he replied. 'Nice. Marilyn and I considered buying a pub once. There was one up Joondalup way, but we never got around to it; no point now, I guess,' Rob said.

I walked over to the sink to wash my hands. Of course, no running water, I thought to myself, looking in the mirror. Dark circles bagged under my eyes. I'm not getting anywhere near enough sleep. 'I'm going back out the front, you two. I'll see you out there,' I said, pushing open the toilet door and walking over to the large counter in the centre of the store, noticing Karly still standing at the front of the shop.

I darted behind the counter to inspect the cigarette compartment. A couple of packs of Benson and Hedges remained. I stuffed them into my pockets without a second thought. I noticed a container of lighters under the counter, too. Why hadn't we packed lighters at our backup campsite down south?

I wandered out to see Karly. 'Hey, look at all these lighters I found! Why didn't we think to pack a bulk supply of lighters?' I grinned. 'Righto old boy, bush survivalist, are we now all of a sudden,' Karly replied with a laugh. 'I'm going to put these in the car. The others are still in the toilet,' I said as I slipped through the doors. The afternoon wind had begun to pick up, causing leaves to blow from the tall gum trees near the petrol station's roof. I jogged over to the car and opened the passenger door.

Immediately, the alarm went off, and the horn bellowed repeatedly. 'Karly! Unlock it!' I yelled frantically. Far out, that was noise we did not need during an apocalypse.

The alarm stopped, and I opened the door, placing the lighters on the floor behind the passenger seat. As I slammed the door shut, I turned back toward the roadhouse when suddenly Karly screamed, 'Drop it! Put it down.' She raised the rifle and aimed it into the shop. I rushed back to the door behind her. As I looked past her, my gaze was drawn to the left side of the shop where she was aiming. A stranger stood there with the largest machete I'd ever seen, holding Rob with the weapon pressed firmly to his throat. Fear washed over me; I was out in the open now, having to deal with a dangerous person.

'What do you bastards want!' yelled the mystery man. 'Where the hell did he come from?' I whispered through my breaths after running over. Karly stepped forward, keeping the gun ready to fire. 'Rob went to have a look over in the Post Office section of the building, so he was probably hiding in there,' she replied. Sophie and Marilyn emerged from the toilet, further spooking the situation. Marilyn shrieked, 'Oh my god, please don't hurt him! We don't want any problems.' Karly and I slowly moved towards the mystery man and Rob.

At that moment, Dan emerged from the toilet, stopped dead in his tracks, and looked around. The moment he saw what was happening, he drew his Glock and aimed it at the man. 'Please don't hurt him; we're okay; please let him go,' Karly begged. 'We're not bandits. Please put the blade down,' she pleaded. Dan stood at the toilet door, his gun aimed at the man. It was apparent he was shaking while holding it. 'Don't come any closer, or I'll kill him if you do. I want all your weapons, so set them down and throw your keys to me,' yelled the man.

He looked at Karly, then at me, then back to Karly, and then Dan. 'This is your choice; you want him to take another breath, then make the right decision,' he yelled, pushing the machete harder against Rob's throat. A small trickle of blood ran over the side of the machete onto Rob's shirt.

I reached into Karly's pocket, out of sight of the man, and grabbed the car keys. I stepped forward with my hands in the air. 'Mate, I'll throw my keys to you, and you can take them, ok?'. 'No, I want all of your shit, including weapons; don't throw,' he was cut short as I lobbed the car key towards him. At the same time, the stranger moved to catch the key as a natural reflex. A single shot rang out from Karly's rifle, hitting the stranger in the chest.

As he fell, the machete swung around and hit Rob on the inside of his left leg. Blood was sprayed everywhere. The spray of blood was immediate and intense, painting the ground in a gruesome pattern. Tinnitus sounded through my ears, deafening me instantly from the gunshot. I could make out both men screaming and yelling. Dan jumped on the stranger and held him down while Rob rolled around on the floor, blood spraying from his wound. Sophie quickly jumped in and helped Dan subdue the man.

I ran to Rob. It was obvious his wound was deep and very serious. 'Marilyn, come and put pressure on this right now as hard as you can,' I instructed her, pushing a rag onto the wound. Blood poured through my fingers. Her face was pale, but she nodded and rushed over, her hands shaking as she pressed on Rob's leg. I raced toward the front doors to get my medical kit out of the car, slipping over on the concrete and landing hard on my elbow. Pain shot through my arm as I held the elbow with my other hand. I picked myself up and got to the car, pulling the kit out and running back toward the doors.

I ran back in through the doors of the roadhouse and over to Rob. Dan and Sophie sat beside the mystery man. It was apparent he had bled out and died. Karly and Marilyn sat near Rob, pressing down to stem the bleeding. He cried into his hand in agony, his face scrunched up. 'Nathan, I have Morphine in the van outside,' he said breathlessly.

I ripped the bag open and pulled the tourniquet out. 'Ok, let me have a look first. Karly, can you get me a heart rate reading, please?' I asked in a hurried voice. Karly removed her hand, and a squirt of blood hit the floor. This was an arterial wound due to its spurting nature and was not good, especially during a zombie outbreak. 'Push your hand back into that', I said to Karly as I slipped the tourniquet up Rob's leg. 'Urgh, far out! I don't feel real good right now; what was I thinking?' Rob questioned himself; his voice was weak, each word a struggle. I stuffed a piece of gauze into his mouth and instructed him to bite down on it as I tightened the strap and twisted it.

Rob groaned at the skin distorting from the pressure of the tourniquet. 'Right, Karly, how's the pulse?' I ran my fingers across Rob's hand and felt his hand grip mine. My heart raced. I wondered what I could do for this man with no medical resources and nowhere to go. 'Pulse is around 46 and weak, Nathan,' Karly said. This was a bad sign; knowing the body fights before it gives up, it had already achieved the giving up stage. Rob sighed and looked at me. 'Hey, Nathan, we all know how this goes; I've lost too much blood.' 'I'm going to do everything I can,' I said as I looked at him.

Desperation clawed at my chest, but I forced myself to stay calm. Marilyn was up at Rob's head with it in her lap, quietly sobbing and rubbing his cheek gently. 'Don't give up; I won't let that happen,' I said. 'But sometimes you can't win, Nathan. I'll give it to you, paramedics. You're stubborn with hearts of gold,' he smiled weakly.

A sudden downpour of rain hit the roof. As I reached into the medical bag, there was a loud bang. 'Karly, what's going on?' I asked. She turned quickly, ducking down and signalling for me to be quiet, a finger pressed firmly to her lips. I looked at Dan and Sophie as they sat there in fear. 'There's a Shreiker inside near the front door,' Karly whispered loudly.

My mouth dropped. The bloody door! I didn't shut it as I came in. The realisation hit me like a punch to the gut. The car horn and gunshot going off probably drew it to the building. Shreiker's were intelligent, loud, and deadly fast. That, coupled with being extremely violent, we were in trouble. I raised a finger to my mouth, gesturing to Rob to keep quiet as he screwed his face up and bit into his hand. Marylin was still quietly crying and didn't even look up. I very slowly rotated on my knees and moved to the shelves. We were only just covered from view. I peered over the top of the shelf, and there it was, standing right at the doors.

It looked like one of the mutated ones we'd heard about overseas. It arched its head forward and sniffed the air towards the roof. Its nostrils flared as it took in the scents, its head twitching with each breath. It moved towards the counter, sniffing the air again. I crouched and slid down the wall, reaching out and tugging at Karly. My hand was trembling as I grasped her arm. After she scurried back, I tugged at Marilyn. She was busy consoling Rob, still gripping his hand for dear life. 'We need to get outside or kill this thing before it kills us,' I whispered. The sound of the pouring rain on the tin roof and the slight ringing in my ears from the gunshot before made me wonder how much noise I was making.

Very quietly, Dan and Sophie helped Marilyn drag Rob around behind the service counter while Karly and I made our way towards the other corner of the dark room behind the shelves. The dim light and shadows provided some cover, but every movement felt perilous. We stopped as the Shreiker jumped up onto the centre service counter and kicked the till off the bench, causing a loud bang. Sweat poured down my face.

The erratic behaviour of this thing was surely going to draw more zombies, I thought. I gripped the wall to my right and grabbed Karly's wrist to the left. Through the stress of all of this, I forgot to breathe. I drew a long, steady breath into my lungs. My heart pounded as I reached for a heavy-looking glass paperweight on one of the shelves. I was dead in the water if it saw me, but it didn't. 'I'm going to lob this', I mouthed to Karly, kneeling beside me.

A small smile crept over her face, and she nodded in agreement. Dan and Sophie joined us. 'We can come back for those two. We need to draw this thing away,' Dan whispered. I peered over the shelves. The Shreiker was still on the counter. I noticed there were now around five zombies roaming outside. 'Right, on three, I'm going to lob this over the other side of the room,' I said. My voice was low but firm. I looked again at the counter, but the Shreiker was gone. A sudden thud noise landed near us, and we all froze.

The Shreiker was now sniffing the pool of blood on the floor from

Rob's wound. Now was my chance. I quickly turned on my knees, inhaled another long, deep breath, leaned out of cover and launched the paperweight as far as I could, hearing it collide with a table long over the other side of the building. Pain shot through my elbow from my earlier fall outside. The Shreiker heard it and twisted around, growling deeply, and raced over to the counter, bounding to the other side of the room like a frenzied animal. I couldn't believe the monster's speed as it tore across the shop.

When it made it there, it flipped two tables out of its way and screeched. If zombies could feel emotions, I would guess it was anger; maybe frenzied was the right word. It looked backwards and forwards, scanning the room. In the growing silence, a whimper came from the left side of the room where Rob and Marilyn were hiding. The monster spun around and snapped its head in our direction, eyes wide.

It came crashing back to our side of the building in a second, jumping straight to the service desk counter and howling. Marilyn screamed as it looked down at them both. 'Hey!' I yelled desperately as I stood, raising my Berretta at it. It launched behind the counter, and a loud screech erupted throughout the shop. A strange noise came from the creature as its last breath was taken. Then, silence again.

We dashed over to find Rob's lifeless body, with a cold, empty stare at the roof, his pupils fixed and dilated. I pulled the machete from the zombie's skull and handed it to Dan. Besides Rob, Marilyn lay on her back with the creature on top of her; the machete taken from the stranger had driven deep into its jaw through to the back of its head. We pulled the beast off her, and she lay there, sobbing and defeated.

She raised her arm and rotated it, a bite visible on the underside of her left forearm. 'I stuffed up kids,' Marilyn sighed. 'I can feel the sickness in me already, coursing through my veins, so it won't be long. My beautiful Rob has passed now anyway,' she said, blankly staring up at the roof, a tear rolling down her face. I wiped the tears away. 'Dan, give me your gun and take everyone away, please,' I asked.

Dan handed me the Glock without question and ushered Karly and

Sophie away, looking back at me briefly before disappearing somewhere in the shop. I looked back at Marilyn. She had rolled over and was hugging Rob. 'Nathan, I don't need you here. Please don't put yourself through this. I know what needs to be done,' Marilyn said. 'Please look through the Winnebago carefully because there are things in there that will help you greatly,' she smiled. 'I've lived a good life, a long life, and fulfilled my dreams and desires. You go on now and leave this place; look after the others. I want my last moments to be with my soul mate,' she sobbed as she reached for the Glock I was holding.

'Be at peace and rest easy; be with Rob,' I said gently as I walked away, fighting back my tears. I'd seen death before, but this was different, closer, and more personal. I walked back to the others standing near the counter in the shop's centre. A zombie stood at the door, wandering mindlessly.

It moaned quietly as it licked between the gap at us, its arms sliding up and down the glass. Further behind it, another eight zombies shuffled near the roadway. 'You okay, Nathan?' Dan asked. I said nothing as I walked towards a shelf with a child's pillow, grabbed it, and walked to the front door. I pulled the Berretta out of its holster, raised the pillow to the gap between the doors, pressed the Berretta into it, and squeezed the trigger.

The zombie's head exploded on the other side through a puff of feathers, and it dropped to the ground in a fleshy heap. That pillow trick muffled the gunshot, and all the other zombies were walking away as if nothing had just happened. 'Let's go, but be on high alert once we're outside,' I said as I unlocked the door and turned to the group. They stood there in shock at what I'd just done. 'Come on, I'm sick of this place. I only needed to stop for a piss, and all shit broke out. Let's go!'

'Can I drive the Winnebago?' Karly said, looking at the group. 'Yeah, of course! Just check before driving. Dan, you can lead Karly and Sophie in the Winnebago in the middle, and I'll follow up behind,' I said. The group agreed as we ran to our different vehicles, the rain still pouring heavily. It slapped against the side of the door and seats as I got in the

Ute. I wasn't going to worry about fuel as we still had full tanks, and apparently, there was a good supply in Donnybrook.

Dan's ute and the Winnebago pulled out onto the highway, with mine following close behind. As we pulled away from the roadhouse, a gunshot echoed inside. 'Rest easy together, Rob and Marilyn,' I thought. 'Copy Nathan,' blared the radio. I picked up the handpiece. 'Hey man, go ahead,' I replied. 'I'm just going to pull up wherever the nearest roadside stop is so we can look through the Winnebago. Also, do you think we bring it with us still?' Dan asked.

I rubbed my elbow, which was sore from the earlier fall. Thank God no one saw it, I thought to myself. I didn't want them worrying about me. 'Yeah, I think so. Karly, Soph, what do you think?' 'Ah, let's decide when we pull up,' Karly replied over the radio. Dan's ute soon cautiously pulled off the road to the left and onto the gravel. Though dark clouds threatened the southern skyline, the rain was now just a light sprinkle.

I jumped out of my ute and walked to the others standing beside the Winnebago. They looked miserable and shocked, the deaths of Rob and Marylin fresh in our minds. 'I'm just going to catch my breath out here after that shitshow. Are you guys alright? I can't believe what just happened. Rob said that he had morphine and other drugs in the van. Can you please look and see if you can find them?' I asked. 'What do they look like?' Dan asked. 'You'll know when you see them. They're in little 1 mL vials, mostly brown glass or tiny plastic containers. They'll be in a smaller bag in a first aid kit or something,' I replied. 'Karly can go with you. She will know what it looks like,' I said, looking in Karly's direction.

Karly walked up and held my face in her hands, looking at me directly and examining me. She then hugged me before turning and following Dan. A wave of exhaustion and shocked reality swept over me, and I could see Sophie coming over.

I took out a cigarette and lit it, taking a deep breath, which caused me to cough as I scanned the road, checking for zombies. My eyes landed on Sophie, who had slumped on the floor, holding her face in her hands.

I was too exhausted to comfort her.

Terror Australis – The Western Front

HOME AWAY FROM HOME

Dan climbed into the Winnebago. The door creaked slightly as it swung open, revealing a well-kept interior. 'Let's look for what we need and get out of here. We need to get back on the road and away from here as soon as possible,' Dan said. Karly agreed with a nod. Inside, wooden floorboards lined the floors with dark cream walls and cupboards, dark marble kitchen top benches, and seating areas.

'Damn, this thing is nice! Why don't we take it?' Sophie said, emerging from the doorway, causing Dan to jump. 'Actually, that wouldn't be such a bad thing. We could shelter in it if there's bad weather coming in at the campsite or flooding', Karly said, her eyes scanning the room and already imagining the possibilities. The bed was still messy, and dirty dishes were in the sink, evidence of Rob and Marilyn's presence.

The rest of the vehicle was clean and orderly. 'What are you looking for?' Dan asked Karly. 'A coffee machine. I wonder if they have a coffee machine,' she replied. 'Who doesn't have a coffee machine? This Winnebago would be worth the price of a small house, yet there is no coffee machine.' Karly exclaimed.

Dan continued looking through the drawers, food, clothes, alcohol, hairdressing kit, board games, cards, books, and other random stuff. His movements were quick but methodical.

He made his way to the back and opened the door on the side of the fridge. Inside were medical bags. He pulled one open and noticed some small pills. Examining them, he entered the bathroom, which was more of a closet with a toilet inside and sat on it. Opening the back zipper, five small brown vials were neatly stowed inside. He gently pulled one out and inspected it. 'Morphine 10 mg/1 mL' was written down the side. Yep, I think this is what Nathan was talking about, he thought.

'Karly! Look what I've found!' Sophie shouted proudly. She turned around, holding a shotgun. 'Oh, hell yeah, that's a nice 20-gauge shotgun! Wicked, plenty of rounds? That might come in handy one day. Anything else in that cupboard?' she replied. 'Nah, usual stuff: clothes, shoes, and underwear. Dan! You got what you were looking for?' Sophie asked, looking towards the bathroom. 'Yeah, I think so. Now, can we get back on the road? Let's talk with Nathan and decide about this, Winnebago?' Dan said as he splashed water from the sink on his face. The cold water was refreshing, momentarily washing away the grime and stress. 'Let's go! Do you think Nathan is okay out there? He was looking very tired and stressed.' Sophie said as she walked towards the front of the Winnebago.

I stood there smoking, looking at the ground, still on high alert. Sophie opened the front door as she and Karly jumped from the Winnebago. I finished my cigarette and stubbed it out. 'How'd you go? Find anything worthwhile in there?' I asked. 'Oh, we found some interesting things!' Karly replied, looking towards Sophie, who was holding the shotgun.

'We found a full cupboard of ammunition for the shotgun and some other things you might be interested in,' Sophie said, pointing at Dan. 'Pretty sure I found those vials you were chasing, man,' he said, handing the medical kit over. 'Wicked work, team, good job', I said to them all.

We all returned to the Winnebago, and I sat at the table. 'Let's look at these vials,' I said, opening the bag. 'What does it say?' Sophie asked, resting her bum on the sink. 'Morphine... 10 mg, 1 mL. I can use this to help us or anyone in serious pain,' I said, looking at the others. 'I'm glad you're here. I can't stand needles,' Karly said. 'So, while you were outside, Nathan, we decided that this would be good to shelter in for extra protection and shelter. We could take it to mum's and the campsite,' Karly suggested.

We all agreed and decided that taking the Winnebago was the best action. Karly and Sophie were happy to stay in the Winnebago and drive there for the rest of the trip. 'I need a serious drink when we get to Karly's mum's mate. Can we stop somewhere along the way? Hopefully, we don't have a repeat of before?' Dan asked. 'I agree with Dan. I'm pretty sure there is a bottle shop along the way, not too far from here, and I could sure use a stiff drink, too,' Karly said. Dan looked towards me and pumped his chest. 'Peace, love, and zombie attacks, bro.' We jumped back in our vehicles, turned them around, drove towards the Southwestern Highway, and then turned left towards Karly's mum's.

It was usually a nice scenic drive down south when we visited Sharon more frequently. We'd never have taken this route, though we did this time as it was further inland and safer from the prying eyes of the undead or, even worse, dangerous people. Australia has strict gun laws.

That being said, we were on farmland, and I don't know many farmers without guns. The roads were long, leaves rolling across them as the trees swayed from the wind, and it seemed to be getting dark early. It was around 4 p.m., and the sky looked darker than ever.

I picked up the radio handpiece. 'Copy Dan. I know you're an adult, but watch out for falling tree branches, if possible,' I said. 'Yeah, copy that man; good call,' he replied with no sarcasm. I think it was apparent we were all buggered after the terrible events of the long day. As we approached the next small town, we noticed a few zombies ambling about and moving aimlessly. 'I wonder what they're doing here already, Nathan. How has it spread so fast?' Karly said across the radio. 'I'm not sure, but it's not a good sign,' I replied. North Pinjarra is only a tiny town with less than a thousand people, and it has no primary road connections to anywhere else other than the central area of Pinjarra. As we continued south, I saw a menacing orange glow to the west.

Fires burned fiercely and hard, throwing embers hundreds of metres into the sky. I looked back to focus on the road and tried to clear my head. Today had been such a heavy day. Our small convoy followed the curves of the road and pastures for a little while before we finally crossed the bridge into Pinjarra.

'Right guys, slow it down through here, I think. There is a risk of zombies and the possibility of rogue survivors,' I said over the radio to the others. It was hard to tell how many people remained in town because a lot left to go overseas when they could. We crawled through the town, trying to reduce the amount of vehicle noise. I couldn't believe it. It was like a ghost town, with no sound except the gentle rumble of our vehicles and the fires in the distance.

Pinjarra was an old farming community with a relatively developed town centre for a country town. We drove past the post office, and a cold shiver ran down my spine. I'm never stepping into a post office again if I can help it, I thought to myself.

We pulled up alongside the bottle shop. We all left our vehicles simultaneously and convened at Dan's ute. 'Right, we hang around here for a couple of minutes before anyone enters that store. After that, we're leaving and not stopping again, ok?' I noticed Dan grinning at me awkwardly, 'What, man?' 'Bro, I feel like a kid, about to go into a candy store and get whatever he wants for being a good boy,' Dan smiled, doing a little dance on the spot. We all quietly laughed. He wasn't wrong; imagine being able to do this in any store, I pondered.

We walked around the back of the bottle shop, which backed onto the sloping park that led down to the river. Karly and Sophie volunteered to be on the lookout. Although the town was deadly quiet, it was better to be safe. Realising the almost military way we went about simply going to a bottle shop made me realise how much we had already changed quickly. The back roller door was free, so we pulled it up about a metre and dove under. 'Only take what you need,' Dan said, looking back at me with probably the most stupid look I'd ever seen on his face, topped off with a wink. I burst out laughing. 'Yeah, right, this is awesome!' I replied.

I found a trolley near the back side of the store. We may as well stock up now because we have some long days and potentially months ahead of us, that is for sure. None of the fridges were working, but that didn't matter. It would probably be too much effort to try to keep beer cold anyway, so we mainly focused on hard liquor. Dan was straight to the top shelf section. 'Man, look at it all! This is sweet,' he said excitedly, reaching for a bottle of Oban Single Malt Scotch Whiskey. He opened the box and pulled the bottle from it, slid the cork out, and took a long swig. Karly would have murdered him if she had seen that. It was one of her favourite drinks.

The store seemed untouched; every type of liquor was there: Jack Daniels, Jim Beam, Tequila, Rums, and so much more. I grabbed four bottles of Bundaberg Rum Distillers Edition, five bottles of Vodka, two bottles of Gentleman Jacks, and three bottles of Drambuie, and then walked to the top shelf section. Two bottles of Johnny Walker Blue Label, four bottles of Oban 14-Year-Old Single Malt Scotch Whisky, and two bottles of Macallan 12. Dan loaded a heap of random bottles into the trolley, and we headed for the exit. On the way out, I grabbed some random red wines.

Karly suddenly appeared. 'Wait, wait, I want to see something,' she said enthusiastically. I followed her over to a locked glass cabinet. A bottle stood there in pride of place. 'The Balvenie 30 Year Single Malt Scotch Whiskey.' I looked down at the price: $1550! 'You don't know how much I've wanted to try this!' Karly said. She broke the glass and retrieved the bottle. 'Let's go,' she said as we turned and headed outside. 'Wait, get some vodka. It can be used as a disinfectant for injuries if needed,' I said, heading towards the shelf. I grabbed a few bottles and continued out of the store.

We back out through the back of the store. The trolley couldn't have made much more noise if it tried. Sophie was leaning against the side of Dan's car. 'Holy shit! You guys are alcoholics,' Sophie said jokingly. 'You'll thank us later, I bet!' I said back to her. 'Let's chuck all this in the back of the Winnebago and get out of here. It's nearly 4:30 p.m., and I don't want to be out in the open when the sun goes down,' I said. We all chipped in, carrying the booze to the bed at the back of the car.

We still had at least two hours to travel to Sharon's. 'Everyone happy to drive in the same order as before? Karly, how is it to drive?' I asked. She grinned and replied, 'It's almost smoother than your ute. I'll keep driving that machine.' I rolled my eyes and laughed.

'Just try and stay out of the Oban Whiskey I got you before we get to your mum's ok.' I said. She laughed again. 'I saw you got me some of those bottles! This is one of the reasons I love you.' I knew that would make her very happy. 'Thanks for all the booze you got us, boys! Where's yours?' Sophie chuckled. 'Mate, you're a two-pot screamer at the best of times,' I called back as Dan threw her a can of UDL.

The town still appeared deserted, with no whisper of a person or a zombie. I jumped back in the ute; its nice leather seats still looked clean and smelled relatively new. I turned on the ignition and grabbed the radio. 'Let's take it easy out of here and no more stopping, hey? Clean run to Karly's mum's house now.' 'Roger, man. You want to lead the way?' Dan replied. I gave a thumbs up through the windshield and put the transmission into drive.

We drove through the first spread of farmlands. Some zombies were out and about as we left Pinjarra, and I saw a few in my rear vision attempting to keep up with our vehicles. The last remnants of the afternoon sun shone boldly across the paddocks. It was a beautiful part of the country, South-west Western Australia.

Sometime later, we came to the outskirts of Donnybrook and turned towards the town centre. 'I doubt much has changed down here yet, but on full alert, please everyone,' I said into the radio. It was different seeing this place with no power. It seemed a little creepy, though it was still a cosy rural town. The service station over to the right and fruit barn were dark.

The shopping area to the left, IGA, was also dark, and no one could be seen. What a weird sight! A dim glow up ahead past the Donnybrook pub illuminated light out onto the street. 'The bloody Asian bakery is open! Oh my god,' Karly laughed through the radio. That place was good for pies and sausage rolls and was always open, even at the end of the world! They must have a generator running, I thought to myself. We drove past and saw a person out front holding a weapon and a sign. 'Trade food, no cash.' I gave a gentle toot of the horn and a wave.

It was around 8:45 p.m. when we pulled into Sharon's driveway. 'Pull the vehicles onto the grass but reverse park so we can leave quickly if we have to,' Karly said across the radio. I pulled the ute out in the middle of the street before Sharon's house and reversed back into the carport. The lawn had been mowed, the trees buttressed, and the garden was green and neat.

A large rose bush stood in isolation beside the letterbox, with an open, sweeping front yard that met at the corner of two streets. I turned the ute off and jumped out of the way before Karly could bowl me over as she ran past. 'Come on, we need to see Mum!' she shouted over her shoulder as she sprinted up the driveway.

Sharon grinned from ear to ear as she came to the veranda fence, holding a rifle. 'Hey, kids!' She blurted out, laughing and crying as she went down the stairs to hug us all. We were excited to see Sharon, a legend of a mum to Karly and myself. She is in her late 40s and full of life, just like her daughter. It's what I loved so much about them both. 'Oh my god, Karly, where did you get that weapon from?' Sharon asked as she hugged me.

'Is everyone okay? Oh, kids, I'm so glad you're all here in one piece,' Sharon said as she looked at the blood on our clothes. 'This is Sophie, Sharon, and you've met Dan before when we set up the main parts of the campsite,' I said, turning an open hand in Sophie's direction. 'Nice to meet you, Sharon,' Sophie said as they hugged.

Sophie's whole body relaxed into Sharon's warm embrace. 'Ok, let's get you settled into your rooms. I've got candles around the house, so be careful with them,' Sharon said as we walked up the couple stairs to the deck.

Firewood lined the back wall over the far side of the deck, and I breathed in the floral scent of the pot plants hanging from the rafters on the long back porch that overlooked the garden. Karly pulled the screen door open and pushed open the glass-panelled wooden door, and we followed her inside. Sharon put a hand on my shoulder and quietly asked me, 'Nathan, tell me straight, what is all the blood from?' I looked at Karly, who was so excited to show everyone her childhood home that she hadn't noticed the conversation.

'There was an elderly couple who got into a bit of strife on the way down, and we helped out. Well, we sort of helped out. We're ok, but they didn't survive,' I replied, looking at the ground. 'Oh Nath, I'm sure you did the best you could,' she said with a gentle, understanding smile and a big hug. As we walked into the living room, we were greeted with the warm glow of candles flickering in the dim light. The room was furnished with a comfortable sofa and a few chairs arranged around a coffee table.

There was also a bookshelf in one corner, filled with hiking, camping, and wildlife books. I walked through the house towards the end of the hallway to the room Karly and I usually stayed in. Dan and Sophie's room was right next door to ours. Sharon had prepared the rooms as she was always very happy to have us, though this time wasn't under the best circumstances. I leapt onto the bed after pulling my shirt off and lay there. Karly knelt on the bed beside me and warmly kissed the back of my head.

'How are you going, babe?' I said in a muffled voice through the pillow, 'I'm good. Today was pretty shit, but we made it. I hope it won't be as hectic down here. I miss normal society already; I'm just over the moon. We made it home, and Mum's ok. I've been dying to see her,' she replied. Karly snuggled with me as I rested my head on the pillow. I'm almost sure we both nearly dozed off before we heard Sharon yell, 'Who wants a drink, kids!? I'm just about to light the fire as well.' I groaned and rolled over.

'Sharon does know that making all that noise soon might serve us up on a silver platter, yeah?' I smirked as Karly hit me with the pillow. I sat up in bed and rubbed my eyes, trying to shake off my weariness. Karly was lying beside me, grinning mischievously as she held the pillow. 'Come on, lazybones,' she said, jumping from the bed.

I got up and walked to the doorway. The room to my right was where we kept food supplies and non-perishables if things got out of hand. Thank God we did that, I thought, looking at it all. There was everything from pasta, rice, and beans to cans of tuna, smoked oysters, and spaghetti. Karly and I loved a good ramen noodle dish, so we ensured plenty of noodles. Cartons of water, fizzy drinks, and cordial; assorted muesli bars; herbs and spices; and tonnes of packets of nuts and pickled vegetables that Sharon had made from her garden. This would keep us going for a while, though we had other means of sourcing food, such as hunting and fishing if needed.

Most of this food was reserved for the inland campsite we had set up months earlier, away from civilization. I shut the door to that room and turned around as Dan emerged from his bedroom.

'You going alright, man? I am so tired,' he said in a drained voice and hazy stare. I could see the dark circles under his eyes. We walked down the hallway in silence to the main living area. The night had settled in deeply, and the candlelight flickered a soft light around the large room. Sophie exited her room and played 80's rock and roll music on the Bluetooth speaker.

'Ah, wouldn't you rather preserve your battery?' Dan asked. 'What, did the USB plug in your car suddenly stop working? Idiot!' Sophie said to Dan, rolling her eyes. 'She has a good point, actually,' Dan said, embarrassed at the foolish comment. 'No, I was just thinking, you know, in case we need to charge our phones or something.' Sophie shook her head, still smiling. 'Don't worry, Dan, I've got it covered. I brought a solar-powered portable charger with me, plus, you know, mobiles don't work anymore'.

Bars had been installed along all the windows on the exterior, good for keeping unwanted visitors out, even the rotting kind. Karly and Sharon stood around the kitchen bench, talking quietly but excitedly as we approached. 'Here, lads, I've poured you both a generous nip of Macallan's. I think we've earned it today,' Karly said, holding two cups in our direction.

'Cheers, thanks,' I said, taking the cup. 'Cheers,' Dan said to her. 'Ok, I've got some food for us, so we will have to heat it over the fire,' Sharon said with a smile. 'I can keep the first watch, sweetie; I've managed fine alone for this long,' Sharon said to Karly. 'Oh, thanks, mum, but most definitely not! I'm impressed you even thought of that, but we will do it in pairs. The house is big, so we can take turns doing perimeter walks,' Karly replied.

'Ok, honey, whatever is best for us was just an offer. But it's been a big day for all of you. Come on, let's go and light the fire and eat!'. We walked outside, and Karly offered me a cigarette as I lit the fire pit. 'Thank you very much; just what I needed,' I said to her. She giggled and took a drag of her cigarette. 'No problem; glad I could help,' she said, leaning back in her chair. She looked relaxed, her shoulders loose, and her eyes half-closed. I threw my nip of Macallan back and drank it down. It was smooth and warmed my throat as the fire pit heated and continued to catch fire.

As we sat around the fire pit, savouring the warmth of the flames, we drank scotch and beer and gobbled down the delicious food Sharon had put out for us. Butcher-style sausages cooked to perfection on the frying pan, their savoury aroma wafting through the air.

It was amazing what a fire pit and a frying pan could deliver, and we were grateful for Sharon's quick thinking to grab some ice before it all melted. Before her neighbour left town, he'd installed a small generator for her to run a freezer. We ate silently, lost in our thoughts and fatigued from the long day. But the quiet was comfortable, and there was a shared understanding between us that words were unnecessary now.

We quietly enjoyed each other's company and the simple pleasure of sharing good food and drink. 'Karly, darling, could I have another bit of that drink we just had? It was bloody beautiful,' Sharon said, breaking the silence. I laughed and said, 'Sharon, you don't have to ask; it's all free, and even if it wasn't, what's ours is yours, so enjoy.' Dan was already standing. 'I'll get it for you, Shaz. Anyone else want one?' We all nodded, holding up our glasses.

The sound of the breeze moving through the trees in the bush opposite the house stirred me from my thoughts. 'I think we should go and check on the campsite tomorrow to make sure it's all good. We've been lucky so far, so I'd hate for it to all come undone now,' I said to the group.

Weary eyes peered back at me. 'Yeah, why don't you and Dan go for a spin tomorrow to check it out, Nath?' Karly replied. I looked at Dan, who shrugged his shoulders. 'I'll never say no to a good four-wheel drive trip.' 'Sweet. I want to sleep in, though, after-night watch. I'm going to head to bed for a few hours. Karly and Sharon, last chance to bail on first watch,' I said.

'Nope, Mum and I have some catching up to do. You guys rest,' Karly said. 'Karly, honestly, it's OK; I can do the first watch myself,' Sharon said. 'Safety in numbers, we reckon, Sharon,' Sophie replied, but ultimately, the stubborn look on Karly's face made Sharon agree. I tipped the rest of the Macallan down my throat and put the glass down.

I tiredly dragged myself out of the chair and walked inside, down the hallway, to the bathroom. I grabbed the toothbrush and scrubbed away, walking into the back room to grab a bottle of water to rinse, the simple luxuries of running water already stripped from us. I was so tired; I don't remember putting my head on the pillow.

Karly woke me a few hours later, around 3 a.m. 'I thought we were doing 3-hour watches. What time is it?' I said to her through a strangled, awakening voice. 'Mum and I lost track of time chatting. I've missed that. We also kept a good eye out; nothing to report,' she said as her head sank into the pillow. Almost instantly, a deep snore came from her.

I smiled at her and gently moved the hair off her face with my finger. Being as quiet as possible, I got out of bed and put on a jumper. The Berretta was on top of the underwear drawer. I didn't like carrying it, but it was necessary. I nearly always forgot our knife-on-us rule as I began to walk out the door. I grabbed it and holstered both the knife and gun.

I quietly walked a few steps to Dan and Sophie's room to wake Dan up for sentry duty. The door creaked slightly, and I paused, holding the door still, listening to see if I had woken anyone. Satisfied I could keep going, I looked up to see eyes staring back at me. Sophie had softly stood up and held a finger to her lip to silence me. She whispered, 'Give him another hour. I'll come with you instead.' I nodded in agreement and went outside while waiting for Sophie to dress.

It would be a lovely morning, but the darkness of the night was still thick. The fire pit flickered gently as it finally died. I picked up some of the wood and added it to the fire. The embers popped as the flames flared back to life, and I watched a single ember spit from the fire and land on my skin, briefly burning me.

I sat down in the chair with my gun on my lap. My eyes scanned along the fence at the back of the yard. I pulled the gun out and began admiring it. The Berretta was black and could fire fifteen shots. It was easy to carry and powerful enough for what we needed.

I holstered the weapon and stood, gazing into the fire pit. Coffee right now would be magical, I thought to myself, and as if reading my mind, Sophie walked out the door with Sharon's camp kettle and placed it on the fire.

Although Sophie was from the city, she could rough it with us camping; she loved it. She often told us stories about her family's trips to show her where her ancestors were from, proudly showing us what we called bush tucker and explaining her aboriginal heritage and how to live off the land. However, she always shotgunned the first warm shower when we returned to civilisation.

With our cups of steaming coffee, we headed for a perimeter walk. I walked down the end of the wooden deck and traversed the stairs. Trees stood beside the house, and around the front, the large garden stood majestically still. I grabbed the torch from the front compartment of my car and walked to the street, skimming the torch back and forth, checking for any unwanted activity. Some houses were lit up further down the street, a long way away from the house.

They must be blessed enough to have generators. We had generators at the camp we would scout out later in the morning, though we decided it would be safer not to illuminate Sharon's house at night. Despite the darkness that enveloped me, I felt a sense of calm and excitement. The prospect of exploring the campsite, returning to nature, and leaving the chaos of the city behind filled me with a real sense of exhilaration.

Nothing interesting happened over the following few hours. Sophie went back to bed, and I had two more coffees, a small bag of chips, and some wrapped salami. My back hurt like hell after sitting in the chair for hours. No noise was heard throughout the neighbourhood at all.

Sharon's house backed onto the bush, so the thought of the unknown in that bush made me slightly uneasy, especially while doing perimeter rounds. Nothing is out there, I told myself. I lit up another cigarette as I walked back onto the back deck. Sophie and Dan emerged from the door. 'I thought we agreed we were doing sentry duty in pairs?' Dan said.

'Yeah, I was meant to wake you when I returned to bed, but I crashed.' Sophie replied. Sophie gave Dan a tired smile as she hugged him. We sat and whispered between us for a while. It was around 5:30 a.m., so we agreed that around 8:00 a.m., Dan and I would leave to assess our campsite out in the bush. 'Yeah, I'm pretty sure we have rested enough. I'm wide awake personally,' Dan said, nodding in agreement.

I handed the Berretta to Dan and gave him a pat on the shoulder. 'Godspeed, my man; hopefully, the hours go by fast,' I told him. He nodded solemnly and pulled the pistol up to his shoulder. I crept back to the bedroom that Karly and I had shared on so many visits before the world's end. Karly was still sleeping.

I dragged my body to the bed and lay on my back, letting out a satisfied sigh. I felt the mattress depress slightly, and Karly put her hand into mine. 'You good, babe?' she asked. 'Yeah, just tired; I will probably snore, so apologies in advance.' Karly chuckled softly; the sound was like music to my ears. 'It's okay,' she said. 'I'll just pretend you're a soothing white noise machine.'

Dan came and woke me. Judging by the sun streaming through the blinds, it must have been around 8:00 a.m. I looked at my watch. Yep, bang on 8:00 a.m. I got up, pulled a shirt on, and walked into the kitchen, where Sophie and Karly sat quietly at the table, coffee in hand. Sharon was sweeping the tiled floor. 'Good to see we survived another night. How was the morning watch? Any issues?' I asked. Dan shook his head. 'Nice, we have plenty of diesel to get around. We can top up at the campsite,' I said as I gulped down some hot coffee. 'Nath, we are all going to come for a drive to the campsite, safety in numbers, plus mum's sick of being all cooped up in the house,' Karly said, smiling at me.

'Sweet, the more, the merrier, I say,' I replied, going over to the breakfast cupboard and grabbing a few small chocolate bars. Sophie sneezed into her elbow three times. I stopped and asked her if she was okay, laughing at how often she sneezed. Karly laughed, too. 'She's had an antihistamine, so that should clear her up soon,' Karly said.

I nodded and finished up the last sips of my coffee. 'I'm excited about today. You know how much I love a good bush bash session, hey? I haven't been down for a while, so I hope no one has found our soon-to-be home while we were away,' Karly said. She seemed in great spirits, though we all were today after finally getting well-earned sleep.

The sun shone high in the sky, and birds chirped in the trees. A gentle breeze rolled up the hill as we walked to the cars. Sharon hopped into the back seat, and Karly was in the front while the others jumped into Dan's.

OLD FRIEND

After a bit of a windy drive up along the dirt road out the back of the house into the bush, we ended up at some farm. It was slow-going. We looked out the windows as a few kangaroos hopped away from us, the crunching sound of gravel and leaves getting quieter as they hopped away. We could feel the warm breeze hitting our faces with the windows down. 'Oh, good to see the Kensington's are going okay,' Karly said as we drove past the house. Everything was nice and quiet, and we could see smoke rising from the chimney of the main house.

This town had lots of smaller, outer suburban farmlands. Peaceful and friendly, this is one of those towns where everyone waves and says hello. I prayed that evil would be contained at that moment before making its way here. 'Sharon, has there been much military presence down here?' I asked, looking back at her in the rear-view mirror.

'Umm, no, not really, just a few. The local police car has made some rounds, and I heard a helicopter the other day, but that's about it,' she said calmly, looking out the window. I was slightly concerned about the possibility of being inundated with zombies making their way from the east.

The dirt road came to a bitumen intersection, so I pulled around to the right and pressed the accelerator. The ute is powerful and reached 100 km an hour in no time. The smooth asphalt and clear signage made navigating easy, even for those unfamiliar with the area. The road twisted and turned through rolling hills and lush greenery, rising and falling with the land's natural contours. I slowed down once we reached the turnoff into the Millbrook State Forest.

The track was pretty smooth for a dirt road; its surface had hardened from years of weather and occasional travellers. Dust kicked up in a cloud behind the vehicle, forcing Dan to back off behind us a little. One section required four-wheel drive mode to get through, as it was quite rutted out. The deep grooves and ridges made the journey feel like a mini off-road adventure.

'Copy Dan. The road might be a problem for getting that Winnebago down this section,' I said into the radio. 'Yeah, we will figure something out,' he replied. Should we need it, we'd previously set up this campsite as an "off-the-grid" location. It was well-stocked and would provide us with months of shelter and food.

The hardware was all in place, from the sturdy canvas tents to the portable solar panels for charging our devices, though a lot of food and perishables were still at Sharon's, stored in the back room. If there were any signs of trouble, two 152-litre heavy-duty storage containers were ready to be loaded and thrown in the back of the ute to get us out quickly.

The journey was relatively quick, and as we came around a bend and over a hill, we were at the campsite. It was a decent size, surrounded by lush bushland, with a rock face drop-off over one side of about two metres to allow for drainage if it rained and a freshwater creek about sixty metres away. 'The camp is going to be great here, running water as well,' Sharon said. 'Yeah, we checked out a few locations, but this one was the best. We can catch fish and probably find a bush track to walk and get some bush tucker,' I said, looking at Karly. In this regard, Karly had more of a knack for it.

Growing up in Donnybrook had its perks, one of which was learning how to shoot a rifle. 'Yeah, we can do that. You can get fish on the sandbar at the beach, hey Nath?' Sharon laughed as she spoke. This was a long-running joke between us all: me standing on the beach, looking out at the ocean, trying to figure out where the sandbars were, and then telling the group. I smiled and chuckled.

I brought some granola bars and gave them to everyone to munch on. Sophie volunteered to be on the lookout with the rifle while we inspected the campsite, her keen eyes scanning the perimeter, the gun steady in her hands. We can never be too safe, even in the peaceful silence of the bush.

As we had hoped, the camp looked untouched. No one had stumbled across our sanctuary. Before the outbreak, a trip to Bunnings was undertaken to get what we needed to set this area up and survive for extended periods. Karly and I set up most of the site, with Sharon's help at times. For shelter against the sun, green shade cloth was strung between the trees.

A twelve-man tent was set up in the far corner, very spacious and surprisingly cool inside. Its thick canvas walls and well-ventilated design made it a perfect refuge from the elements. There were also three 4-person tents around the clearing.

To protect those tents, six three-metre gazebos were constructed above them and another for general shade. These allowed us to sit under them when it was blistering hot or kept us dry from the rain. The gazebos had a large, waterproof canvas on the bottom and a light material above it, including LED light strips on the framework on the undersides for lighting. A small water collector was neatly constructed.

It fed down a pipe from a good-sized rock ledge down the creek, where it collected in a hidden water tank. Dan's ute also had a rooftop tent on it. There were two 4-stroke generators and a few 180-watt solar panels. A creek ran into the river about a kilometre further downstream, and this was a great swimming hole. The transparent, cool water was always inviting, making it the perfect place to relax and refresh after a long day. The creek was stocked with various fish, like bream and trout, making it a good source of fresh food.

There were two 152-litre storage containers, one with tools and equipment like an axe, machete, binoculars, glowsticks, chainsaw, shovel, a fire extinguisher, and anything else we could find value in. We had a handful of LifeStraw's items, which we used to drink from most running water sources, automatically filtering out nasties that may make us sick. A large campfire area in the centre of the camp has a solid steel campfire cooking plate, kettle, cast iron pots, and other cooking implements.

A large metal waste container was around 50 metres away, which would allow us to burn any waste. A 208-litre drum and a broken-down diesel ute were nearby, full of diesel, and parked a little further away for fire safety. Other pieces around the campsite included camping chairs, batteries, rope, hunting equipment, fishing and crabbing equipment, a fold-out table, and a composter to help us grow vegetables.

As I mentioned, we did not mess around when we set this up. 'Hey Nath, do you want to go and just grab the Winnebago now to try and get it past that rut in the track up there rather than worry about it if we're in a hurry?' Dan asked me.

Karly shot him and me a look and pointed sternly backwards and forwards at both of us. 'You look after my Winnebago champs; she's done us well this far.' I rolled my eyes and raised my eyebrows at Dan with a grin. 'You three want to wait here or come with us?' I asked. 'Yeah, too easy, we will wait; we can check the fences and that here while you two do that,' Sharon replied.

We used thick metal wire drilled into trees to create the perimeter, and from these lines hung metal cans to help us hear over the low babbling noise of the creek nearby. Karly had put together a device to make it electric—nothing that would totally stop a zombie or person, but enough to give them a shock or force them to make noise.

Dan and I jumped in his car and cruised back along the track to the bitumen road headed towards Sharon's. 'How are you and Karly going, man?' Dan asked. 'Great man, yeah, really good, been stronger than ever. This zombie bullshit doesn't help any situation, though we've grown stronger together. Well, that's how I feel anyway.' 'Good to hear, man. It looks like you two are solid,' he replied. 'What about you two?' I asked. 'We're going well, too, and I feel like I connect with Sophie. Plus, the sex is amazing!' he exclaimed. 'Ha-ha, I don't need to know, but I'm happy for you. Maybe rubber up so we don't have to bring a baby into this world yet, hey?' I said as we both nervously chuckled at the idea.

'Looks like another storm is rolling in, so let's get this bloody Winnebago down there and get back to Sharon's to chill,' Dan said. I nodded in agreement as we exited the dirt track behind Sharon's. A vehicle was pulled up along the verge. I instantly burst out laughing because I knew who it was immediately: 'Chance, you son of a bitch!!!! Yes! He remembered, how good!' I yelled in happiness, shadow punching the air. We swung into the driveway as he stood there looking prouder than ever.

We jumped out of the car and ran over to him, hugging him and laughing joyfully. 'I told you, maggots, I'd make it! Right, what needs to be done? I'd love a beer, but it looks like we have work to do first?' The grin on his face was huge, and we were both happy to see him. Explosive expert and ideas man, or self-proclaimed anyway, he would be an asset to the group. 'No time to discuss the Perth crap. We can do that later tonight. I'll drive the motor home. Where did you even get that from, rob someone's nanna?' Chance chuckled. 'You can drive, man, no worries, but just be mindful that Karly may hurt you if you crash it,' I warned. Chance nodded, looking impressed.

'Well, it's a step up from my old beat-up car,' he said, glancing over at his old car. 'Anyway, let's get to work. What's the plan?' I explained to Chance what we had in mind for the campsite and the equipment we had already set up. He listened carefully, nodding and occasionally asking questions. Chance shared his ideas for improving our security. He suggested digging trenches around the perimeter and filling them with sharp objects like broken glass and nails, which would deter anyone from trying to climb over or dig under the fence. Dan sarcastically said, 'Shit, I knew we forgot something. Where did we leave the excavator and broken glass?'

Chance jumped in the Winnebago as we got back in Dan's ute. We headed back the way we had come until we got to the rutted-out area. Dan and I hopped out and grabbed the recovery tracks out of the back. 'Follow my guidance so it doesn't bottom out. It doesn't matter if it's a one-way trip for this thing; it's just providing shelter from heavy rain, but we can't have it bogged and blocking the road for us,' Dan reminded us.

We gathered some sturdy, good-sized branches and placed the recovery tracks on top. 'I'll just take it nice and slow,' Chance said. 'Man, it's probably best if you drive; even if you break it, Karly won't care seeing you driving it,' I said. The Winnebago made it through the rutted section with no trouble. 'So, dare I ask where you got this from, medic man?' Chance asked over the radio. 'You don't want to know,' I replied, as Dan and I shared a knowing look.

We came around the corner and into the campsite area. The Winnebago pulled up onto the area near the fence line. 'Chance!' Karly squealed as she ran over to him, giving him a big hug. 'Nice to see you too!' he replied, returning the hug. 'I'm happy you're here, but you know how hectic the end of the world makes things. You bring a level of danger, no matter how good a guy you are,' she said.

'Without me, the end of the world would continue. I want to think I hold the fate of humanity in my hands,' he joked. 'Brave words, man, really?' Dan said, giving him the thumbs up. 'How are you two anyway, all good?' Chance asked us. 'Super great, apart from the end of the world happening, but we always joked about it, so shit happens really,' I said. 'Chance, this is Sophie, my girlfriend,' Dan said as Sophie gave him a polite nod while Chance walked up and hugged her. 'Pleased to meet you, Sophie,' he said. 'I know what you're probably thinking—yeah, yeah, what a legend, but it's true what they say,' looking towards Dan and me for confirmation.

Chance was a great guy, but damn, the crap that would pour out of his mouth was incredible. Then again, we all fuelled each other in the shit-talking department. 'Everything okay here?' I said, looking around at Karly and Sharon. 'This site is good to rock and roll; let's hope we don't need it. I prefer my bed', Karly said.

We all chatted about what else we could do for safety or checks before we left. As we made our way towards the cars, the weather seemed to be taking a turn for the worse, with a chilly wind cutting through the site, causing Sophie to sneeze and cough. Her cough sounded more profound and more laboured than before.

I glanced at her, noticing the telltale signs of illness: droopy eyes and a flushed complexion. A sinking feeling settled in my stomach. The last thing we needed was for one of us to fall ill. As if in agreement, the storm clouds overhead rolled in faster, casting a dark and overcast pall over our surroundings. We quickened our pace, eager to reach the safety and warmth of our cars before the weather took a turn for the worse.

The trip home seemed to take forever; the bumpy track was angrier than the previous two times. The wind had picked up, and the sky had become menacingly dark. We pulled into Sharon's house, happy to be home. Weather systems could be crazier down south this far compared to Perth, but a bit of rain never hurt anyone. I find it quite relaxing.

'I think I will go and lay down for a bit, Nathan. Do you have anything for my head and throat? They're starting to hurt,' Sophie asked. 'Yeah, I'll take your temperature, and we will watch you. I'll grab some paracetamol and lozenges, too. Rest is your friend now,' I said.

I gave her Paracetamol and took the temperature. 38.9 degrees was read on the scanner. 'Yeah, you've picked something up. Plenty of water and paracetamol will help relieve your symptoms'. Dan walked Sophie inside as Chance came over to Karly and me. 'So, you two want a game of Fuck the Dealer?' This is a card game where you start as the dealer and guess the dealer's next card. If you're wrong, you get a second guess. If you're wrong after the second guess, you drink the difference between the cards.

The dealer stays in for three incorrect guesses and has four drinks if the person guesses the card on the first go and two on the second, and the dealer count resets to three. You're screwed if you don't have many cards left at the end as a dealer. We played a few rounds and talked mountains of crap. I had four beers and then opened a rum bottle, sipping it with coke. Sharon stood and went to light some candles inside, checking on Sophie on the way through. We lit the fire and sat around it. We reminisced about the good old days and our times as children, telling each other stories.

I pushed out of the chair and stood up. 'Crap, in all the excitement of seeing Chance, we haven't had anyone on watch. I'll go first,' I said. I picked up the rifle and walked up the side of the house, then up the other driveway that faced the bush.

Even at dusk, the bush seemed eerie, as though someone or something was watching me. Maybe I was getting paranoid; who knows? Old mine shafts could be found in that section of bush. It was creepy to think about. It reminded me of Tolkien's Lord of the Rings and the orcs in their underground fester pits. Somehow, that seemed more appealing than zombies.

I walked about twenty yards into the bush, looking through the rifle's scope like a navy seal. I can thank alcohol for that. I returned to the road as the rain settled into a drizzle. I was grateful Sharon was still around and didn't leave when the chance came. It's suitable for Karly and all of us; family is what matters, especially during times like these.

Mum and Dad escaped to the safety of London, although I'm glad they left, considering what may lay ahead of us. Dan and Sophie are great, and so is Chance—good people to have around for the end of the world. I walked back down to the house and went through the door, heading straight for the bathroom to use the toilet.

When I arrived, I remembered that we had no power, so I headed back outside to the bush. Lucky for us, it was only number one that needed to happen. I finished and walked around the corner to the other side of the house. Chance emerged, beers in hand. We cheered each other, chinking bottles and taking a sip. 'So, what happened, man? Also, it's great you're here,' I said happily. 'Me too, brother, me too. Ahh, it went to crap up north. Our house got overrun, and I had to leave quickly. I honestly had no idea what to do or where to go, but then I remembered you saying, here is where you all would be, so here I am. The others didn't make it.' He smiled as always, but I could see sadness in his eyes.

'Well, you have us now, so that's all that matters; at least we're not zombies. Yet.' We talked a bit longer about random things: how we thought the zombies came to be, old pets we had loved, and what we thought the world would be like in a few years. I finished what remained in my beer and looked out over the dark eastern skies.

'Oh man, I need another one. I'm going to check on the group,' I said. 'Yeah, I'll come with you,' Chance said. 'Actually, I'll give this sentry thing a go. Hand me the rifle,' he said with an outstretched arm. 'No worries, man, it should be pretty chill this far south, but we must remain vigilant. We've all seen too many zombie films to realise that.'

MEDICATION MISSION

Karly and I were up early the following day, sipping black coffee and talking with Sharon in the kitchen. The aroma of freshly brewed coffee mingled with the cool morning air, creating a comforting start to our day. 'Do you even know how to kill a zombie, Nathan?' Sharon asked me, looking at Karly also. 'Pfft, easy. I have a TV. World War Z and Zombieland taught me how to be a warrior. Just incapacitate the beast by driving something into its brain,' I laughed, hugging Karly and then rubbing her head.

'Hey! I'm not a zombie,' she cried. Dan walked through the back door to where we were sitting. 'Hey Nath, can you come and have a look at Sophie? She looks terrible.' 'Yeah, of course, where is she?' I probed as I stood up. 'In the bedroom,' he replied, pointing down the hallway.

Sharon stopped me, holding out a face mask. I walked through the house to their room and knocked on the door. 'Hey Sophie, are you okay?' I asked as I opened the door. 'Wow, Sophie! You look awful.' Hearing the urgency in my voice, I composed myself and touched the poor girl on the arm and then her forehead. She looked very unwell as she raised her head from a bucket, which was one-third full of vomit.

The acrid smell hit me immediately, making me grimace. I left the door open slightly to allow some putrid smell to escape the room. Dan came up behind me and closed the door softly. 'Yeah, her temperature is 39.9 degrees. She hasn't been eating or drinking. She doesn't even feel like she can get up'. 'Oh God, I must have picked up something in Perth; I feel like crap,' she grimaced, closing her eyes and lowering her head back over the bucket. 'Maybe she has an infection,' Dan said.

I put my hand on her forehead. She was burning up, and her symptoms pointed towards an infection. 'Are you coughing up any green or yellow phlegm?' I quietly asked her. 'Yeah, I am,' her soft voice managed through pants and dry reaching. Each breath she took seemed laboured and painful. 'Ok, possibly an infection; she has no injuries though, and I'm not sure why she's spewing so much, but she needs antibiotics,' I said, looking up at Dan.

I grabbed the blood pressure cuff and wrapped it around her arm while placing the stethoscope in my ears. I made Dan write down her results; her blood pressure came back at 92/58, and she had a heart rate of 130 beats per minute. My brow furrowed, concerned by these unsettling numbers. I held the stethoscope on her back and listened to her lungs.

As I pressed the cold metal instrument against her skin, I heard an alarming sound—unequal air entry. It was as if one lung struggled to function correctly while the other attempted to compensate. I looked up at her, meeting her worried eyes with a reassuring smile. 'We're going to get you the help you need,' I said, hoping to instil some calm in her. But inside, I was racing to devise a plan to treat her and praying it wasn't too late.

'She's lost a lot of fluid from vomiting and has become dehydrated. I'm going to grab the medical kit out of the car', I said, standing up and heading out of the room. I walked out the back and to the car, pulling out my medical kit. As I turned back, Karly was by my side and touched my shoulder. 'Everything ok inside, babe?' she asked, looking concerned. 'We have a problem. Sophie's gone downhill really quickly, and it appears she has an infection of some kind. I'm going to put an intravenous line in her hand and give her some fluids because her blood pressure is quite low. I need to be mindful of sepsis as well. Let's grab my medicine bag from wherever you threw it after the zombie attacked me. Would you please? I need antibiotics.' I came to Karly's side to find the bag's contents strewn across the back seat as she was madly searching, reading the labels out loud. She looked up with what looked like tears in her eyes. 'Nathan, I, they, when,' she started, stumbling on her words. Finally, taking a breath, she said, 'They aren't in there. I mustn't have picked them up after the attack.'

'If she goes into shock, then we're in a world of trouble,' I continued over my shoulder as I walked back towards the house. I opened the medical box and rifled through it, pulling out a 20-gauge needle, a bag of saline, a Tegaderm, a bung, gauze, and a 10 mL saline flush. Dan was by Sophie's side, stroking her hair, which comforted her. I pulled out a mask for Dan and another for myself. 'Just a precaution in case she's infectious,' I said. 'Does that mean, like, infected? She won't turn, will she?' Dan shot back at me in a worried tone. 'No, no, like the bacterial infection type, not the zombie type,' I said reassuringly.

I gently touched Sophie on the arm. 'I'm going to put this needle in your hand, ok? After I give you some fluids, everything should start to feel much better. There is going to be a little scratch on the back of your hand, though,' I said to her, but she was so sick she barely nodded. I applied the tourniquet near her wrist. I opened an alcohol preparation pad and sanitised the back of her hand. As I took her hand, I said, 'Okay, just a little scratch,' and I pushed the sharp edge through her skin and into the vein. Blood flashed back into the indicator, and the catheter was advanced into the vein.

The bung was applied, the tourniquet loosened, and a Tegaderm clear window was placed over the top of the injection site. The 10 mL saline flush was drawn into a syringe and gently pushed into the bung opening, a successful placement as no resistance was felt. 'Perfect, got it in nicely. Dan, can you pass me that bag of fluids, please?'.

As I worked away, the bag was lobbed over, setting up everything for Sophie. Saline raced through the tube, and air bubbles were flushed out of it. I connected the line to the bung and set the drip rate. 'Right, I've got that bag to run over three hours, but we have a bigger problem than that,' I said quietly, looking at Dan. 'She needs antibiotics, Dan. They were lost at the house when the zombie attacked me, and the only place we're going to get them is at a hospital. I'd say the local chemist, but I highly doubt that stuff would be left lying around; surely, it would have been cleared by now. Come outside with me,' I said, gesturing for him to follow me.

As we left the room, Karly stood there, anxiously waiting. 'How did it go?' Karly said, squeezing Dan's arm reassuringly. 'Yeah, she's hooked up to an intravenous line, so she should feel a little better. Someone will have to keep an eye on her. More importantly, she needs antibiotics.'

We entered the kitchen, where the others were waiting. 'Sharon, have you got any antibiotics in the house?' I asked. 'I'm not sorry, hun. Well, I'm sure I don't, but let me check.' 'Donnybrook Hospital may have been cleared out, but it's worth a shot. What sort of medicine do you need?' Karly asked. 'I think she has a chest infection that may cause systemic issues, so preferably Amoxycillin or Augmentin Duo Forte will work the best, and if you find Ceftazidime, grab that too'. I spoke quickly, knowing the urgency in my voice conveyed the gravity of our situation. 'Ceftaza what?' Karly asked me. 'All good, I'll write it down.'

We discussed our options. It would be the first time we had ventured out of the house and back in the direction of town and possible trouble. 'Hell. I'll drive around Donnybrook Hospital and look to see if they have any there,' Chance said. Sharon spoke up quickly and said, 'Yeah, I'll go with Chance and have a look. It's only a smaller hospital, so there shouldn't be any drama, and I know my way around. You guys stay here. We won't be long.'

I really hoped Donnybrook Hospital would work out, but I dreaded the thought of going to Bunbury due to its greater population. Nowhere near as large as Perth, though big enough to pose a real threat should the zombies have made it there. 'Ok, if Donnybrook doesn't have antibiotics, the closest hospital to us that will have this stuff, hopefully, will be in Bunbury. We can head there through the back roads to Boyanup if we have to, get what we need, and come straight back,' I said to Karly.

'Dan and Sharon can stay here and look after Sophie, and we'll head up with Chance when he and Sharon get back,' I said, looking at the group. Karly nodded in agreement, her face determined. It sounds like a plan. We'll have to be careful on those back roads, though. Who knows what we might run into,' she said, her voice serious.

Sharon got in the driver's seat as Chance slammed the passenger door shut. 'Can you remember what medication Nathan said to grab?' Sharon asked. Her hands gripped the steering wheel, her knuckles white with anxiety. 'Amoxycillin and some other drug; I honestly think whatever we find there will be a miracle,' Chance replied as Sharon pulled up to the stop sign. 'Sounds like Nathan, always optimistic,' Sharon chuckled. 'You're telling me,' Chance replied.

Donnybrook sure was quiet that morning, with no people nearby. 'Love these old country homes,' Chance said, peering out the window. 'Yeah, it's so nice down this part of the world', Sharon replied. The ute pulled up to the Donnybrook Hospital. 'This is the hospital. Really?' Chance said, pointing out the window. 'Regional Australian hospital, what'd you expect?' Sharon chuckled. 'I'm surprised the place even has a door at the front,' Chance commented as Sharon shook her head and rolled her eyes.

They got out of the car and approached the front door. Birds chirped in the trees overhead. 'We should be careful going in,' Chance began to say at the same time as a brick went sailing through the glass panel, shattering the glass into the hospital administration area. 'That works too,' Chance said, shrugging his shoulders. They both walked in, scanning the small reception area. 'Let's look around first,' Sharon said. 'Yeah, let's just search as we do that. The place looks pretty locked up.'

Chance and Sharon stood there in silence for a few moments. 'Righto, it seems clear; just be vigilant,' Sharon said. The main area had little to no use. Chance grabbed a box and threw in some spare bandages, splints, and Paracetamol. 'Told you,' Sharon said, emerging from a back room, 'gutted, nothing left. Oh well, worth a shot.' 'Let's head back then,' Chance replied as they left the building.

Around ten minutes later, they pulled into the driveway. Sharon and Chance got out, their faces sharing the disappointment; the weight of their fruitless search was evident. 'Nothing, literally nothing, was left in that hospital. And I mean nothing at all, man,' Chance said sadly. 'Ok, well, let's not wait any longer; Bunbury it is then,' Karly said. The three of us got into my ute. Karly and I had our weapons, though Chance was unarmed, apart from his belt knife. I reversed out of the driveway onto the street and took off. 'Bunbury isn't far away. It should take roughly thirty minutes as long as nothing unexpected happens.' I glanced at my watch. It was only 930 a.m.

The morning was still young. 'Yep, sweet. Beautiful day after all that rain.' Given the current circumstances, I was glad to be out in the sunshine because I felt scared being out at night. It felt like our lives were more threatened at night—weird people out and about and zombies. Urgh, gross, I thought to myself.

Goosebumps ran through me despite the warmth of the sun beaming today, with not a single cloud in the sky. It's a welcome change from the rain we've been seeing lately. 'You used to live here, hey Nath?' Chance asked from the back seat. 'I never did, but mum and dad did! They loved it there. It was great always visiting them; I wish I could drive past and see the house. I could have grabbed Dad's home distilling gear,' I replied. 'I used to come to Bunbury a fair bit when I was at school,' Karly said. 'The Donnybrook school only went to grade ten, so senior years were in Bunbury. Victoria Street is nice to see, and I stayed in a few hotels in the past,' she said, gazing out the window at the trees whipping past.

'The speedway coming up is sweet; there are plenty of events on there, like dirt bikes and car races,' Karly said. 'Did you come for the dirt bike races?' I asked. 'Yeah, plenty of times, never a dull moment,' she said with a huge grin. 'I'm not a fan of dirt bikes. I'd legit kill myself by accident,' I said. Karly laughed. 'You just need to get in touch with your inner daredevil, Nath.' 'I'd have one of those cool old CBRs if I had a bike again,' Chance replied. I couldn't help but feel a twinge of envy as I thought about Chance's love for motorcycles. I had always wanted to ride one but never had the courage to try.

We drove on towards Bunbury, past the speedway on the left. The familiar sight brought a wave of nostalgia. 'Damn, I used to love going there and watching the bikes race back when I was younger,' Karly said. As we came around the bend, a military Humvee tore towards us, veering onto the wrong side of the road and flicking its high-beam lights at us.

I jumped on the brakes, bringing the car to a halt. I could feel Karly gripping my arm as Chance whispered, 'Seriously.' The military Humvee pulled up close to us. Both the front and rear passenger windows were rolled down.

A microphone boomed to life. 'Driver and passengers, hands out the windows and keep them there as we approach, or we will open fire'. We all put our hands out as heavily armed military personnel walked towards us, rifles drawn. 'What do you think you're doing?' a heavily muscled man asked us through Karly's window.

His voice was gruff and no-nonsense. 'Our friend is sick, and we are trying to get antibiotics, hopefully,' I blurted out, attempting to finish the sentence before I was interrupted. 'You are not permitted any further. We have lost control of greater Bunbury and are setting Deflector Points up ahead, so turn around and go back to wherever you came from,' the soldier barked. 'But we really need antibi--,' Chance was immediately interrupted by the soldier at my side of the car.

'Turn around, or you will be detained. Driver, leave now!' he yelled at me, raising his rifle to my head. I put the car in reverse and backed away slowly before doing a U-turn and driving off. 'Alright, here's the situation. We're trying to get to the northwest side of the speedway where the hospital is. It shouldn't be too much of a problem. We park the ute somewhere out of sight, cut through the speedway, past the airstrip around the back of College Grove, past the university, and into the hospital grounds,' Karly explained. 'Ok, that sounds good, but what about the soldiers?' Chance replied.

'If any soldiers are out there, then they will be at the deflector point unless you have a better plan.' I thought the plan through, and all I could think was, 'What the hell is a deflector point?" Chance shrugged his shoulders and looked at me with a stupid look on his face. 'Sorry, does it look like I work in the army?' he asked, laughing with his usual grin.

Karly got out of the car and opened the big steel fence gate. Large advertisement signs dwarfed the raceway, along with tall lighting towers. I pulled the ute around the back of a building, parking between two abandoned cars, to try and conceal it. I got out and walked around the vehicle. 'Right, the car's locked; let's go. We need to be super alert while this happens. I dread to think about what would happen if we got caught,' I said.

It was quite a dense bushland behind the speedway, though a clearing up ahead made us all stop quickly. A helicopter was coming to land beside two military jets, which were parked up.

Around a dozen soldiers were standing near the hanger on the far side. We watched as the team from the helicopter made their way towards the hangar, escorted by the group of soldiers. There was an air of urgency and tension among the group, and we couldn't help but wonder what was happening.

'Let's just keep to the bush as much as possible and get past the airport,' Karly said, barely audible against the helicopter's noise. The dense foliage offered some cover, and the thick underbrush slowed our progress. We continued for about five minutes, noticing we were at the boundary fence of the airstrip. The boundary was marked by tall wire fencing, partially obscured by the overgrown vegetation that clung to it.

We glanced back, checking we weren't being followed or noticed, before quickly running through the bush. The bush around us was teeming with life—the rustle of leaves underfoot, the distant call of birds, and the occasional crack of a twig breaking. Around ten minutes later, all three of us stopped, bent over, panting, trying to catch our breath. 'Holy shit, I'm unfit,' I said, looking at Chance. 'Yeah, same here. Too much booze, I reckon,' he replied while Karly laughed. 'What do you two mean, the absolute picture of health,' she said sarcastically through pants of breath.

After catching our breath, we stood near the bush edge, scoping out the road. 'About thirty metres, we must run across the road in the open. You two going to be alright doing that?' Karly asked, a mocking smile spreading across her face. 'Yeah, one at a time, I think, in case one gets caught. Anyone disagree?' I asked. 'Nah, that's easy. It'll be me that gets caught if anyone,' Chance chuckled.

We waited a moment longer, and I ran across the road with no sign of anyone. The sound of my feet pounding the dirt road seemed unnaturally loud. I made it to the bush and peered up and down the road. 'Clear?' I yelled. 'All clear. Karly's next,' Chance called back. Karly took off from the bush cover and made it across the road.

After Karly, Chance followed quickly. I'd never seen Chance run before, and it was quite amusing, almost awkward, particularly when he stumbled and his arms flailed before catching balance.

HIGH ABOVE THE HORDE

'See, not so hard, princess,' Chance announced, and Karly rolled her eyes. We walked another ten minutes or so through bushland to the back of the hospital. The grass was long and itchy to walk through, and the morning was heating up. My shirt was becoming sweaty from the heat, and my heart was racing a million miles an hour.

Crickets jumped in the long grass as we disturbed their morning rest. 'What's that noise?' I said to Chance. He didn't reply. I caught up to him and noticed he was cringing and slightly tipping his head to the right side, listening. I did the same. It didn't sound like the wind, and it wasn't that rustling sound dry trees make. It sounded more like something alive and moving.

A feral cat appeared briefly before sprinting away from us. 'That scared me for a second,' Chance said. We stopped, just in the confines of the bush, as the hospital stood before us. The building loomed ahead, a stark, imposing structure against dense foliage. The hospital, a two-story brick building with white-framed windows, looked unnervingly quiet and abandoned.

The silence around it was almost deafening, broken only by the occasional rustle of leaves and distant bird calls. 'Ok, through the back door is a garbage chute. That should take us down to the chiller room. We don't want to walk around the front if we're spotted. We also don't want to go any further than the chiller room, and we need to be extremely stealthy and quiet. We stick together and stick to this plan,' Karly said. 'Where to from there?' I asked.

'Well, I'm not sure, but that'll get us in. I'd hoped you would have some sort of idea where they kept the drugs.' 'Ok, I'll have to get a basic look at what's around. It shouldn't be too hard, but there will more than likely be soldiers in here, I reckon. Also, I know a pharmacy is attached to the hospital somewhere, but that'll surely be heavily guarded. Medication will be in other locations around the wards; I just need to find where, but when I see it, I'll know,' I said.

We cautiously approached the back door, bracing ourselves to push it. The old, weathered door creaked slightly as it swung open, unexpectedly unlocked.

I didn't think it'd be that easy, but low and behold, it was unlocked. We all entered the hallway, and just like that, we were in! The usual hustle and bustle of a hospital, now silent, was uncomfortably quiet. The door to the chute was sealed shut, so we decided on an alternative route.

'Ok, let's stay together and search rooms as a group; no splitting up.' We crept into the next ward, praying there were no soldiers as we entered the double doors. No one is in sight. The hospital lay bare, usually full of patients, visitors, and staff. It was a weird sight.

Gurneys and medical carts stood abandoned, with paper charts scattered on desks, left in haste. We turned the corner and started searching through the rooms. The air was stale, filled with the faint scent of disinfectant and the underlying mustiness of neglect. I kept my eyes on Karly and Chance. I glanced around all the rooms. 'Where could it be? Maybe they moved it all,' Karly said; her voice was a hushed whisper, tinged with frustration. 'No, there must be some of what we need here somewhere.'

As we continued to search, a large roar, more like a screech, echoed down the hallways. My eyes widened in fear as I shot around to look at the others. 'What was that!?' I mouthed. Their faces mirrored my terror, eyes wide and breaths held.

We stayed there, crouched, frozen in fear. I crept over to the door, gesturing for the others to follow. I peered around the corner and down the hallway but could see nothing. I quietly moved out of the room towards two large double doors with round glass windows in them and rose slowly to look through.

A trolley with a white blanket over something large and wriggling burst through the doors at the other end, wheeled by four soldiers. Their movements were urgent, almost frantic, as they steered the trolley. They trundled it into the room and out of sight. The creature roared again, a terrible and horrifying noise. A glass panel in the door exploded, and a soldier came through it, slamming into the wall across the hall. Gunshots rang out as weapons were unloaded on whatever it was they'd brought in.

Two soldiers came out, speaking frantically on their radios. 'Bunbury One, Bunbury One, this is Hotel Team Seven. Two soldiers are down in the research unit. Over'. A moment of silence was followed by a response: 'All units, all units, proceed to the north-east deflector point. We are losing control. Authority to use lethal force approved. This is not a drill.' 'Bunbury One acknowledged. On our way,' the soldier yelled into the radio. They ran off without a further word, leaving the other soldier lying motionless in a pool of blood.

'What is in that room? I really need to see this,' I said, gently pushing through the doors. Karly suddenly grabbed me. 'Are you out of your mind? Don't bloody go up there. It could be alive, whatever it is!' she exclaimed. 'Just trust me, this is important,' I whispered back. I glanced back at Chance, who nodded, telling me he had my back. I crept further along the hallway. The heat from the outside sun and the lack of air conditioning made the hallway stifle, and beads of sweat lined my hairline.

I approached and opened the door slowly to reveal a giant, writhing mass of something under the sheet. The source of the screaming, but what was it? I wondered. I walked closer to the door, awed by the size of whatever it was. Chance quickly joined me. Bullet holes were peppered up one side of the sheet, and another soldier lay against the back wall in a large puddle of blood from her severe, gruesome injuries.

'What in the hell is it?' I said, staring at the table. 'I don't have a clue, man; aren't you the paramedic?' 'Geez, I must have missed that unit while attending university. My apologies. How to identify aliens and zombies. I'm sure it'll be in the future curriculum, though,' I replied. The attempt at humour was hollow, a defence mechanism against the terror we faced.

'This is an absorber type by the looks of it. See the large, whip-like tentacles and the huge ovals on them. It literally feeds off other zombies and gets larger. I think they're slow, but the bigger they get, the larger the whip gets.' I remembered hearing about these; the first one mentioned on the news was being marketed as a "new hope" or solution. Anywhere there was an outbreak, they planned to transport absorbers and let them eat the others, and once done, the government would kill them. The question was, where did they come from? 'We need to get the hell out of here, but medication first. Anyone see a dispensary unit anywhere?' I asked the group as my hope began to fade. 'Yeah, there's one inside the room back there,' Chance replied.

We peered around the doorway and exited to the left, following the wall to the next room. As we entered, the dispenser unit was immediately to our left. 'Paramedic Nathan, you'd have a password for this, wouldn't you?' Chance asked stupidly, looking to Karly for support, her eyes still darting back to the creature's room.

I stood up and walked over to it. 'If I have ever heard a river of shit flow from someone's mouth, it is your chance,' I said as my eyes scanned over the unit. 'This is going to be hard to get into,' Chance said. As he said this, I stepped back, kicked out with all my strength, and toppled the dispenser over, spilling nearly all its contents on the floor. 'Damn, that's going to be a hell of a hard job to replace,' Chance said in dismay. Scattered on the floor were needles, medications, and liquids, as well as what I was looking for—antibiotics.

'Yes! Right, we are looking for a drug called Augmentin Duo or Amoxicillin tablet, but preferably injectable stuff; don't worry about that other one I said earlier. I said as we panned our hands through the contents. We found it eventually on the other side. 'Okay, plenty more here could help us, so grab whatever you can carry too,' I said. 'Ok, what about here?' Chance was pointing at a shelf. 'Nope, that is just any other over-the-counter crap,' I replied, grabbing the bottles and packets of medication vials. Get stuff with "prescription only" written on it.

The air was filled with the sound of machine guns firing somewhere well away from the hospital. I suddenly hear a small smash sound behind me as Karly accidentally broke a vial on the floor with the weight of her foot. I turned around and noticed the broken glass. 'Be careful, Karly; the vials are made of glass, which is really fine,' I said as I picked up the remaining vials. 'I'm all good,' she whispered back quickly.

'Let's go!' I said firmly, opening the door. We ran down the hallway and back through the double doors, back past the chute and to the rear doors. I cracked the door and peered through, slowly pushing it open. We all exited without a word said. We ran across toward the small building next door. 'Nathan, we have to look at whatever that is,' Chance said over the now near-deafening sound of machine gun fire and the occasional explosion.

Karly pointed to a ladder on the side of the building. 'Can we go, please? I don't want to see this.' 'Yes, we won't be long.' Karly drew her gun to stand guard, unwilling to see what was coming. The ladder was a service ladder, luckily still in decent condition. Chance went first, racing up the rungs. I pulled myself up behind him and onto the roof.

I noticed Chance standing there with his mouth on the floor as I appeared. Tanks and soldiers formed a blockade about one hundred metres away. Beyond that, thousands, and I mean literally thousands, of zombies trudged towards them. There was a pause as the soldiers appeared to be having difficulty controlling them. The soldiers started shooting again, mowing through the zombies. The tidal wave of zombies continued streaming as far as the eye could see. 'We can't do anything; we have to go now, Chance,' I said frantically.

Chance didn't appear to hear me. He was sitting down now, his head in his hands. I rushed over and grabbed his arm. 'We can't stay, Chance;

now come on!' I yelled as I shook him again. Chance's eyes were still fixed on the carnage unfolding at the deflector point.

As we stood, I, too, was paralysed with fear as we watched the zombies rush through the defensive lines of the military. They were everywhere, swarming like ants, relentlessly hungry for flesh. Screams of terror and pain filled the air, mingled with the groans of the undead. It was hard to tell who was alive and who wasn't, as bodies lay scattered on the ground, some still twitching in their final moments. The smell of death and decay was overwhelming, making me gag and cover my nose with my shirt.

My attention was drawn to a helicopter in the air near the right side of the checkpoint, which seemed to be in trouble. The aircraft struggled to maintain altitude, swaying violently as it dipped and weaved through the air. The sound of its rotors chopping erratically filled the air, a harbinger of impending disaster. Something was dangling from the bottom of the helicopter, but it was hard to determine what it was. Suddenly, a loud explosion ripped through the air, shattering the tension. The helicopter's erratic dance ended abruptly as it plummeted towards the ground.

The chopper hit the ground with a deafening crash. The impact sent shockwaves through the air and a blinding flash as it exploded. A bright orange ball of flame erupted from the wreckage; the heat was intense even from a distance.

Shrapnel and debris flew in all directions, the sound of metal twisting and fuel igniting, creating a symphony of destruction. A plume of black smoke rose into the sky. I tapped Chance on the shoulder as I approached the ladder. The military was obviously losing the battle and now was the time to leave. We had a decent amount of ground to cover to return to the ute.

'Karly, are you okay?' I asked as I got to the bottom of the ladder. 'Yes, I am. What did you see?' 'Lots, we need to get moving; it's a slaughterhouse back there.' All three of us ran around the side of the building and headed back towards the bush. I led the way and made a point with Karly and Chance. I heard the low sound of the gunfire about thirty metres to our left, and I assumed they were shooting at more zombies heading in our direction. We approached the opening.

'We don't have much further to go, but we have to get on the road and then to the other side of it,' I yelled. Karly and I both moved ahead, but neither of us said anything. 'Right, let's just all run. We don't have time to wait to go one at a time,' I said, panting. The others agreed, and we all took off across the road. We made it across and continued without slowing through the bush.

A branch whipped my face, instantly inducing a painful burning sensation, but I had to keep going. Around five minutes later, we could see the ute. I hurriedly reached for the door handle and opened it. I got in the passenger seat, gesturing to the others to 'hurry'. Karly got in the back seat, and Chance took the driver seat. There were no discussions, no questions, and no arguments. It was a rush of adrenaline.

'Karly, if we are going to make it, I need you to guide me there. I don't know where the hell we are,' Chance said between heavy breaths. 'Just drive! I'll guide you!' Karly blurted out, buckling up her seatbelt. Chance floored the accelerator, and dirt spat from the back tyres. 'Turn right here. There's a small road on the left-hand side,' Karly directed. Chance nodded and made the turn. We were now on North Road. 'Keep following this road straight through the roundabout up ahead,' she said.

We were on the main road that would take us back to Donnybrook. 'Holy crap, that was a shit tonne of zombies. I think we're in trouble,' I said, still panting through breaths. 'Yeah, that reminded me of Perth when I left. I'm not sure how I made it down here without running into a herd that big,' Chance said. 'Let's get back to Donnybrook, sort Sophie out, and see how things are in town'. 'Yeah, we will always use a sentry now, even during the day, and go for quick scouts around town,' Karly replied more as a suggestion.

We felt the car's rumbling as we raced down the road, looking back to see large fireballs filling the sky a fair distance off. 'I love the smell of napalm in the morning,' Chance said. 'Nathan, have you still got the drone in the back?' Karly asked. 'Oh, shit yeah, Chance, pull over.' The Ute came to a skidding stop on the side of the road as I jumped out, heading around the back of the Ute to grab the drone case. "Mavic Air 2" was written on it. I pulled it out and took out my phone. 'How do you have a charge on your phone, man?' Chance asked. 'Well, see, that thing we've been driving in, with the wheels, still charges phones too, funnily enough,' I replied sarcastically. 'Have you tried?' 'Yes, there's no reception anywhere or internet. I have tried making calls, but it's all down. Nothing works; trust me,' I said, interrupting Chance. I connected the phone to the drone and attached it to the controller.

The drone whirred to life—quite a noisy little thing, but with good flight time and range. 'How much charge is in the batteries?' Karly asked. 'So far, about twelve minutes, and it can go 5 km at a max speed of 65 km. I haven't really tried it too much,' I replied. 'Well, let's see how it goes. At least we can gauge what we're potentially up against.' The drone took off straight, about ten metres above the treetops.

It cruised effortlessly through the air like there was no breeze at all. The drone sped past the last of the bush and into the clearing. I slowed it down to stationary so we could have a good look around. There were literally tens of thousands of zombies in huge herds that made one massive one. 'Holy. Fuck,' I said, stunned. Military units still fought the hordes, and fires burned in overrun areas.

It was a devastating sight to witness those poor people. A lone rocket deployed from somewhere behind the field of view of the drone glided over the hordes and slammed into a large group of zombies, sending bodies and body parts flying. The military units were severely outnumbered and overwhelmed, and as we watched, some began to retreat. 'I suggest we get some distance down the road before any zombies head this way,' I said, pressing the return button on the drone screen.

'This is bad. This is bad. What are we going to do?' Karly said, looking at us for a miracle. 'I don't know, one step at a time. Let's just head home for now,' I replied. The drone zipped down and landed on the road in front of me. I picked it up and put it in the case, returning it to the Ute.

93

HOOK, LINE AND SINKER

I got into the driver's seat and turned the vehicle on. This was now becoming too real, I thought to myself. There are so many zombies that we wouldn't stand a chance against them. We possibly had a few days left at Sharon's, and then inevitably, we'd have to retreat to the camping ground. How long would we have there? Where do I go from there? All these questions raced through my head as I sped down the road.

We could head even further south if needed, but we would wind up somewhere near Albany and against the coast, with nowhere else to go. Of all the stuff we relocated, why did we not consider a boat? We were too far inland from the coast, I guess, but damn, why didn't we think of that? We pulled into Donnybrook and drove along the main street. A few random people were walking around armed. They wearily looked at us as we drove through. I drove to Sharon's house and reversed into the driveway.

Dan came out to greet us. He was pacing, his hair ruffled and clearly concerned. 'She's going downhill really quick, man,' he said. I grabbed the antibiotics from the pile of drugs. 'Is my medic bag still in the room?' I asked. 'Yeah, I haven't touched anything since you guys left,' Dan replied as we walked up the stairs and into the house. Dan was a few steps ahead, anxious to get back to Sophie.

In the darkened room. My mask did little to hide the stench of vomit.

'Man, can you open a window? We need to air this room out,' I said as I plunged the sharp through the rubber bung on top of the antibiotic vial. Sophie looked as pale as ever, making a raspy noise with every breath she took. I just hoped it wasn't too late, I thought as I administered the medication.

'This should take effect pretty quickly. I'd expect to see improvement by tomorrow morning,' I said, hoping I was coming across as confident, throwing the syringe in the bin. 'Thanks again, Nathan; I really appreciate you doing this for us,' Dan said. 'No problem; just pray it works. I'm not an antibiotic expert, but I think it will do the trick.' I stood and left the room, walking down the hallway and outside, where Karly and Chance were waiting.

'She's going to be okay. Hopefully', I said. Karly came over and hugged me, pulling me close to her. Her smell distracted me from the world falling apart for a few brief moments. 'I love you. We will get through this,' she said. 'You're amazing,' I replied into her ear.

'Right, about that major issue, those herds. I think we will be alright at the camping spot. It's remote, and the terrain would be difficult for zombies to traverse,' I said. 'Yeah, that or we will get an avalanche of zombies coming in unexpectedly at some point,' Chance said.

Sharon walked over with a friendly smile on her face. 'Sharon, we'll have to leave here at some point very soon. Zombie numbers are far greater than we expected, and I don't really have any other solution right now,' I said. She looked sad momentarily while she took in what I had said before restoring her comforting smile.

'Yeah, ok, well, I trust what you guys have set up at the campsite, so let's just do things one step at a time,' she replied. 'Right, well, let's get the temporary stuff packed up. We must get the ute packed with the large eski and the food supplies. I think that's a priority. We need our supplies,' I said. 'If you guys don't care, Mum and I will continue to watch the perimeter,' Karly said.

'Yep, that sounds good. I'll start sorting the food. We should stay here while we can, especially while Sophie is recovering, but we leave at the first sign of trouble before it's too late. Sentry duty is more important now than ever, so go for it,' I said. I walked over and gently kissed Karly before heading inside with the others.

I slid the 152-litre eski out of the pantry, and Chance helped lift it. We walked it down the end of the house to the far room, where all the supplies were. We lowered the eski to the ground and opened the lid. 'I'm stressing about how many zombies there were in Bunbury, mate,' Chance said, looking at the floor. 'How many is "many"?' Dan had appeared at the door.

I looked up at him, shaking my head, before responding. 'Thousands, man, probably closer to tens of thousands.' 'Jesus, that's not good; what a shitshow. Whose idea was it to stay again?' he asked.

No one spoke for a minute as we decided to stay. Why didn't we leave when we had a chance? What made us think we would be safe and put our trust in a government that had contaminated our country with zombies when we were one of the few safe places in the world? We began piling food into the eski. 'Let's quarter fill it, take it out to the ute so it's not too heavy, and walk the rest out.' 'Yep, that sounds good,' the guys replied.

I looked at a bag of spiral pasta and laughed. 'Who would've thought, lads, here at the end of everything, and we somehow survived this far anyway?' Chance held out his fist for a fist pump, which I acknowledged. 'Yeah, man, it's crazy. I wouldn't want to do it with anyone else. Peace, love, and zombie attacks, lads,' Dan replied with a wink. 'Nathan, seriously, smoked oysters? Doesn't your butthole turn into a putrid toxic wasteland when you eat these?' Chance asked. I laughed, too. 'Want to starve or eat ass? Just don't tell Karly, or she'll hide them from me.' I replied.

Funny how, after everything we had just witnessed, we chatted and laughed, trying to keep the mood light. When the eski was about a quarter full, we carried it out the side door to the ute and lifted it into the tray. It wasn't too heavy, but still, it was heavy to lift.

'I think I saw a wheelbarrow in the shed earlier,' Chance said. Dan went and got the wheelbarrow from the shed, and we used it to carry the rest of the food from the room out to the ute. Karly and Sharon appeared from around the side of the ute. 'How's it going, Nathan?' Sharon asked. 'Yeah, getting there. One more load and we will be done.' 'Any signs of zombies out there, Sharon?' Chance asked. 'Nope, not around these parts; very quiet.' 'Peace of mind would be nice, but that probably won't happen though,' I said. 'Come on, let's get this done,' Dan encouraged, reminding us of our mission.

It was around 5 p.m. when the ute was fully loaded. All the supplies were where they needed to be in case a rapid exit was required. Chance emerged from the house with some whisky and walked over to us. 'Good work, lads! Let's chill for a bit and relax while we still can,' he said. I took a swig of the whiskey. 'A nice cold beer would be good about now.

I loaded Sharon's small generator as a backup for the campsite, so no joy,' I said. Dan laughed. 'How's the irony? We're at a house and can't have a cold beer yet. When we get to the campsite, there are cold beers all around. Pretty sure there's a fridge in the Winnebago, too,' he said.

'That'd be right. We need to find Chance a weapon. The machete is too close range, and your knife is really only a last resort,' I said. I took another swig of whisky and eyeballed Dan. He was clearly worrying about Sophie, so I gave him a nudge to bring him back to the conversation. 'Yep, I'm sure we will find something,' he replied, taking a swig of his whiskey.

The setting sun painted a red and orange pattern on the horizon as the wind blew gently over us. A comforting feeling permeated as we all silently stood there on the driveway. Tomorrow, we would face whatever was ahead of us, but for now, nothing seemed to interrupt us in this moment of calm.

'Chance and I can do a sentry watch tonight if you all want to get some rest first,' Dan said. 'Ok, sweet, thanks, gents. I'll check on Sophie on the way through. Come wake us, and Nathan and I will do a second watch,' Karly replied. 'Sounds good,' I was already thinking of the comfort of bed. We walked inside and went to the kitchen, quickly scoffing down some canned food. I don't think any of us were really fussed at that point and were keen to get some sleep. I said goodnight to Sharon before going to the room and undressing. I would love a shower, I thought, smelling my underarms.

We had buckets of rainwater and a camp shower, but it would have to wait until tomorrow morning, I thought to myself as Karly entered the room and closed the door. 'Sophie is looking much better already; good work, babe,' she said. We climbed into bed and faced each other. 'What's on your mind, babe?' Karly enquired. 'I'm a little stressed about what we saw in Bunbury, if I'm totally honest. That was a lot of zombies. It really brought our position into sharp focus for me. We need a backup plan. I think we may be right at the camping ground, but what if we aren't?' I replied.

Karly looked at me and smiled. 'We need to be prepared for worst-case scenarios. Hmm, I wonder...' Karly suddenly shot upright. 'What about Rottnest Island!' she exclaimed. I grinned and replied, 'holy shit, holy shit! That would make so much sense. There's no way zombies could reach us there!' Rottnest is an island off the coast of Perth, about a thirty-minute ferry ride away.

'But we need to remember how good the camp setup is. It would take a lot to try to get to Rottnest. We don't have a boat, and the campsite has so much equipment. It is an option to keep in the back of our minds, though,' she said proudly. This idea eased my worries slightly. It was a possible alternative and potentially a very smart one. We hugged and closed our eyes, drifting off to sleep almost immediately.

I woke suddenly, looking around, although the room was still dark. I could've sworn I'd heard someone laughing. I continued to lay there listening, partly scared, partly intrigued as to what it was that woke me or if I was dreaming. Then I heard it again—unmistakably, a laugh. I quietly got out of bed, grabbed my Beretta, and walked down the hallway. The laughter rang out again, and it appeared to be Chance.

I walked outside into the cool early morning air, guessing it must have been around 4 a.m. Dan and Chance stood against my ute, snorting about something. 'Hey!' I startled them. They both swung around; Chance almost lost his footing and stumbled sideways. 'Are you drunk, Chance!?' I asked. 'He is, but I'm not. He only started having some swigs again about an hour ago. Did we wake you?' Dan asked.

'I'm not going to give you two a lecture, but there are potentially thousands of zombies heading our way, and what is Chance going to be able to kill besides himself in this state?' I gestured towards a stumbling Chance, gripping the ute to steady himself. 'But whatever, go to bed, you knobs! Karly and I will take it from here,' I said, trying to calm myself.

I knew that fighting amongst us would cause so many more issues, but after what we had seen today so close to home, it was hard to keep the angry undertone out of my voice. Dan helped Chance as he staggered inside. I walked back inside and into the room, gently waking Karly. 'Hey, it's our turn to take watch,' I said miserably. 'Urgh, is it cold outside?' Karly's croaky morning voice returned. 'No, it's a nice morning. The sun's not yet, but you shouldn't need a jumper. I'll see you outside,' I said, getting up off the bed to head back outside, hoping the boys hadn't missed anything.

It was a quiet morning, and the country air was crisp and fresh as I breathed in. Karly joined me a moment later, still half asleep and yawning. Her hair was tousled, and she rubbed her eyes, trying to shake off the remnants of sleep. As I looked over, she grabbed my hand, turned her head to the side, and said, 'Okay, spit it out.' When I remained silent, she said, 'Nathan, I know that look. I have seen it a million times when the TV remote won't work. You're annoyed about something, so spit it out.' I briefly told her about Chance's drunken state, although Karly remained calm, easing my mind. I could see from the small crinkle in her nose that she was annoyed. 'C'mon, let's do a perimeter walk. I doubt the guys could have done one for a while,' I said, standing.

As we walked around, Karly asked, 'How long do you think we have here?' 'I think at least another twenty-four hours, surely. At the first sign of any zombie activity, we bail out of the campsite. What do you think?' I asked. 'Yeah, that makes sense. What did you want to do today?' I thought about it briefly and replied, 'I don't know. What is there to do but wait and watch?' 'Oh, I know! Let's go hit up Macca's farm. Remember that landing I showed you? You can get Marron from there! Plus, we need more guns, and I know where the gun cabinet is. They took off a while ago, so we should be safe,' Karly replied. No way was I going to argue with a feed of marron because they are amazing to eat. 'Umm yes! That sounds like a great idea,' I replied enthusiastically.

I suddenly became excited because I loved fishing and catching marron, and I knew for a fact that Karly did, too. Over the next few hours, Karly and I talked between ourselves about the good old days, watched the sun rise, and even engaged in a bit of flirting. It was nice spending some quiet time alone with her.

Around 7 a.m., Sharon appeared on the deck, announcing her arrival with a loud shout directed towards us. 'You two lovebirds want some toast?' Without hesitation, we signalled our affirmative response with a thumbs up and then slowly returned to the house. Once there, we eagerly began to munch on the freshly heated toast that had been prepared for us over the fire.

It was a simple yet satisfying meal of Vegemite and butter as usual. 'What's on for today, kids?' Sharon asked, sipping her coffee. 'We were discussing it earlier. I think we have a chill day and head to Macca's farm to get some supplies and marron to eat for dinner. Pretty sure we could all do with a nice crustacean feed,' Karly replied. 'Oh, awesome! Yeah, bloody oath!' Sharon said ecstatically.

'I've got two yabby traps in the shed and two crab pots if you want to use them. I don't want to rely on all their marron nets still being in good order,' Sharon said. I think she was more excited than us. The rest of the group joined us as they woke up, and we shared the plan for the day. Chance wasn't as excited about catching Marron as everyone else, and I wondered whether he had a headache. We agreed he and Sophie would stay at Sharon's, leaving only a single vehicle, especially with Sophie still not being 100%.

Chance was happy with the arrangement despite being hungover.

With some colour back on her face, Sophie was finally looking far better than the previous day. If anything happened, he would drive straight to where we would be after Karly showed him how to get there on a map. Macca's farm was east of Donnybrook, straight down Boyup-Brooke Road, and in the Glen Mervyn area.

We all got dressed and gathered what we needed for the day before meeting at our cars. Karly wanted to drive, so Sharon sat in the back of the tray with me while Dan sat up front with Karly. The road was flanked by gravel on either side, and the towering gum trees soared above us, making us feel small in comparison.

The scenery was classic Australia, with lush green fields stretching out on some farms while others appeared dry and brown. The occasional cow grazed lazily in the fields, and we couldn't help but marvel at the vast expanse of farmland that seemed to stretch out endlessly before us.

'How are you and Karly going, Nath? You look after each other, ok?' Sharon yelled over the wind whipping against our faces. 'Yeah! I think we're going well, given the crap circumstances at the end of the world, but there's nowhere else I'd rather be. I'm grateful for everyone that's here, including you!' I replied, sharing a smile with her. 'How about you? Are you going, okay?' 'Yeah, yeah, well, what do you do? Things could be worse,' Sharon replied.

I had a worrying thought flash through my brain momentarily, remembering back to yesterday's herd encounter. Don't stress, I told myself. Karly applied the brakes, a little too hard. Sharon and I turned to each other and burst out in laughter. Karly could 4WD like a natural; she just had a brain for off-roading, but get her in traffic, and she hated it.

We had an ongoing joke about her hitting kerbs and calling them "whoopsies." Through laughter, Sharon said, 'Some things never change,' and for a second, I forgot it was the end of the world. The ute turned left into a driveway.

We followed the dirt track through a vineyard and over a steep hill. The view was breathtaking, with the land stretching out in a tapestry of green and brown. When the car came to the summit, you could literally see for miles. Beautiful green and brown sweeping hills lead off into the distance.

At the bottom of the hill, about three hundred metres away, there was a decent-sized house with a large dam out the front. Several posts stood around the house, marron nets hanging off them. 'Straight ahead, that is Macca's farm, Karly said out the window, smiling. We slowly drove off the road and over the hill along the dirt track that led to the dam. Some kestrel hawks flew overhead as we pulled up to the house. 'How nice is this place,' Dan said as he inspected the area.

Karly walked over to the jetty, looking down at the water as she headed straight for the small shed beside it. A few seconds later, she came out with a bag of marron pellets for bait. She was quite the keen marron catcher, which was exciting to watch. The nets were set up and thrown into four different areas around the dam.

The two yabby traps were set, and the crab nets would have to be checked every thirty minutes or so, and we made sure to use the marron nets we found hanging. We stood around, talking. It would be a great place to stay, but the likelihood of people finding and raiding the farm was far too high. Karly and Sharon walked around the other side of the dam to explore. 'Can I pull the net yet?' Dan asked eagerly. 'Yeah, man, the crab nets can be checked.' We walked a short distance to the first one.

He pulled it up quickly, revealing nothing in the net. The next crab pot was pulled up, containing one marron. 'Quick, quick, pull it up,' I yelled. The pot hit the jetty, and I reached down and took the marron by the middle of its body. The marron wriggled in my grasp, its claws snapping menacingly. I was careful not to let it pinch me, as that hurts like all hell. The crab pots were thrown back in, and I walked the marron over to the ute and dropped it into the large bucket. 'Well, that's one. We need a few more if we want a good feed,' I said.

Karly and Sharon had been to this farm for a lot of parties and, in the old days, to help out when needed, so it should have come as no surprise when Sharon joined us, saying, 'There's a bulk diesel tank around the other side of the old hay shed. Let's leave the nets in and fuel the car up before returning to check the nets and gather supplies'. Everything was overgrown from months of abandonment, so Karly drove, knowing the way around after years of driving the property.

We stopped at the old workshop shed, once manned by a mechanic I had met years ago and even become friends with. I chuckled, remembering the grumpy old man in grease-stained clothing wandering around complaining about how he had no help and then not letting me touch anything when I offered. We found some spare tyres, which Dan and Karly chucked into the ute tray. I wondered if there was anything else useful when the smell hit me.

I tentatively walked towards the smell, holding my knife out, not wanting to alert the others yet. There he was, the old mechanic—not a zombie, but certainly dead. Clutching a bottle of rum, he slumped in his old camping chair, facing a dusty TV. There was a note next to him. Filled with sorrow, I read on as the note outlined why he had taken his life. He wasn't willing to wait around and turn into a monster, but he couldn't leave his home. The sight was heartbreaking—a lonely end to a hard life.

I carefully folded the note and put it in my pocket. He deserved to be remembered. Before anyone noticed I was missing, I rounded them into the car, and we went to the diesel tanks and then back to the dam. Once we returned, Dan suggested that now was the time to go find the guns and any more supplies that we could around the house. Karly and Sharon waded into the dam to clean off while I went with Dan.

We walked over to the front of the house, past the large shelter near the jetty, and peered through the glass doors. Nothing obvious stood out. It looked like the house had been left in a hurry. Clothes were on the floor, and dishes were still in the sink. 'Look!' I said, pointing to a rifle leaning against the safe inside.

I grabbed a rock and smashed a glass pane in the front door, unlocking it. We walked over to the safe, where the old hunting rifle was leaning against it. 'Karly will know how to use this properly, man? Let's have a look for ammo,' I suggested. We had a bit of a look around the house, but there was nothing useful. However, we did locate a box containing rifle rounds.

We walked outside and back to the undercover area, where the others were drying off. 'Oh, nice rifle. That's an old Winchester, good for medium-range shots,' Karly said. 'We got some ammo as well.' Dan stood, smiling, holding the box up. 'Good work, let's pull the pots, hey?' Karly asked. We all walked over to the first pot. Karly grabbed the rope and pulled hard on it. The pot was empty, surprisingly, seeing as though they'd been in there for 35 minutes. Sharon pulled the second pot and seemed to struggle a little, with Karly coming to give her a hand.

As the pot came to the surface, I could see that it was full of marron, much to our joy. 'Woohoo!' we all cheered. Six marrons in total, plus the one from the crab pot, made seven. We collected them up and loaded them into the bucket. After packing everything up, we left the farm, driving back over the hill and down the road. The hill seemed steep, driving back down it, but we made it without a problem.

I stopped at the road, checking both ways for cars, realising that if there was, in fact, a car, it could mean trouble. The sun was still high in the sky as we cruised along the road back towards Sharon's. 'I hope Sophie is feeling better,' Karly said from the back seat. 'What do you think it is, Nath?' Sharon asked me. 'Not too sure, but it really knocked her around, whatever it is—maybe something bacterial?' I suggested. 'Just need to be mindful around her in case whatever she has is contagious,' I cautioned.

We pulled up in Sharon's driveway around midday, jumping out happily and bringing the marron container onto the deck. Dan checked on Chance and Sophie while Karly, and I set up the fire pit and lit it. It had to be roaring to boil the large pot of water, so it would take a while to get to the right temperature. We carried the large metal pot out and filled it with water, some salt, chilli flakes, and lime fresh from the small tree in the backyard. The fire caught and was burning nicely.

We lifted the pot onto the metal frame and waited. Karly went and lay in the hammock while I sat near the fire. Chance came and joined me. 'How's the hangover going, man?' 'Ah, not too bad,' he replied. 'You seemed to be having a ball last night,' I said as Chance looked down at his feet. 'Look, mate, after what we saw in Bunbury,' I started but was interrupted. 'I know, I know; trust me. Sophie doesn't talk much when she is sick, so I had plenty of time to feel bad,' he said, looking up with a short smile. 'She said that I was a great nurse, though.' I laughed, shaking my head.

I went inside, unfolding the note from today. I re-read it and said a small goodbye. I don't know why I hadn't told the others about him; maybe it was to protect them, but that was his home, and I didn't want to disturb his peace. Folding the note and tucking it into the side pocket of my bag, I headed back out into the fire, the flames licking at the pot's base. 'Let's get the marron in. The water's boiling,' I said. Karly came over as I quickly placed them into the boiling pot. It only takes six minutes for them to be cooked through, from deep black to dark red when cooked properly. 'Dan is also doing sentry at the moment,' Karly said.

Sharon came out with old newspapers and laid them out on the table for me to put our freshly cooked dinner on. Karly went to get Dan, who came back out looking at our feed and said, 'Where's the vinegar?' That's when we heard the soft voice of Sophie standing in the doorway.

'You aren't getting any. The vinegar is for pickling vegetables.' We all looked up and laughed as Dan walked over and hugged her, saying, 'Ladies and gentlemen, she's back!' We got stuck into eating the marron, barely letting them cool off. They were so damn delicious.

After we finished eating, we sat around, relaxing while we still could. Karly began snoring from the hammock while Sharon and Chance talked at the fire. Dan and I were checking the house's fortifications, the windows, and the gates, ensuring we could leave at a moment's notice if we needed to. We cleaned and oiled the weapons and sharpened everyone's waist belt knives. It made us feel useful amongst all the waiting around.

WHAT LURKS IN THE SHADOWS

The afternoon sun slowly faded over the horizon as we began discussing the sentry watch and what we would do for the evening to keep ourselves entertained. 'We should definitely make a damper at some point,' Chance said. 'Or a spit roast, but we'd need to go hunting,' Dan added. I remember Karly saying she had a spit roast unit at their old place back before the apocalypse. A pig was placed over the open fire lined with hot coals and cooked slowly to perfection.

Nothing beats a BBQ, especially if it involves a spit roast or any smoked meat. 'We should have planted vegetables and fruit at the campsite to be a bit more self-sufficient. That would've been great, but oh well,' Sophie said. 'They would have died while we were away, but we have seeds there waiting for us; don't worry,' Karly responded with a gentle squeeze on Sophie's arm and a knowing smile. She was an idea's person, that's for sure. 'Okay, we'll make a damper for sure, and yes, we will need to hunt and fish also. We can't survive on canned food and pasta forever,' I replied.

I placed a few more logs on the fire as it was beginning to get dark. 'What are we doing tonight, guys?' Dan asked. No one seemed to have an answer. We all just stared at the fire without saying much. I guess surviving the end of the world was pretty mentally and physically draining. 'Listen, I'll take the first watch. It's nearly nine now, so you guys go and get a good night's sleep,' I said. 'Oh, I'll join you for the first watch, hey?' Karly asked. 'Yeah, of course, that sounds good!' They all agreed and slowly dispersed to their bedrooms. I could hear the chatter fading as they walked into the house together. We sat peacefully, looking up at the stars.

A cool evening breeze drifted the heat from the fire over my body. It was a calm and relaxing evening, with no sign of any foul zombies. 'Suppose we should go for a walk around the perimeter then,' I said with little enthusiasm. We got up and walked to the front of the house. 'Let's chill in the ute for a bit. We can still see most of the property from there; at least, we will be comfortable. Roll the windows down so we can hear anything,' Karly said. We sat in the car, holding hands, not saying much. We didn't need to; we just enjoyed the silence and watched the night sky roll by. 'I'm getting tired, babe,' I said, looking over at Karly. Her eyes looked heavy as she nodded in my direction in agreement.

I woke suddenly, still in my seat. I must have fallen asleep. Dan was standing next to the window, asking me if we were ready to go. 'Where are we going again?' I asked, stirring to life. 'We decided to go to Bunnings in Busselton, remember?' he replied. 'No, but ok, jump in,' I nodded, feeling a sense of Deja vu wash over me. I turned the ute on and off, and we went.

The trip seemed rather quick, and before I knew it, we were turning into Bunning's parking lot. Deserted as expected. As we pulled up and turned the vehicle off, a police cruiser parked in front of us. What the hell was this police vehicle doing here? I thought to myself. An officer jumped out and walked over to the window. 'What are you lot doing?' she said. 'I'm just grabbing some supplies for our campsite. Do you mind if we go in?' Dan replied. 'Not at all; just do the right thing and leave supplies for others,' she said. These were the rules. You could take things as long as you didn't go overboard.

Every shop was a free-for-all, basically, unless it was an essential service. The police cruiser drove off slowly. We walked over to the entrance, which was boarded up. Surprisingly, the first board we pulled on came loose, and we slipped through the gap, heading inside.

Bunning's was a traditional one-stop shop. It had everything from building materials, tools, BBQs, security items, and camping equipment. It always had a great sausage sizzle in the good old days, which I remembered hungrily grabbing my stomach.

I couldn't remember exactly what I had to get. Dan and Karly seemed to have a plan, taking off in separate directions with trolleys before I could ask again. I headed straight for the tools section. It was packed with tools, which may come in handy. I wandered back over and grabbed a trolley from the entrance, quickly returning to the power tools section. I grabbed a chainsaw, a drill, a portable radio for music, a few spare batteries, and a charging station. Surely, these could be used with the solar panels at the campsite.

I headed around to the lighting section and grabbed some solar-powered camping lanterns. There were around fifty aisles to explore, so I took the trolley back to the entrance and grabbed another. As I stopped the trolley near the door, I noticed something out of the corner of my eye. Go-carts. Go-carts! 'Karly! Dan! Come quick, I've found something amazing,' I yelled at the top of my lungs. They came running over.

'What! Since when did Bunning's sell go-carts? We should use these to drag the trolleys around with supplies,' Dan yelled excitedly. 'Let's have a race around Bunnings. It's wide enough, and who cares if we wreck anything? I think we've earned a bit of fun,' Karly said happily. It was a wicked idea. 'I got dibs on the pink one,' Karly yelled, jumping in the seat.

As we turned the engines over, they spattered briefly and then started. We lined up next to each other. 'On my mark,' Dan yelled, 'Go!' It was amazing as we all laughed and overtook each other around the corners. Dan slid out into a pile of buckets, taking last place. If ever I wanted to do something in Bunning's without an adult telling me no, this was it. Ironic. I used to be an adult in the public eye, but now I do not care the slightest.

We stopped where we started. Dan peered over with an evil look in his eyes. 'Want to have a joust off in these?" he smirked as he said it. 'Oh, hell no, I'll referee that,' Karly reacted. 'Sir, I challenge you to the death,' I said poshly. We decided that no items we found were suitable for jousting sticks, so we found welding helmets and fluorescent light bars. These would be our swords, like true knights. Holding a makeshift flag, Karly instructed us that when the flag dropped, it was go time. We drove about fifty metres apart and turned the go-carts around. I couldn't see shit out of the welding helmet, so this would be interesting.

I stared eagerly through the helmet and saw the flag drop. I pushed the accelerator and hammered towards Dan with the light tube in my left hand, raised in the air like Mel Gibson leading the battlefront charge in Braveheart! As Dan's go-cart approached, I swung hard, smashing the tube into his helmet around the same time his splintered over mine. I couldn't contain the laughter as I pulled up.

I jumped out and removed the helmet, dusting off the shards from the light while still laughing. I turned around and looked towards the others, who were both standing frozen and staring at me. Suddenly, an unmistakable zombie growl erupted behind me. I turned around to see an undead creature pushing itself out from under the aisle, mouth wide open, ready to chew my face off. I noticed more emerging from all around the store. I instantly felt engulfed, surrounded by death and decay, like the store was swallowing me.

A wave of zombies blocked me from getting to Dan and Karly. I took off running. 'Run!' I yelled, sprinting as fast as possible towards Dan and Karly. I turned my head to look back over my shoulder. Zombies were quickly gaining pace on me. As I looked forward, I tripped over something hard, causing me to fall and slide along the smooth concrete floor in pain, coming to a stop on my side. I rolled onto my back to catch my breath.

Karly was standing over me. She bent down, grabbed the front of my shirt with both hands and yelled, 'You need to wake up!'. 'What?' I replied, confused more than ever. She reached around the back of her pants and pulled out the Beretta, aimed it up past my head, pulled back on the hammer, and screamed, 'You need to wake up,' and squeezed the trigger. Time stood still. I could see Karly's mouth moving, but all I could hear was a ringing in my ears.

I snapped out of my trance-like state at the sight of the gnashing jaws of a zombie up close to my face, its hands wrapped around the front of my shirt, pulling me closer to it. Half of its face was missing, and its rotting teeth and foul breath were horrific. A single gunshot went off beside my left ear with a deafening ring. Blood sprayed the inside of the car and over my face, as the zombie loosened its grip on me and fell to its knees beside the car.

I peered across to see Karly opposite me with blood splattered on her face, both hands shaking as she aimed the Beretta at the window. 'We fell asleep!'. I kicked open the ute door, and the zombie hit the driveway. Another three zombies were staggering up the road towards us.

'That gunshot noise wasn't good,' Karly shouted. I could barely hear what she was saying through the continued ringing in my ears. We'd fallen asleep on watch at possibly the worst time ever; I couldn't believe it. Without a word said, as though we'd read each other's thoughts, we ran towards the house. As we ran up the stairs to the deck, Chance came outside wide-eyed. 'Zombies!' I yelled. 'Get everyone up.'

Two zombies began to make their way onto the deck, their eyes vacant and their movements jerky. We froze, unsure of what to do next. But Chance was quick to act. He ran over to the pile of weapons we had collected and grabbed the machete. His eyes were locked on the approaching zombies. He delivered a single strike to the first zombie with fierce determination, hitting it straight in the head.

The sound of metal cracking through bone echoed across the deck, and the zombie fell to the ground, motionless. The second zombie was still approaching, its arms outstretched and its mouth open in a grotesque grin. Without hesitation, Chance swung the machete at the zombie's neck, aiming for the spot where the spine met the skull. The blade sliced through the air with a satisfying whoosh, and then it connected with the zombie's neck, severing it in one clean stroke. Blood spurted out of the open slash, splattering across the deck and onto our clothes.

I ran inside, grabbing the towel hanging on the railing and wiping my face as I headed towards the bedrooms. Everyone was awake from the noise outside. 'Nathan, Nathan, are they here?' Sharon shrieked from the hallway, stumbling as she pulled her shoes on and grabbed her knife.

The glass in her room's window shattered as a zombie tried to force its way in. 'Weapons up, everyone! Be careful what you're shooting; make sure it's not each other,' I yelled out as I ran into Sharon's room and kicked the zombie trying to get in. The kick didn't have much effect apart from pissing it off. Sharon let out a sob.

It wasn't just that there were zombies; the one I had kicked used to be her neighbour from down the road. We didn't have time to worry about that now. We were no longer safe. I left the room and headed back outside, closely tailed by Sharon. 'Let's go,' Chance said as six zombies staggered around the far side of the deck.

We all ran frantically to the cars. I sat in the driver's seat and turned over the ignition. Karly and Sharon got in the back seats as Dan, Sophie, and Chance entered his car. I shoved the gear selector into drive and pushed on the pedal hard. A zombie landed on the bonnet and punched the windscreen, cracking it. 'That's one of those Shreiker zombies!' I shouted.

My heart was pounding in my chest as I pulled the pistol out of my waistband. The zombie was right before us, its decaying flesh glistening in the moonlight. I aimed the gun outside my window towards the bonnet, taking a deep breath and trying to steady my hand.

The first shot went wide, hitting the pavement with a loud bang. I quickly regained my composure and fired two more rounds, aiming for the zombie's head. The first bullet missed, grazing its shoulder and sending it stumbling backwards. But the second shot hit its mark, striking the zombie in the head and causing it to collapse onto the bonnet of the car.

It screeched loudly, thrashing around as its body convulsed. I placed the pistol on the passenger seat and slammed my foot on the accelerator, driving forward at full speed. The car lurched forward, hitting another zombie who was shuffling towards us. The impact was enough to send the zombie flying. I felt a sense of grim satisfaction as it disappeared under the vehicle and was sprayed out of the back tyres.

As I pulled out onto the road, my heart still pounding in my chest, I glanced down the street to the left. A single house was burning brightly against the night sky, the flames casting an eerie glow over the surrounding area. Watching the burning house, I saw something that made my blood run cold. A person was running from the house, screaming for help. But they were quickly overtaken by a group of zombies, who grabbed hold of them and pulled them to the ground. A wave of despair washed over me as I realised that there was nothing we could do to help them. We were on our own in this world, fighting for survival against an enemy that never slept and never stopped. But, despite the odds, we had to keep fighting. It was the only way to stay alive.

I grabbed the radio. 'Dan, I thought there'd be more zombies, but there's not too many. Stay alert and focus on driving. Let's get to the campsite,' hanging the handpiece back up. Shit, I thought to myself, hitting the steering wheel a few times, furious with myself for falling asleep. Karly had her head down, and I could see she was angry with herself, too. I grabbed the radio. 'I'm so sorry, guys; we fell asleep. I don't even know how it happened,' I said into the handpiece. 'Oh my god,' Sharon whispered. Sharon asked, panicky, making her voice crack. 'Are you kids, ok?' Sharon asked, panicky, making her voice crack. 'Yeah, we're ok. It's not our blood. I thought that was it for us, Mum. It scared the shit out of me,' Karly said to Sharon, who grabbed a tissue and wiped some blood off Karly's forehead.

'How could you not have been scared?' Sharon responded. 'But we are all still here, and it will be okay.' 'I am so sorry I fell asleep.' Karly was still looking down, and we felt the weight of responsibility for what had just happened. 'These zombies are out of control if I'm going to be honest, and I don't want to cause too much stress, but there were so many zombies it was terrifying to see when we were in Bunbury,' I said, looking at Sharon. 'It was terrifying, but I think adrenaline kept us going to get away from there,' I continued, glancing into the rear-view mirror.

The vehicles flew down the road, their high beams illuminating the countryside. Heading south, I expected there not to be as many zombies, but after that, it would be a death sentence if I didn't remain vigilant for any coming from the east.

We hadn't gotten far along the road when we saw five zombies stumbling aimlessly. Both vehicles pulled up as I jumped out of the car and walked around the front of it, pulling out my pistol and firing at the first zombie that approached my direction. Dan shot at the same zombie I was firing at, knocking it down to its knees.

All five were now heading in our direction. Chance joined us and took to another zombie, cutting it down violently and causing blood to spray across the road. A blood-curdling screech rang out from a field adjacent to the road that instantaneously sent shivers down my spine. I was now scared for my life, and everyone else's around me.

The worst-case scenario was being out fighting zombies in the middle of the night. I was angry at myself for falling asleep. What was I thinking? Then again, I'm only human. Chance yanked the blade from a zombie's head as it lay motionless on the road. Its shirt was torn, and its pants were hanging off it. 'We need to keep moving; it's too dangerous out here at night in the dark!' I said with a shaking voice.

As we walked back to the utes, everyone turned around when we heard a slapping noise from one of the zombies that we had just cut down. We all held up our weapons, unsure of what we were looking at. A snake-like object slapped against the ground, protruding from its back. I suddenly realised it must be an Absorber zombie.

The snake-like whip arrowhead penetrated deep into the skull of the zombie lying beside it. I pulled the Beretta out of the holster and walked over to it. Another whip appeared, standing upright like a snake, poised and ready to strike. I aimed the Beretta and squeezed the trigger. It clicked, but there was no bang, and no ammo was left in my gun! The whip slewed forward at me as I dodged out of its way.

Chance jumped towards it, cutting deep into the fleshy tentacle and dismembering it. The Absorber zombie was lying on the ground, sitting upright and growling at us. We stood there stunned; it had just healed itself from the other zombie's body. It was time to leave. We all ran back to the cars and locked the doors. The car wheels screeched as we sped off, hitting the absorber as we left. We weren't hanging around to see what that thing was all about.

A HOME AMONG THE GUMTREES

Soon enough, we turned off the rugged dirt road towards the campsite. I prayed that there was enough distance between us and those disgusting, foul creatures. When we arrived, we walked over to the main area and sat down as I turned on a single battery-powered lantern.

We were all on high alert and still nervous about what had just occurred, jumping at every noise. I doubt there will be much sleep happening tonight. I unzipped my backpack and took out a cigarette, offering everyone else one.

'Ok, well, while it's fresh in our minds, do we want to discuss what we just saw that Absorber do?' Chance asked us all. 'Yeah, you cut it down, and it fed off another zombie with those tentacle things to fix itself,' I replied, staring blankly at the ground.

'As if regular zombies aren't enough, these things have some nasty surprises up their sleeves,' Karly said. 'We are basically screwed if we lose this campsite. What are we going to do if that happens?' Sophie asked. 'We just need to keep doing what we're doing, sticking together, and having rostered sentry breaks so at least two-thirds of the group can pay attention properly and never let our guard down again,' I said. '

We need to devise some rules for this campsite, like no fires during the day and in the evening. When the fire goes on, it must be lit hard and fast to reduce smoke visibility. Not so much from zombies but from any weirdos that might be about'. We discussed rules and safety and came up with a list that we called the golden rules. They were written on the side of the camper.

1. Two minimum on sentry duty, and both have guns

2. Fires only at night, lit hard and fast to reduce smoke, never during the day

3. Chores and tasks to be spread fairly

4. No single-person activities away from the camp

5. To reduce noise, no guns to be shot at camp unless the situation is dire

6. If you are bitten, you're put down humanely

These were the main rules. Number six was a given but helped reinforce the need for vigilance. We all talked for hours as the sun began to rise, discussing the new laws we would live by and how to make the camp run most efficiently. Around 8 a.m., someone suggested we go and have a wash down at the creek. No one argued with this idea. In fact, it was probably the best thing I'd heard for a while, eyeing off the group who were covered in blood and looking utterly exhausted.

I reached up and felt the soft, pillowy bags under my eyes. We slipped through the wire ropes at the back of the camp and headed down to the creek, most of us stripping down to our underwear and jumping straight in.

The water was refreshing, and I could feel my muscles starting to relax, showing relief. Karly splashed me in the face, so I returned the favour, and a water fight ensued. We washed ourselves and cleaned our hair. I pulled myself out of the creek and grabbed a towel. As I was drying myself off, we discussed gathering more firewood and what was for dinner that night.

Chance was craving some meat instead of canned food, and he let us know, eagerly looking around for signs of wildlife. I didn't want to burst his bubble by asking how he planned to get it so quickly. 'Hey Karly, do you remember that swimming spot in Millbrook? Had that high cliff face overlooking it?' Sharon said. 'Oh yeah! Nathan, remember me telling you about that?' Karly asked. 'Ahh, Hidden Falls. That place sounded awesome!' 'We should go check it out at some point!' Sharon said.

The day was off to a good start, and we had some laughs trying to keep ourselves going to distract ourselves from the carnage. Sophie said she was feeling nearly 100% better, so she and Dan were setting things up and reinforcing fences around the camp. Karly and Sharon collected more firewood while Chance and I were on sentry duty. We wouldn't normally have done sentry during the day, but given the high risk of zombies, nothing seemed silly or far-fetched at this point.

'Man, I'm over this shit already. Can't they just drop a nuclear bomb or something on them?' Chance asked. 'Yeah, on the whole world, start over. Maybe this is God's way of resetting the world,' I replied. 'Probably,' Chance said with a shrug of his shoulders. 'So, back at Sharon's, we may or may not have fallen asleep in the car on watch.' The memory was still fresh in my mind, and the guilt lingered.

'No shit, Sherlock, but it's fine. No one died; you just buggered our quiet escape plans,' Chance said with a wink. 'I was dreaming that Karly, Dan, and I were in Bunnings, helping ourselves to some things, and I found go-carts. We were racing them around the store, flogging each other with fluorescent light tubes. Then zombies came out of nowhere, and I tripped over them. Karly shot me in the frigging head, man.' Chance chuckled to himself.

'Surely you would've survived catching a bullet even with that noggin, hey? Anyway, serves you right for not bringing me to Bunnings in your dream,' Chance replied, now laughing out loud. 'I must have forgotten the invite. Your mum was there, though,' I joked back to him. We did another perimeter walk and spotted a rabbit—a good sign of food around, I thought. 'Let's go for a walk around camp and see what everyone's doing,' I said.

'Does Nathan or anyone have an alternative plan, Karly?' Sharon asked. 'I know we all hoped we would never actually have to use this campsite, and this really was the last option, but for now, we're stuck here. We can test the radio every now and then to see whether the military gets control, and then maybe we can return home. I heard a non-military plane escape when it went to hell in Australia. I think it was the one we heard about where the really rich paid thousands for a late evacuation. They had been planning it for ages, but maybe we can get it if we hear about another one on the radio. Although I did suggest to Nathan earlier that heading to Rottnest Island might be the go. Just unsure where we could get a boat from,' she replied. 'That's smart, my girl! You're a thinker. Yeah, how could we get a boat?' Sharon said, looking around the group for more suggestions.

'Actually, I think Nathan's cousins have a boat at their place on the canals back up in Mandurah, though a wave of zombies probably stands between us and the boat,' Karly said, not looking up as she neatly stacked the kindling, keeping herself busy. She often did this when she wanted to avoid a situation. 'I don't know; we'll figure it out. I'm sure we will get by if we remain positive,' Karly said. 'We should have a group discussion about it this afternoon,' Sharon said.

A kookaburra laughed loudly in the trees overhead. What a perfect metaphor, I thought as it laughed down at us, almost mockingly. The Kookaburra was introduced to WA from the East to help control snake numbers, but over time, they started to prey on our native species. When will we ever learn? As we looked up at the kookaburra, a magpie landed near Karly. 'Oh, look, how lovely,' Sharon said with a big smile. Karly bent down and put her hand out, though the magpie was hesitant and flew away.

They watched it fly to the top of a tree and settle into position. 'How's the morning treating you two?' I asked as we approached Karly and Sharon. 'Just talking about boats and stuff.' 'Just stuff, huh?' I said. 'Yeah. We're all thinking about boats, especially after I mentioned that your cousins might have one,' Karly replied. 'I'm sure we can figure something out.' I knew we had to think about alternatives, but for now, I was happy to be feeling semi-safe where we were. The magpie flew down and landed on the branch next to the one it had been perched on, watching us. It chirped, almost like it was talking to us. 'That magpie sure likes you,

Karly,' I said.

'How's sentry duty going? No sign of any fester heads?' Karly had come around, hugging me as I stood watch at the perimeter of our campsite, scanning the tree line for any signs of movement. 'All quiet on the western front,' I replied, trying to sound confident. 'We should grab the drone and look around from the skies. It never hurts to be careful.' Chance and I made our way over to the solar panels that had been put up on stands, grateful for the extra power they gave us.

'Geez, these came in handy,' Chance said, admiring the sleek design of the solar panels. I picked up the battery charger and removed the drone battery. 'Drone is in the Ute still,' I said, heading towards the car. I grabbed the drone and slid the battery into it, pulling my phone out of my pocket. 'I've only got 14% battery left, so we must be quick,' I continued.

Chance grinned and replied, 'What? Have you got someone to call or a dinner reservation booked somewhere?' Chance never failed to lighten the mood, or at least try, no matter what happened. 'Yes, Chance, actually, I'm catching up with your mother for a dinner date at that Italian restaurant in Leederville; you know the place?' We laughed and pretended to box each other as we walked over to the side of the camp and up a slight hill. Chance got the drone ready while I connected it to the phone. 'Alright, mate, let's go find out what's out there,' I said.

The drone's blades whirred rapidly as it lifted off the ground and shot up into the air. Dan walked over to us to see what we were doing. 'Good old drone, ay? See anything?' he asked, his eyes squinting up at the tiny speck in the sky. I continued to fly the drone for another ten minutes, covering a large area in all directions from the camp. The lush green bush below stretched out as far as the eye could see.

It was peaceful up here, with only the distant sound of birdsong and the occasional rustle in the leaves to keep us company. Suddenly, out of nowhere, a hawk appeared on the horizon. It swooped towards the drone; talons outstretched as if to attack it. I quickly manoeuvred the drone out of its path, narrowly avoiding a collision. 'That was close,'

Chance exclaimed, a look of relief crossing his face. 'Damn, that was lucky. I nearly lost it.' The drone returned to us and shut itself down just as it landed, its blades slowing to a stop as we gathered around.

Chance went to pull the drone case bag open, jumping back suddenly and shrieking. A snake slithered out of the bag, stopping and lying motionless, staring at us, licking the air with its tongue. 'That's a Southern Death Adder,' I breathed, standing frozen. 'Highly venomous; don't move, or it won't be good news for you.' It was patterned with magnificent colours, light and dark brown lines, separated by black lines with a skinny tail at the end, managing to camouflage. It was a reminder that zombies were not our only danger.

The snake eventually got bored with us and slithered off away from the camp. 'That was close,' Dan said, watching to ensure the snake didn't turn around. We headed back into the main part of the camp, putting my phone and the drone battery back on charge. 'We nearly lost Chance to a Death Adder before,' I said cheekily to Karly and Sharon.

On hearing this, Chance puffed out his chest and, of course, made up a story of how he single-handedly fought to save all our lives. We watched, laughing and rolling our eyes at him. Sophie walked over and joined us. 'Oh, where did it go? Do you think we should maybe, you know, get rid of it so it doesn't come back?' she said quietly.

I was surprised to hear that from Sophie, the quietest of us all and always wants to protect animals. 'It's getting cool, so let's get the campfire going and continue our chat about the next steps,' Sharon said. 'Sharon! Fires only at night,' I said back, secretly longing for the distraction.

'I've got a nice surprise for us all also,' Dan said, excitedly walking off, then returning moments later with a plastic bag. I watched curiously as he rummaged through the pack, my mind racing with possibilities. What could it be? Snacks? A game? He produced an ice-cold beer. 'Where did you get these from?!' I jumped from my spot to grab one. 'Man, I forgot about them; they were in the Engel fridge in the back of my ute,' he replied, handing them out.

Sophie waved Dan off, opting out, as I took my first sip of the ice-cold liquid. I had to force myself to stop, so I didn't finish it all in one go. Sharon jokingly asked for a stubby holder, to which Dan held up a finger and pulled one from behind his back with a grin. It's the only one, though, so use it well, he joked. Dan was quieter than Chance and less assertive than me, and he didn't often joke as much. He was usually content to sit back and watch those around him. He made a noise as he leant back and took a swig of his beer, clearly content in this moment. We settled in, and as it got dark, it made our fire feel like any other camping adventure.

'It's all a waste of time. I appreciate what we're doing, but it doesn't look good for us all. We really need to discuss options. What's the point anyway!?' Sophie broke the silence. Those words shook me. I couldn't understand because we had all tried to stay positive, clinging to the hope that our camp would keep us safe.

We had this camp that we had planned out. I had watched our group survive the impossible; the idea of giving up now after all this felt like a black cloud in my head, but what were we doing? As I looked around, I could see Sharon sitting up straight, Chance was shifting uncomfortably, and Karly started fiddling again.

There was a clear shift in the group. It was obvious that they felt as I did. 'What's gotten into you?' Dan snapped. At that instant, she got up and stormed away from the campfire, retreating to a tent. 'Everything alright there, Dan? She mentioned something or...' Chance quietly asked Dan as we all sat in shock, absorbing what had been said.

'Anyways, children, we're all adults here, so let's respect what was said but focus on the positives. Karly mentioned you have cousins that live in Mandurah, Nath,' Sharon said, turning her attention towards me. 'Yes, I do. There's a boat on the canals there, which is already in the water or should be anyway. I wouldn't know where the keys are, though. We must look after the boat if we take it,' I replied.

We discussed other options, such as travelling even further south or heading inland towards South Australia. However, we constantly came to the same conclusion, being met with zombies heading from the IPRC.

The night deepened as we talked, and we realised that we had really thought of this campsite as an end game. As the night went on, we talked about more options, with Sharon, on occasion, having to quiet us down as we got heated about our ideas, talking over each other. Dan produced more beers as we quieted down. We concluded that sticking it out at the campsite off the grid was ideal for now. We had plenty of food and decent shelter. We opened some cans of fruit and beans; it was a boring dinner, but it filled us up.

I walked over to the tent that Sophie was still in. 'You ok, Sophie?' She didn't answer me, but I could tell from her breathing that she wasn't asleep, so I left some food at the door for her. I took the trash over to the large metal container for food scraps and threw the trash in. Sophie eventually emerged for sentry duty with Chance, not joining in the conversation. Sharon and Dan were up next; we had already agreed on this order, so I was glad Sophie had come out so that Karly and I could have the night off. We retreated to the campervan. 'Few rounds of cards, Nath?' Karly asked. 'Yeah, why not?' I replied.

We played a few rounds and had an early night. It was just after 7 a.m., and the morning promised to be another beautiful one—dead quiet and bathed in sunlight. I woke up before Karly and sat, reminiscing about those weekends when she would sleep in while I was home.

Back then, I would tiptoe into the kitchen to make her coffee, knowing she was a light sleeper who kept her eyes closed until I returned. I'd come back to find her smiling and lean in to kiss her softly, savouring the warmth of her lips and the sweetness of the moment. When Karly woke, we shared a breakfast of cashews, munching on a few handfuls before sealing the rest back in the container.

For a time, this was our life: eating, swimming, drinking, and relaxing, with little concern for the passage of time. We created a makeshift calendar to keep track of the days. With his typical flair, Chance labelled the day he found us 'Victory Day,' while Dan dubbed our escape 'D-Day.' Taking on the role of our chronicler, Sophie marked the days with an air of authority and relief, seeming to find solace in each passing day that we were safe.

We diligently checked the fences daily and inspected the new defences we had crafted. Sharon had ingeniously dammed off an area, making it easier to catch marron, and we became adept hunters, setting snares and traps to conserve our bullets and avoid noise, although we didn't hunt every night. I vividly remember the morning we caught our first kangaroo. It was around 4 a.m., and I was on sentry duty, our rotations having been reduced to one person at a time. I found the kangaroo lying there, undisturbed by my approach.

The animal was swiftly dispatched. 'Sorry buddy, it's you or me,' I said before hoisting it over my shoulder. I walked back to camp, knowing this would be a feast. The next day, Sophie found some instant mashed potatoes, and we prepared a true meal together. We had all lost some weight, but that day, we shared a meal that felt like a celebration of our survival and resilience.

I woke to another sunny morning, unsure of what day it was. We had decided to go to Iron Gully Falls today, so I got up and dressed for the day. Karly came over and helped me pull some more stuff out of the back of the ute so the others could sit in the back when we went to Iron Gully Falls. As everyone emerged from their tents, they got changed into swimwear, and we got in the car. Dan and I were the only ones inside the vehicle; everyone else wanted to lap up the views of the trip and the sun's rays. 'This is the life, isn't it?' Chance said, leaning back against the side of the tray, his face turned to the sky.

Sophie laughed, adjusting her sunglasses. 'Sure is. It beats being cooped up indoors, that's for sure.' 'Remember when we used to do this back in the day?' Chance continued. 'Just driving out to nowhere, finding a spot to swim and relax?' Sophie nodded with a nostalgic smile on her lips. 'Yeah, those were the days. It's nice to have a bit of that normalcy back, even if it's just for a short while.'

It was only a twenty-minute drive, and that's as far as we could take the car due to the track becoming very rugged and inaccessible. I pulled up, and everyone piled out of the tray, flies instantly upon us. Sharon stepped forward, pointing out towards the distant cliffs. 'We just have to walk up that ridge, then another, and it's over the side of the second one,' she explained, her voice filled with confidence.

A track was already cleared through the bush as it was a popular swimming hole back before the world's end. The path was dirt in most places, with odd stone steps in others. The bushland here was thick, and the flies were out in force already. They had to be constantly shooed away. I turned back to Sophie as we walked and said, 'Hey, everything's going well, ok? You seemed a bit down and out the other night.' 'Yeah, sorry about that. I was feeling a bit hopeless. I didn't mean to kill morale around the group,' she replied.

'We came up with some good ideas anyway. If anything goes wrong, we have a plan of escape, but all is well. I am just checking,' I replied. We carried on our trek along the trail towards Iron Gully Falls. Just as I was about to ask if we were nearly there, we came to an opening, and a gorgeous big swimming hole stood before us. 9 a.m., a perfect swimming time, I thought to myself. The sun was reflecting down over the waterhole, and it looked beautiful. The swimming hole wrapped around a large rock face and was nearly fifty metres deep.

We dumped the bags and jumped in the cold morning water, splashing about and laughing, exploring what the area had to offer. 'Righto, whoever can swim down and grab a handful of mud wins the honour,' Chance called. We all dove below the surface towards the bottom, and though it was dark, I pushed down a little further. The water became colder as my hand touched the bottom. I grabbed a handful of mud and pushed it to the surface. Karly and Chance had already surfaced, winning our little tournament. We explored one of the side caves. The water was shallow here, and the bottom was smooth like ice. 'Hey, who's going to make the jump?! You love heights, don't you, Karly?' I asked, pointing up to the southern side of the water hole.

A narrow shelf led out over the water on the side of the cliff, around twelve metres high. 'Ha! That's got nothing on Sophie's apartment!' Karly replied. Chance, Dan, Sophie, Karly, and I made our way out of the water and around the cliff wall. As we walked around the top, Sharon waited in the water, calling, 'bugger that.' I stopped at the end of the wall and looked down. The shelf continued out over the water and was around fifty metres long.

'Who's first?!' I yelled, getting ready to run. Dan was the first to run, and he took off, sprinting past everyone. I saw him grinning at me as he got to the shelf. Dan jumped and spun around, flipping us all off with the middle finger. The splash and slap of water sounded painful, and as he surfaced and yelled, 'Ow! My back!' Everyone erupted in laughter.

I peered over the edge. It was actually higher than it looked. Suddenly, my sissy instinct kicked in, and I didn't want to do it. Karly could clearly see the hesitation in my eyes. 'Didn't you go cliff diving in Ibiza with a Red Bull dive master?' she asked. 'Yes, but I was about five beers deep,' I said, looking back at the water below. I thought you got this; just count to three and jump. One, two, three.

Chance came flying off at the same time as me, and the rush was amazing as we hit the water, jetting liquid up my nose and what felt like into the front of my brain. I surfaced and flicked the water from my hair and my eyes. 'Woo-hoo!' I yelled up at the girls. I really wanted to jump again, as always, when I put the big boy pants on. We stayed in the water and egged the girls on. 'Jump, jump, jump,' we chanted.

They held hands and jumped simultaneously, hitting the water below. The force of the water tore Sophie's bikini top off, apparent as she surfaced, breasts out. 'Boobies! Boobies out for the boys, ha-ha,' Chance responded, laughing. 'Nathan! Close your eyes!' Karly laughed as she roared at me. Sophie found her top, and Karly helped her put it back on. We each had a few more cliff jumps, and Sharon even jumped from one of the lower levels. Everything was beyond amazing, full of energy and excitement.

Around 1130 a.m., we were all pretty worn out, so we lay on the large rocks to dry off in the sun, admiring the beauty of the landscape. At midday, we gathered our things and walked back towards the vehicle. Karly looked at me and said, 'So, what did you think of the place?' 'I loved it; I've never felt so good in my life. Everything was amazing; even the cliff jumping was epic,' I replied. It felt quite humid walking back along the track.

We got to the high point at the track and noticed dark clouds beginning to form far off the coast. 'Oh, we might get a bit of rain this afternoon,' I said. 'Righto weatherman,' Chance said as he walked past. I quite enjoyed the little digs we'd have at each other, which kept the brain healthy for the next payout.

STAR STRUCK

We made it back to the car. I wrapped a towel around myself and pulled off the wet underwear, throwing them in the tray and pulling on my shorts. We all piled in and headed back to camp; almost everyone sat in the car, feeling tired. A great day spent by the water—these were the good days to live for. The black clouds were higher now, and they began to show their true colours, a blackish grey moving swiftly. We heard the first distant rumble of thunder, and the wind started to pick up, making the trees sway. The warm day had dropped in temperature a little, and leaves blew through the camp.

We decided to clean up the campsite as best as possible and put anything that might be damaged undercover, in tents, or in the Winnebago. All the firewood was moved under the marquees, and loose objects were secured. A good afternoon storm in Australia is quite spectacular and often puts on a good show of Mother Nature's force. We faced a problem tonight. Due to the noise of the storm, it would be next to impossible to hear or see any unwanted guests approaching.

Dark clouds filled the sky as we put dinner together around 3 p.m.; it was probably easier to do it earlier than during the impending storm. 'How are we going to do sentry tonight if it's pissing down?' Dan asked. 'Umm, I'm not sure,' I said as I put the last of the wood under the tent.

'I think a majority of us should sleep in the Winnebago to avoid being crushed by falling tree branches,' I said to everyone in earshot. 'Why don't we have a person on sentry in the Winnebago? You can still see out of it, and there are two in a ute near the top of the camp. Just not Karly and Nathan together,' Dan said, smugly shooting me a grin. 'Yeah, that's probably the easiest,' I replied.

As the deep rumbling of thunder began, the entire campsite filled with an air of anticipation. The temperature dropped rapidly, and the wind picked up, chilling our spines. We looked up at the darkening sky, knowing that the storm was about to hit. Just then, a loud boom of thunder shook the campsite, making it feel like it struck the very ground beneath us.

We rushed to secure our belongings, attempting to put up some last-minute tarps to protect our campsite from the impending downpour. Large, heavy rain drops began to fall, hitting the dry earth with a satisfying thud.

'Damn, I love the smell of rain; you can smell the summer's heat in the water when it hits the ground,' I exclaimed to Karly, who nodded in agreement. Despite the rain, we were all filled with a sense of excitement and energy. This was the Australian bush at its finest, untamed and unpredictable. We huddled together under the tarps, watching as the rain intensified and the drops came down faster and harder.

As the storm raged on, we could feel the electricity in the air, the hairs on our arms standing on end. Lightning flashed overhead, illuminating the sky in a brilliant display of splintering light and power. Eventually, the rain began to subside, with the drops slowing down to a steady drizzle.

We looked out at the world around us, the landscape transformed by the storm. The air was fresh and clean, and the smell of rain lingered in our nostrils. Karly headed for the Winnebago, seeking refuge from the dampness of the storm. I grabbed my sunglasses and followed her, eager to get out of the rain and dry off. As we settled inside the Winnebago, we could hear the rain continuing to fall outside, the sound of it thrumming against the windows like a gentle lullaby.

Sophie and Karly were on the first watch for the next four hours, then

Dan and I. It was cosy in the Winnebago, with everyone being spacious enough to accommodate us easily. Rain noisily peppered the sides and roof of the Winnebago. It was a beautiful sound and quite relaxing. I laid my head back on the pillow and stared up at the roof, soaking in the moment of peace while I could.

We had a round of cards and discussed the plan for tomorrow, and everyone agreed to go to the beach if it wasn't raining. Sharon suggested a hunt for some fresh meat. The rain picked up a little more, and we turned out another round of cards. It was a pretty good night until it was my turn to do sentry duty with Chance.

The ute pulled up alongside the Winnebago, and the girls jumped out and ran inside. 'It is pouring down out there. Don't think I've seen rain like this for ages,' Sophie exclaimed, wiping water off her arms. 'Yeah, we couldn't really see beyond the confines of the camp, but it was an alright vantage point,' Karly replied, peering through the Winnebago window at the sheets of rain.

'Ah well, Chance, are you ready for this?' I asked. We got up and ran out the door to the car, getting in quickly as it was still raining heavily. The sound of the rain pounding against the car's roof was deafening, making it difficult for us to hear each other.

I pulled the gear selector in reverse and inched back until I had enough room to turn around. I pulled the vehicle up at the sentry point and turned it off. As the droplets of rain came crashing down against the windscreen, lightning flashed across the sky in jagged streaks. 'Least the weather is putting a show on for us,' I said.

Chance seemed lost in his thoughts as he spoke, 'This world can be a very cruel place. It's sad to see what's happened. After all the life goes on, what will be left? How would the world be if we somehow won this, if a miracle happened and we beat the zombies?' I turned to face him. This was a hard one to answer, I thought. 'What's truly important is survival; what's the point of being tough if you die along the way? People will kick their heels for a bit, but it will pass. People are resilient; it's just that you have the will to fight for life and win,' I replied.

'I'm surprised they haven't just dropped a nuclear bomb on us yet, like, what is the rest of the world doing while we're being swarmed?' he considered acquiescently. 'Pretty sure there isn't much of the world left, man'. 'Imagine finding a cure! Now that'd be epic,' I said.

We continued discussing what the world may look like if we won, and it gave us some sort of hope talking about it. I looked around at all the trees and the campsite down from us, which had a shiny coat of rain on them. It made them look a little unnerving in the darkness of the rain. There was more chance of a zombie sneaking up on us in this weather.

I highly doubt it will happen, though. Just try not to think about it, I thought to myself. The rain eventually stopped around 3 a.m., thirty minutes before our watch ended. I drove the ute back to the Winnebago and opened the door to find everyone in bed sleeping. Chance followed me in, and I could see the redness in his eyes. He looked like he wanted to fall asleep immediately. I woke Dan and Sharon and told them the rain had eased off. I said goodnight to Chance and jumped into bed.

The next morning, the sun broke through the clouds, casting a warm, golden glow over the campsite. The air was crisp and clean, carrying the freshness of last night's rain. Birds began to chirp, bringing a sense of normalcy to our makeshift haven. It was a perfect day just to relax and enjoy life's simple pleasures, even amidst the chaos of the world around us. Karly and I set up some folding chairs and settled down to enjoy the morning. 'Today feels like a good day just to chill,' Sophie said, stretching and yawning. 'Maybe we can take a break from all the stress and just enjoy being together.' 'I agree,' I replied, sipping my coffee. 'We need days like this to keep our spirits up. Besides, we can't always be on high alert. We'd burn out.'

After breakfast, we decided to split up and take care of small tasks around the camp. Karly and I collected more firewood, ensuring we had enough for the next few days. Chance and Sophie worked on reinforcing the tarps and tents, making sure they were secure in case of another storm.

Dan and Sharon took inventory of our supplies, noting what we might need to scavenge on our next outing. By midday, the sun was high in the sky, and the temperature had risen to a comfortable warmth. We gathered by the table with a deck of cards and some snacks. A friendly game of poker ensued, filled with laughter and light-hearted banter.

In the afternoon, we decided to explore the area a bit more. A small creek was nearby, and we thought it might be a good spot to catch some fish. Armed with homemade fishing rods and a bit of bait, we made our way to the water. The creek was serene, and the water was clear and cool.

We sat by the bank, casting our lines and chatting about old times. 'Remember that time we went camping in the Blue Mountains?' Dan asked. 'We got lost for hours trying to find that waterfall.' 'Yeah, and then we found it just as the sun was setting,' I replied, laughing. 'It was beautiful, though. It's totally worth getting lost for.' The hours passed peacefully, and we caught a few small fish. It wasn't much, but it would add some variety to our meal. As the sun set, we returned to camp, feeling refreshed and content.

We prepared a simple dinner of grilled fish and vegetables at the campsite. The evening air was cooling, and we huddled around the campfire, enjoying the warmth and company. As the night grew darker, we decided to call it a day. We took turns keeping watch, ensuring that our little haven remained safe.

I woke slowly, and the sun shone through a crack in the curtain. I rolled onto my back. I looked up at the roof, my mind blank and calm— not a worry. 'You're so perfect when you sleep,' Karly said. I laughed as I looked towards her. She was lying on her side, head in hand, like Rose's pose when Jack sketched her on the Titanic. I rolled my eyes. 'Go on then, say it,' I said through chuckles.

'Paint me like one of your French girls,' she laughed and grabbed my leg, dry-humping it. We lay there in silence again, staring up at the roof. 'Least the rain has stopped. It really rained cats and dogs last night, didn't it?' I said.

'Mm, what time is it?' Karly asked. I looked at my watch. 'It's 1000 a.m.,' I replied. 'Great, what are we doing with the day?' she asked. 'Don't know. We need to go hunting at some point, I think. I'd love for some rabbit or something meaty to eat.' Now, all I could think about was food. 'Remember all the smash burger places in Pert. Those double beef patties, dripping with cheese and sauce,' I said with a sudden hunger in my stomach. 'Ha-ha, gosh, you're lucky those things didn't give you a heart attack, but yes, I will admit, they were great,' Karly replied.

Chance shot up suddenly and looked around, still half asleep. 'Did someone say they were doing a run to get smash burgers?' he said. What remained of the morning rolled slowly, and we discussed what was in store. Dan and Sophie left for a swim, and Sharon said she was feeling lazy and would get some sun. I suggested we hunt for some food, and Chance raised his eyebrows. 'I guess I wouldn't mind some food myself, though,' he replied. 'Aren't going to find any burgers out there, Nath,' Chance said smartly. 'Yeah, I know, but maybe if we're lucky, we can catch a rabbit or two,' I replied.

'Anyone knows how to make a rabbit snare, actually?' I asked Karly and Chance. 'Yes, I do,' they said simultaneously. 'We just need some wire from the toolbox, the hammer, and the drill. We have a drill, right?' Chance asked us. 'Ah, yeah, I'm pretty sure we do,' I replied, walking over to the toolbox. I pulled the lid open, looking around inside. 'Jackpot! Yes, we do!' I said it excitedly as it gave off a mechanical whirl.

'Let's go then; grab some nuts from the food container, and let's get going,' Karly said. We grabbed our stuff and headed off. 'Sharon, we're going to try to get some tucker,' Chance said as we passed her. I stopped briskly and turned around. 'Come on guys, rule number 4. There are no solo activities, so, unfortunately, Sharon, you'll have to come with us, but it'll be fun.' 'Oh kids, how bloody far away are you going? I'll be fine here; you'll probably be within yelling distance anyways,' Sharon replied. 'Fine,' Karly said, rolling her eyes, 'but any sign of trouble, please yell out,' Karly said.

We walked away from the camp, following a thin track that skirted into the forest, with tree roots sticking out from the exposed soil. We walked through thick undergrowth over tiny boulders filled with thick crevices and silt until we reached a small clearing. We stopped at the edge of the clearing to inspect some bright yellow flowers. Karly picked one up and held it up for us to look at. 'At least beautiful things remain through the chaos,' she said softly. 'This will be far enough; we don't want to be too far from where Mum is,' she stated. 'I'm going to cut off a length of wire and shape it; do you want to help?' Karly asked. 'Sure,' I replied. 'Oh, I'll need more wire than that,' Karly replied, holding her hand out towards me.

'Ok, so we need a stick about forty centimetres high with decent thickness. I need that driven into the ground with a small hole drilled through it. The other stick must be straight with a small nook hanging off it. The wire is passed through the drilled hole and twisted back onto itself. Before that is done, a loop needs to be made at the other end of the wire. This is then fed loosely over the length of the wire. Rabbit comes bounding along and jumps through it, snaring itself as it knocks the wire,' Karly explained. 'I'm not really good at visualising things, so you'll have to show us the first one,' I replied.

Karly laughed and shook her head at me. 'If you hold the other end of the wire in your hand, I'd like you to take the drill and clamp it onto the main stick. Twist the wire back onto itself,' Karly said as she walked over to Chance and held the wire in her hands.

She took the drill, dropped the end through the top of the main stick, and set it down on the ground. She picked up the hammer and drove it into the ground. Chance and Karly laid the traps as I uselessly walked around the small clearing. 'So far, so good, guys; these are all good, so now we just wait,' Chance said.

We heard a rush of wind through the trees and leaves rustling. It was quite loud and close by. Chance jumped at the sound and dropped the wire. 'Was that what I think it was?' he said. 'Yep, that'll be a kangaroo; if it is, we've just set up three rabbit traps,' I said. 'You've got to be joking,' Chance and Karly said in unison. I looked at Chance, 'Yeah, man! Why didn't you set up a kangaroo trap at the same time?' I said through a short chuckle.

The day wore on pleasantly; it was not too windy, and the sun radiated a good amount of heat. We sat near the edge of the clearing, almost in total silence. It was around midday, and I had filled my stomach with some of the nuts we brought, which were quite good. There was no sign of any animals anywhere. I sighed, 'I think it's time to pack up and head back.' 'God, we've only been here a few hours; patience, my young one,' Chance replied. 'Alright, we'll just wait a bit more,' I replied. Nobody talked or moved. 'Hey Chance, Karly, do you guys have any snacks...?' I asked as I looked around me. We hadn't moved since we sat down. The sun had dropped a few centimetres past where I was sitting, and the sky had turned a pale blue behind the trees. The birds were still chirping. I went to say something to Karly but stopped suddenly.

We all heard it. A faint yet very distinguishable blaring of music. The music rapidly got louder, pouring through the trees and bouncing off the rocks. Chance jumped to his feet with a fearful expression on his face. 'What the hell,' he said through gritted teeth. 'Oh no! Mum is back at camp by herself! We need to go right now,' Karly said. We all stood up without a second thought and started running through the bush toward our camp. We slowed the pace as we approached our campsite.

'I wonder when Dan and Sophie are due back?' I said to Chance quickly. We crept behind the Winnebago, where men's voices could clearly be heard. Karly was closest to the corner of the van, and she peered around the corner of the vehicle. She turned back to us. 'They've got mum tied up, but she looks ok,' she said desperately, peering around the side of the van again, trying to get a better look at what was happening.

'Stand up slowly, with your hands in the air,' a deep voice said menacingly. I closed my eyes and sighed. This might be a problem, I thought to myself as I slowly turned. A man with dark hair and a neatly shaved head stood over us, his firearm aimed at Chance. He looked slightly older than me, maybe in his mid-thirties. He was wearing a black leather jacket, jeans, and boots. We all stood up as he flicked his gun sideways, indicating that we should move into the main camp area.

'Ok, slowly now, no sudden movements,' he said. We did as he said, keeping our hands up. Karly cried out, 'Mum,' and ran forward, kneeling down and hugging Sharon. I saw her scrunched face, and she appeared to be crying. 'HEY! I make the rules now! Get up, or you'll be shot like a dog,' the man barked brutally. A second older man emerged from one of the tents with what looked like an AK-47. He must've been in his sixties. He had short, dark hair and a prominent scar on his neck, which I guessed must have been a knife injury from years ago.

'Well, quite the setup you guys have here—not bad at all. Very well-maintained camp, solar power, and fences even, I'm impressed. I could see us living here, but that leaves us with one large problem,' the younger man said cheekily, shooting the older guy a smirk. 'See, you guys don't understand. A large problem that requires you to die. Probably,' the man said, waving his gun around without a care. 'Get in a line on your knees over near her,' the man said, using his gun to gesture towards Sharon. She whimpered and also complied with his command. 'So, what's your name, fella?' I asked angrily as I got to my knees in line with the others. 'Oh my gosh, I must apologise for my rudeness,' he laughed. 'I'm Damian,' he said as he gazed over our faces.

He had a white T-shirt underneath the black jacket. His eyes were focused on me, and he appeared to be assessing us. For what, I wasn't sure. Goosebumps ran across my body and into the back of my head like an icy hand running up my spine. He had quite literally told us we were all about to die. I had to come up with a plan quickly. 'The gentleman over there is Mark. He looks nice, but he is a murderer and rapist, so watch him,' Damian said with a raised eyebrow.

'Also, I must say sorry, we never knew you were here. We have a little settlement north of here,' he said, kneeling down in front of Karly. 'There's another problem, though,' Mark said, aiming his sidearm at Karly's throat and using the barrel to try and raise her face to look at him. She briskly spat in his face as I yelled, 'don't you fucking touch her, or it'll be the last thing you ever do, you pig.' Mark got up and drew his arm backwards and then firmly backhanded me with his gun.

I let out a groan as I fell sideways onto the dirt. Instantly, a hot, searing pain radiated through my skull like lightning. I could feel warm blood on my face before I even began to attempt to sit back upright.

I returned to my senses as Mark tugged me to my feet, dirt and small twigs falling from my hair. I groaned as everything began to swim before my eyes. Everything was a blur; my eyesight turned black and red as the colours shifted. I squinted around to see where I was. I saw Damian looking at me, but his face was just a blur. He grabbed his jacket and pulled it back into position while clearing his throat. 'Hey! Anyone else who wants to fuck around will have a bullet buried between their eyes! Well, faster than I thought you would anyways,' Damian yelled at us.

'Now, as I was saying, the other major problem we have is that there is one big ass horde moving this way, a couple thousand strong if not ten thousand. Obviously, we were moving them away from our settlement, so, our bad,' he said snidely. 'Now, before we proceed with any further formalities, does anyone have any last words?' Damian asked. Shit, I thought to myself. Come on, think, think, think. Mark walked over to me and raised his firearm at my forehead. I then remembered the gun in the Winnebago, under the mattress.

'Wait!' I yelled as my eyes flinched at the sight of the gun barrel staring me down. 'I have information in the Winnebago that I can show you. It might be important information for everyone's survival,' I said hesitantly. 'Get up then; let's see it,' he said, his gun aimed tightly at me still. I struggled to my feet, blood running into my eyes and pain soaring through my head once again.

'I need my hands, please,' I said, not expecting it to work. Mark walked over quickly and cut them loose with side cutters. 'One move, and you're dust. Move it,' Damian said. I walked towards the Winnebago, wiping my forehead with my hand. A large amount of blood smeared the back of my hand. I pulled the door open and stepped inside. 'You guys do realise that music will probably draw a lot of zombies, right?' I asked, glancing back at my captor. 'Shut up and move,' Damian replied as I walked up the steps into the Winnebago.

Damian stepped in with his gun trained on me. I breathed heavily, looking around. 'Be quick, my friend; we do not have much time,' Damian said intimidatingly. I bent to my knees to look under the bed while sliding my hand under the mattress. I blindly fumbled around for the gun, though I couldn't find it. Fuck, I thought! Dan must've taken it; now I'm screwed. 'What are you doing with your hand?' Damian yelled.

He took two steps over and reefed on the back of my shirt, sending me off balance and causing me to fall backwards. 'Time's up. Fuck your information,' he yelled, reaching down and lifting me by the front of the shirt with incredible strength. He turned with me towards the door as I was about to get my footing. 'Join the others,' he said calmly, raising his gun and smacking me in the forehead for a second time.

He pushed me out of the Winnebago, and I hit the ground hard as I fell backwards. My vision was totally blurry, a pain shot through my head like I'd never felt before, and the wind left my lungs. I cried out as I rolled over, blinded by blood filling my eyes. Damian made his way out of the Winnebago.

The hammer of a gun was suddenly heard. 'Drop your gun right now, you piece of shit!' I glanced over to see Dan standing there at the side of the Winnebago, his barrel pressed against Damian's head. 'Oh, a straggler, I see,' he said. 'Sophie! You all good?' Dan yelled. 'Yep, I've got his gun,' Sophie yelled back as she disarmed Mark.

Sophie kept the AK-47 aimed at Mark as he kneeled while she unclipped everyone. Sophie came over to me, lying on the ground. 'Are you ok?' she asked with a horrified look on her face. 'I think so, mate,' I said, wincing as I stood up. I was whacked in the skull twice, and my head is burning.' Dan still had his gun trained on Damian. 'You are outnumbered; drop it now or you're done,' Dan said hurriedly. Damian stood there in silence, gun in hand. 'You won't do it; it'll attract too much attention,' Damian sneered. 'Are you a serious idiot!? We heard the music from miles away. You've already drawn attention to us!' Dan yelled at him. 'Dan, they've drawn a horde towards us,' Sharon screamed, pointing towards the hillside.

Around thirty zombies were slowly staggering in our direction. Damian took the distraction as a moment of opportunity and quickly aimed towards me. A gunshot rang out through the bush. Blood sprayed from Damian's skull as Dan released the trigger, killing him instantly. Sophie screamed and jumped back in shock. 'You good man? He didn't shoot you at the same time, did he?' I said it frantically.

'No, he didn't, man. Are you okay?' Dan asked. 'Nope, all is well, I think. My head bloody hurts, and I think it will need stitches,' I replied. Dan helped me to my feet. I felt dizzy standing. 'We need to go,' I said. 'Mum, Sophie and Chance start gathering critical things—weapons, medical supplies, and whatever food you can throw in the ute trays,' Karly yelled.

'Nath, you go sit in the front passenger seat. You probably have a concussion, ' Chance said as he glanced at me. 'We'll sort this.' I stumbled over to the car, grabbing the handle and glancing at the hill. Hundreds of zombies were pouring over the ridge. I was about to head for the driver's seat when Chance pushed me out of the way. 'If anyone is driving, I am. It's also not safe for you to drive right now; I'll be right behind you, though,' he said. 'Let's go, people, please hurry up,' Chance demanded as things were thrown into the back of the ute. Dan ran over to the car and gave me three Paracetamol.

I threw them down my throat. 'What do we do with this old prick?' Dan asked me. 'Leave him. He's a sex pest and a murderer. Tie him to the tree and leave him one bullet on the ground, just out of arm's reach but close enough so he can reach it with his foot if he really tries,' I replied. 'Damn, but yeah, you're right,' he said, closing the door.

I put the seatbelt on and cracked the window for some air. I heard Dan speaking to Mark, 'You have wronged people both before and during these times. You chose wrong, so this is as far as you go.' He handed Mark the firearm as he begged to be freed. Dan zip-tied his other hand to the tree and placed a single bullet in the dirt. 'If you're smart, you'll know what to do with this,' Dan said, turning his back on the disgusting human.

Karly and Sharon jumped in the back, Dan and Sophie into their ute. 'Let's go,' came over the radio from Dan's ute. 'Shit, we only have a quarter of a tank of fuel left,' he said. 'Why don't we just head to Mandurah and get a boat? We can leave for Rottnest Island. Surely, zombies can't swim. I don't have any other ideas on where we can safely go,' I said.

Karly looked at Sharon and shrugged her shoulders, 'not the worst idea, bugger it, let's just do that,' Karly said as Chance quickly reversed the car. The car moved forward as zombies began entering the camp. Chance stopped and stared at Mark.

The old man looked on in horror as he desperately tried to reach the bullet with his foot. Zombies edged closer to him as he whimpered. He finally managed to flick the bullet close enough to grab it. He slid it into the chamber and cocked the hammer. He slowly moved his finger to the trigger, putting pressure on it. Taking a deep breath, he brought it to his eye level and aimed at the distant figure moving towards him.

He turned the weapon on himself, looked up to the skies, and squeezed the trigger. The gun made a clinking sound, indicating the firing pin was bent. He quickly racked the slide back, seeing that the bullet was still there. That was it then; the pin was bent. The old man looked deeply saddened; his last moments on Earth were to be spent with nothing to defend himself. He was completely vulnerable to the zombie horde.

He began to scream as the zombies approached. 'Let's go, Chance, he's done,' I said as Chance hit the accelerator. I glanced back briefly, seeing many zombies sinking their teeth into his flesh.

RUN BABY, RUN

Chance roared through the bush, unsure of where he was heading. 'Turn right here!' Karly said urgently. Chance reefed the vehicle around, narrowly avoiding a large tree, but smashed the side mirror. We wove around a few more trees, and Karly shouted out again. 'Straight through here, turning right a bit earlier,' she said. Chance followed her directions, and soon enough, we were on the deserted highway again. 'Everything we do turns to shit; when can we get a damn break?' I said in a frustrated tone.

'At least we're still alive,' Sharon replied. 'Those men were pigs back there; I'm glad they're dead now,' Sharon said. This was a pretty extreme thing for Sharon to say, which slightly saddened me to hear, but she was right. 'Ok, so if we head the back way through Glen Mervyn, through Collie, and along Tallanalla Road, it should take us to Mandurah on the back way through Pinjarra, Nathan. Can you remember your cousin's address?' Karly asked.

'Ah no, I can't. It's on the canals, though, and I'll be able to recognise it,' I replied. 'Wait, why are we going to Mandurah again? Surely it'll be crawling,' Sharon asked. 'My cousin has a house on the canals; there's a boat. I'd love to think they'll be there waiting for us, but I think they left for overseas a few years ago. We can take their boat to Rottnest Island to get away from all this,' I replied, staring blankly out the windscreen, pain ripping through my head.

Zombies littered the highway, sometimes having to go completely off-road to get around mini-hordes of them. The roads were graveyards for cars, all abandoned, while others had been driven off the side in the hope of escape. I glanced up at Chance as he dodged zombies by the dozen. He kept his eyes hard on the road, driving us towards Mandurah. 'Brace!' Chance yelled suddenly as an object hit the front of the car and went under it. The car lurched forward, and we could feel the impact reverberating through our bodies.

I looked back to see what had happened, and I saw a zombie lying motionless on the ground. 'Jesus! You reckon that'll buff out?' Chance laughed as the rear wheels bounced over the zombie. We all laughed. What a weird thing to laugh about, I thought. Were we all going a little crazy? I glanced back, saw Sharon shaking her head at me, and laughed again.

We cruised at a decent speed for the next hour and a half until we came into Mandurah. I was in and out of sleep. Chance kept shoving me, trying to keep me awake. As we continued to drive, I couldn't help but notice how much we had all changed since the outbreak began. We were all a little crazier, a little more paranoid, and a little more desperate. Our relationships had also changed, as we relied on each other more than ever to survive.

There were dozens upon dozens of zombies, no matter where you looked. They wandered aimlessly along the roads and out of buildings with no purpose. 'These poor people,' Sharon said sadly. 'I know Sharon, but we just need to remember that they aren't people any longer,' I replied.

We pulled into the school grounds of Glencoe Primary School and quickly jumped out. 'Right, we need to get some supplies, and Chance, you're going to have to stitch this gash in my head back together,' I said. He agreed, and we all darted across the parking lot as quietly as possible.

The sun's dying light glared horizontally across the walls of the school. Around ten zombies moved towards us as we approached a door. I turned the knob, and surprisingly, it opened. 'Sweet,' I said as I pushed the door. We all went inside, and I locked the door behind us.

We were in what appeared to be a sporting supply shed. This school was quite large and felt eerie, devoid of people. I thought it was like something out of a movie as we moved quietly towards the end of the shed. The orange afternoon light pierced through the windows, casting shadows across the floor from the zombies looking in.

'Why do we need to be in here?' Dan asked. 'Aren't you a Paramedic? Don't you have stitches in your kit?' 'Nah, man, the big difference between nurses and paramedics; we don't stitch injuries; the nursing station may have some around here,' I replied. Karly pushed the next door open, and we entered a long hall with numerous offices down the right side and a large reception office at the end.

'I'm pretty sure there's a nurse station at the end of the hall in that large office,' I said. 'If these are the teachers' quarters, one of these teachers will surely have some alcohol,' Chance said. 'Really Chance? Really? Do you think now is an appropriate time,' I whispered loudly at him.

'Oh my god, you're an idiot; it's for you and your head for when I shove a needle through it a dozen times. Those blows to the head did not knock any sense into you,' he said with a grin in response to my accusation. I grinned, 'Yeah, whatever, let's keep looking.' He was spot on, though; I wasn't thinking clearly.

We moved forward quietly in the direction of the main office. The doors were closed on each basic classroom, a faint haze of orange light shining through into the hallway. We came to a U-turn with a small flight of stairs opposite the main hallway. 'Left side first,' Chance whispered. We each took a door on the left side. I opened mine and peered into the shadows. I could make out the desks. 'Nope, go back to the main office doors first,' I whispered to the group. The glass doors opened quietly as we entered. 'There,' I said, pointing to a door with a vent in it.

'That'll be the nurse's office.' We moved forward and into the room. The sun had nearly completely vanished from the horizon now, making the office extremely unnerving and deadly quiet. I opened the cupboard, revealing a good supply of medical equipment. 'There we go,' I said happily, pulling a suture kit from the cupboard. 'Ha-ha, of course, the nurse has Vodka,' Chance said, having a swig. He handed me the bottle, and I took a large mouthful.

Karly emerged at the doorway, holding a packet of little metal-cased candles so we could see what we were doing. 'We're going to wait out here if that's ok. I can't stand what you two are about to do,' Karly said. 'Yeah, fair enough,' Chance said, lighting the candles with my lighter.

I walked over to the door and closed it; the rest of the group was quietly sitting around the large fishbowl-like exterior. Dan and Sharon were crouched over a couch, peering outside at the small groups of zombies passing by. I walked over, and Chance handed me a vodka-soaked piece of gauze.

I applied it to my head, and once again, a searing pain shot through my skull. 'Damn, that really hurts! You know what to do?' I asked Chance. 'No, tell me, nurse,' he said. 'Right, the sharp hook needs to go about half a centimetre into the tissue; it then wraps back around itself, and you continue to do that down the gash with about half a centimetre gap between them,' I said. 'Righto, let's just get it done,' he said. He lifted the tweezers and hook to my forehead. I felt it dig in and slide through my skin.

I sat there patiently as he continued to push the hook through my forehead, pulling the wound closed. 'When you're done, tie the end off around itself,' I said. Chance worked on me for another ten painful minutes or so as I swigged the vodka. 'There we go, princess, good as new,' he said, proudly looking at my forehead. I got off the bed and looked in the mirror. 'Not bad at all, my man; good work.' The wound was sutured well enough, so I just had to watch it now for any sign of infection.

I popped my head out to where everyone was waiting. 'Oh, that looks alright,' Karly said, looking at my head. She gave me a big hug and thanked Chance. 'So, the cousin's place is about three minutes from here down McLarty Road and then onto Old Coast Road. The house is on the estuary, so I said, hopefully not too many zombies. We slowly left the school grounds and headed for the vehicles. Chance jumped in the driver's seat again, and Dan was in his. 'You feel okay, babe?' Karly asked me from the back seat. 'Yeah, I feel a bit nauseous, but I'll survive,' I replied. 'Don't you have Ondansetron in your paramedic kit?' Karly questioned.

I was impressed she remembered the drug; she always took a liking to the things I talked about when I did paramedic work full-time. 'Nah, I'll hold off; it's not too bad, just concussed, I think,' I replied. Once again, the streets were loaded with zombies as Chance carefully drove between them, being careful not to hit any and destroy the ute.

'There it is, Nathan! Amity Cove Road is the street; turn left!' Karly yelled excitedly, pointing to the top left of the windscreen at the street sign. 'Thank god your memory is better than mine, I couldn't remember the street name,' I replied. Chance pulled the ute into the driveway and turned it off. 'We leave the keys here hidden somewhere; I think that will be safest. At least we have a vehicle on the mainland, and we know where it is,' I said.

I walked up to the front door and attempted to open it. 'Dammit locked,' I said to everyone quietly. A screech rang out from down the street, which made us all jump. 'Let's get up on the brick wall and jump out into the backyard. Everyone, eyes open, and stay vigilant,' Dan said.

We all climbed up on the high brick wall one by one and walked along the length of the house, stopping by a corner that offered a view of the jetty where the boat was tied off. A skittering sound came from near us, and we all looked around but couldn't pinpoint the source. Suddenly, a figure passed the house out on the street. It ran dangerously close, so we all crouched down and hid from view. Whatever it was, it hadn't seen us.

I jumped from the wall and landed in the overgrown grass, turning around to help Karly, Sophie, and Sharon down. My cousin's house was a single-story brick house that backed right onto the Mandurah Canals, a really lovely spot. You can walk right out the back door, across the sloped lawn, down some stairs, and be on the jetty. The high ceilings inside met elegant light fittings, with large windows across the back with a view to the river canal.

It truly was an amazing property. Hard work gets you to a place like this, I thought. I approached the glass-panelled back door, praying that it was unlocked. I couldn't bear the thought of smashing their glass. I gripped the knob, closed my eyes, and turned it. It continued turning, and the door opened. I fist-pumped the air in celebration and turned back to the others. 'Ok, we're looking for boat keys.

I think they should be somewhere obvious,' I said through whispered breath. We all entered quietly, but from the sounds coming from the street out front, it sounded like more activity was occurring outside. 'Chance! Stay out the back on watch. Shoot anything that moves if it goes for us. Karly, give him the rifle, please,' I whispered shrill. We crept slowly around the abandoned house, each step taken with the utmost care to avoid making any noise that could potentially alert unwanted guests.

The heavy silence in the air only added to the sense of danger permeating every corner of the house. As we cautiously made our way through the darkened rooms, we also searched for any signs of useful items that could help us survive a little longer. Sharon emerged from a room. 'No keys here,' she whispered, her voice barely audible above our breathing. I headed cautiously towards the front door, where I could see a set of keys hanging on a hook.

My heart raced as I reached out and grabbed them, the jingle of the keys sounding like a gunshot in the silent house. I grabbed two sets of keys. One was clearly for a car, but the other two sets had multiple keys on them, so I took them all. We didn't know what they were for but couldn't afford to leave anything useful behind. I crept over to Dan. 'Man, to have a night in this house,' he said wistfully, looking longingly at the very welcoming-looking bed in the corner of the room. 'I'd kill for a proper bed.' 'Wouldn't we all!' I replied.

I headed back to the back door. Chance was standing on the brick wall, looking out into the darkness of the yard. 'Keys?' he said. 'Yep!' I held the keys up to him. Karly was by my side out of nowhere, which made me jump slightly. 'Let's have a quick look to see if there's any food still here,' I said, looking into Karly's eyes. We both nodded and headed back inside. I grabbed a backpack that was already in the kitchen and put all the food in it. I kept an eye out the front windows, ensuring we weren't attracting unwanted attention. Two others also took the time to search for food and other items we could use.

I slung the backpack over my shoulder and stopped suddenly as I heard something. I stood in silence as I heard panting heading in our direction. I wasn't sure what it was, but at that moment, glass from the front door panel suddenly exploded, and a zombie landed in the front hall. I stood there frozen and terrified; my breath left my body in an instant. The foul beast got up, looked straight at me, and sprinted towards me. Two shots were fired from behind the kitchen counter, hitting the beast in the head and neck and spraying blood around the room.

The stink of rotting flesh and coagulated blood filled the air. Before I knew what was happening, another six or so zombies were attempting to push their way in. 'Karly! Go get the boat going!' I yelled, throwing the keys at her. 'Chance!' she yelled as he entered the back door with the rifle, poised and ready to shoot. Another window smashed into one of the other front rooms. Chance fired three rounds from behind us, not hitting a single zombie. 'Chance! Breathe and focus!' I yelled. We needed to hold them off for as long as possible while Karly got the boat going. I prayed there was fuel in it. I stood looking at the window separating the kitchen from the hall.

I raised the Berretta and started to fire. A headshot was my primary target, but it was difficult under pressure, especially with a shaking hand. My first shot hit the hand of one zombie, making it turn to face me. I managed to shoot it in the head with my follow-up shot. I fired at another one, which didn't work. I turned to call Chance, but he was busy shooting behind me. I shot a beast in the left cheek; it fell over and got back up, but then was hit in the head by Chance's bullet. The front door was almost completely smashed in; knuckles were pushing through the wood.

'We need to go! They're coming through the side gates!' Chance yelled. I didn't need to be told twice. I raced towards the back door behind Chance. I was the last one out. Chance swung his machete high and buried it in the skull of a zombie who almost flanked us, spilling its brains onto the blade. We ran towards the grassy slope as a child's screams from the house right next door filled our ears. I felt sick to my stomach. Zombie children, bloody hell—how much worse can it get? Chance looked back at me as we hit the jetty, and he looked like he was overwhelmed by terror.

As he looked at me, he quickly looked above me into a tree on the shoreline and raised the rifle as a zombie threw itself at him, knocking him to the ground. Chance hit the jetty hard, causing the rifle to bounce off the jetty and into the water. Karly and Sophie were screaming at us in fear. I quickly approached the zombie that was trying to get up and squeezed the trigger four times, unloading the rest of the magazine into its rotting head.

I squeezed the trigger a fifth time and heard a clink; I was out of ammo. I helped Chance to his feet as more zombies crashed out of the house's back door. 'We need the gun!' Chance yelled. 'Leave the gun, it's gone! Get in the boat!' Dan yelled frantically. The engine sputtered and groaned as Karly frantically turned the key, but it refused to start. My heart pounded in my chest as I looked back towards the abandoned house we had just left.

The hair on the back of my neck stood on end as I saw movement in the corner of my eye. I turned slowly, my eyes widening in terror, as a zombie child stumbled down the grassy slope towards us. Its flesh was heavily decomposed, hanging off its bones in ragged strips. Its vacant eyes stared out from a face covered in black and red blotches, and its white dress was torn and stained with blood. I felt bile rise in my throat as the stench of decay filled my nostrils.

This nightmare came to life, a scene from a horror movie that had somehow become all too real. My mind raced with panic, and my thoughts were jumbled and incoherent. I wanted to scream, to run, to fight, but all I could do was stand frozen in terror, staring at the zombie child as she closed in on us. The boat finally roared to life, and Karly slammed the throttle forward as the boat accelerated away from the jetty. The lifeless child stood at the end of the jetty, staring at us, not a sound coming from it.

'Holy shit, that was close,' I said breathlessly. 'Could they own any more keys? Three-quarters of that time, I was trying to find the right key. Sorry guys,' Karly said. 'Not your fault, honey; you did good,' Sharon said, hugging her. The tears were running down Karly's face as Sharon held her tightly. I could see the sheer relief on her face. My adrenaline was still pumping, and I hadn't caught my breath as I walked over and comforted Karly. I think we all thought we would die back at the jetty. 'Those zombies sure seemed much more violent than usual, don't you guys think?' Chance said.

'The first one, though, had to be a Shreiker; that level of aggression isn't normal in zombies. But then I'm pretty sure all his friends came to the party when they heard the gunshots,' I replied. Sophie leant against the boat, shaking both hands in front of her. 'I feel disgusting,' she sobbed. 'That poor child, no one gets out alive by the looks of it.' I had never seen anything as terrifying as that or heard its scream; that was a sound I would not forget anytime soon.

Karly steered the boat out of the inlet, past the Mandurah and Halls Head foreshores, and into open waters. 'I think we need to stop doing things at night. It seems way more dangerous, and the zombies appear to be more aggressive at night,' I said over the noise of the boat, thinking back to what had just happened. 'Yeah, I agree. We have less cover during the day, but things seem easier," Sharon yelled. 'I mean, we didn't really have a choice thanks to those fools earlier,' Chance said.

The morning air whipped against us as we cruised along the coast north towards Perth. It was impossible to hear anything from the roar of the engine and the hull hitting the water, but small herds of zombies were visible along the coast from time to time. 'Would you look at the devastation?' I said, staring in disbelief. Some herds were moving; others were just standing on beaches doing nothing.

Chance stood beside me, 'probably ran out of shit to break or lives to ruin,' he said, staring at a group of zombies staring back vacantly at us. The sound of Karly's voice panicked me out of my thoughts. 'Are you ok?' she asked me over her shoulder as she guided the boat. 'Yeah, just annoyed that whatever we do falls apart, it's always something.

Look at them all, standing there like Muppets; just die already,' I said in a frustrated voice. She hugged me and looked up at me. 'We're going to be okay,' she said. I loved every part of this girl; she was so strong and held us, especially me, together like the group's glue. I kissed her forehead and stared blankly at the coast.

We continued to cruise along the coast, past Fremantle. I remember Fremantle, the old, historic part of Perth, with its hipsters and overpriced beers and ales. It sure was good for a Sunday session, though. Fremantle Prison was in there somewhere, built in the mid-19th century to house hardened criminals. Rottnest Island was around eighteen kilometres off the coast of Perth.

The sea was calm, thankfully, and the boat was not a bad size, but I dreaded thinking about how it'd go against waves, not to mention the shark-infested waters around these parts. 'Does the darkness and not knowing what creatures are underwater at night have a name, Nath?' Dan yelled at me.

'Yeah, from memory, it's called thalassophobia.' The thought of treading water halfway to Rottnest Island, not knowing what was below, made me shudder. 'What do you think we will find at Rottnest?' Dan pondered. 'Don't know; seeing if it's inhabited will be interesting. Surely it will be,' I replied. 'Yeah, people will definitely be there. Think about it; it's probably one of the safest places on the planet right now. No way zombies can get to it; unlimited seafood supply; plenty of firewood; the list goes on,' Karly said.

'Just as long as whoever is there is friendly. We don't want to be walking into a death sentence,' Sharon yelled, the wind whipping her hair across her face. 'For all we know, this is our last resort. I think we can assume that the mainland is lost. Or, if not lost, difficult to traverse due to that massive zombie population,' Dan said. 'Yeah, I think it's safest to assume that,' Karly said.

CHALET 153

As we drew closer to the island, the boat engine backed off a few gears as we cruised slowly into Thomson Bay towards the jetty. A single gunshot cracked through the early morning darkness, hitting the water ten metres before our boat. Sophie screamed and jumped up. A blinding light was aimed at us. 'Driver, kill the engine and hands up everyone in the boat,' a loud voice boomed across the ocean at us through a megaphone.

We all immediately put our hands in the air. 'Do you have any weapons on the boat?' it blared at us. 'Yes!' I yelled, 'We come in peace though!' 'Driver, restart the boat and drive slowly towards the jetty; no funny business or I will shoot,' the man behind the megaphone yelled. Dan turned the engine over and drifted towards the jetty slowly.

A single soldier stood at the end, aiming a firearm at us. 'We don't want any trouble, sir,' Sophie said. He lowered his weapon and holstered it. 'Ok, can you guys move over to the jetty and step off the boat one at a time? I need to see what you have on board,' he said, securing the boat and jumping into it. We stood in silence, watching the soldier inspect the boat. He climbed back onto the jetty and looked at us.

'Where have you come from?' he asked. 'We were in Perth when it all kicked off, then we went down to Donnybrook and have been hiding out there, but the zombies made it that far south too, so we left. This was the last place we could think of as a realistic and safe option,' I said. 'Ok, well, I'm Sam anyway. 'I somehow managed to escape the bullshit military operations going on over at the mainland.'

Obviously, this guy had been in the military for a while, as he stood proud and had a serious-looking sniper slung around his back with his uniform neatly pressed. He was a dark-skinned lad with short hair, a stubbled face, and muscular stature. 'Thanks for helping us, Sam; this was literally our last resort as somewhere to survive," I told him. He nodded to acknowledge my comments. 'Right, I need you all to line up along the end of the jetty, facing in my direction. I have a device developed by the Hostile Organism and Pathogen Unit that will scan your retinas to determine infectivity levels. When you've been scanned, move behind me up the jetty and wait at the box over there,' Sam said as we lined up.

He pulled the device from his utility belt and walked up to Karly. A funny electronic scanning noise rang out as green and then blue lasers rapidly scanned her eye. The screen on the device turned green. It was my turn next, the laser seemed to peer deep into my soul. 'I didn't know that technology existed yet,' Chance stated as Sam held the laser to his eye. 'Now is not the time for questions and answers will come later,' he replied.

Sharon blinked repeatedly as the laser did its thing. 'You ok, mum?' Karly asked. 'Yeah, hun, I just felt weird having my retina scanned,' Sharon replied with a quick laugh. Next was Dan, followed by Sophie. 'Basketballer, this one for sure, damn son, you're tall,' Sam said to Dan. I laughed, and Dan rolled his eyes as the scanner shone green.

Dan walked towards me as Sophie had her eye scanned. BEEP, BEEP chimed the scanner; a red alert flashed on the screen. 'WHAT! I'm not infected,' Sophie yelled in shock. 'Sorry, lady, it is what it is,' Sam replied, drawing his sidearm. 'Wait! Please, she can't be infected. Scan her again,' Dan said frantically, pleading with Sam. 'Fine, if you shut up and let me do my job!' Sophie stood there shaking, tears welling in her eyes.

The laser ran over her eye a second time. The machine paused briefly and then shone up a green screen. 'Well, I'll be damned; you live to see another day,' Sam said in a surprised manner. Sophie ran to Dan and cried into his arms. Sharon shot me a look, the type that symbolised, did we just make a mistake coming here? 'You haven't been bitten or anything, have you?' Sam asked Sophie. She shook her head.

Sam walked past us, nodding in the direction he was heading. 'You lot could probably do with some rest, by the looks of you. I'll take you to one of the chalets just up the road, and we can reconvene in the morning,' he said as his flashlight swept along the concrete jetty. 'There are other survivors here too, so in the morning, come back down along this path to the main area,' he said, pointing at the Thompsons Hotel.

A quokka ran across the path in front of us. 'Oh, how lovely,' Sharon said, turning back to look at us with a smile. A quokka is a small fury animal, about the size of a small rabbit, native to Rottnest Island. The only place in the world where you will find them. The sun was just beginning to shine through the morning sky as we arrived at Chalet 215 and 216. 'Split up, grab a bed, and I will see you later in the morning,' Sam said. 'Thank you; we really mean it,' I said as I walked past him. He turned around and walked back down the road without saying a word. We had stayed in these chalets before. 'Guess what! We get to sleep in a bed!' Karly said with a huge smile. It was a very welcoming sight as I kicked off my shorts and jumped into bed.

I woke around nine hours later. Everyone else was still sound asleep, so I quietly got out of bed and walked to the back screen door, which I opened quietly. It was almost like being on holiday here; the sun shone brightly high in the sky, and the ochre, yellow brick chalet formed a small area out the front that looked straight across to Thompson Bay. Its crystal-clear water made it very tempting to go for a swim immediately. Large trees and island pines provided a little shade beside the chalet. The water was about twenty meters from where I stood. I walked over to the wooden fence and leaned against it.

The water was so clear that you could see the reef and underwater features for about one hundred meters off the coast. Many boats were moored and sat peacefully bobbing in the glassy water. A stingray cruised the sea floor in very shallow waters before scooting off to the deeper areas. The whole bay was a marvel, a peaceful sea, and a beautiful environment. You could see right up the coast as it bent around on itself, as far as Bathurst Point. The screen door shut behind me as Dan and Sophie walked over; Dan finished pulling his shirt on.

'How nice is this man? We've never actually been here before. Not sure why we haven't,' Dan said, staring out at the water. 'I always wanted to come here,' Sophie replied. 'That's a quokka,' Dan said, pointing up at the small brown creature that was stretching a tree branch along the fence. 'Cool animals. Can you pat them?' Sophie asked, realising she hadn't seen one before. 'No, it's discouraged. They are pretty nice; you can walk right up to them; they're really tame,' I replied. 'The fishing here would be sweet, man. We should organise that,' Dan said.

'Oh, mate, it's wicked fishing here, especially if you go off the coast a little with a boat. There are plenty of bays around the island, too; Salmon Bay and Geordie Bay are beautiful to swim in. One has a large flat rock and coral formation you can swim to and walk along,' I replied. 'Sharks aren't really a bother here, but we are off the coast a fair way, so they are still a danger,' I said. 'What kind of fishing do they do here?' Sophie asked. 'All types; there's plenty of bait fish and such to get you started. It's just fishing, unlike anywhere else,' I replied.

I watched the multi-coloured fish swimming about in the shallower areas, mostly just eating the baitfish that were drifting up and down. Very mesmerising and calming indeed. We walked back inside as everyone else started to get up. 'I'm still tired. Can I sleep some more?' Karly said it through tired eyes. 'I know, babe, we all are. But let's go to the Thompsons Hotel and see what the go is,' I replied understandingly.

We gathered our things and headed out the back door to the road. All the roads on the island were quite narrow due to the lack of vehicles, except for an ambulance and a police car. The walk was nice. We didn't say much as we approached Thompson's Hotel. This was a modern pub with a large outdoor area. Giant umbrellas covered the tables where people usually sat. Sam, the soldier, gestured for us to approach him as he sat at a table with two others. We walked over and sat down at the large table.

'This is Michelle and Steve,' Sam said. 'Michelle is the island caretaker, and Steve owns one of the boats off the coast and keeps a steady stream of food coming in from the ocean.' We all said hello and smiled politely. 'I look after the vegetable crops and other various things to help us survive out here,' Michelle said. 'Numerous other people around the island are doing their jobs, which we are all assigned. Now, tell us a little about yourselves,' Sam said. Dan started, 'I'm Dan, and this is Sophie. We both used to work in hospitality and pubs and are dating. '

Chance rolled his eyes as he looked at me with a smirk. 'I'm Chance, and I worked in mining and have a thorough knowledge of explosives and random shit,' Chance said sternly. Sam had an impressed grin and then looked towards Sharon. 'Hey everyone, I'm Sharon. I also worked in mining and am good with heavy machinery,' she said. Sam then turned his attention towards Karly and me. 'I'm Karly; this is Nathan. I have also worked in mining, as a safety advisor and a good trades assistant. Nathan is a paramedic and firefighter. He was in mining also,' Karly replied.

'It's lovely to meet you all. We can utilise a good range of skills here on the island if you want to stay. Everyone pulls their weight here and chips in, so we can go about life as normally as possible,' Sam said. 'During the week, you're expected to do your tasks, whatever they may be assigned. Saturdays and Sundays are for relaxation, but he said that sometimes Steve will go out on the boat, weather dependent, based on what he has caught during the week.' 'There's a few of us here who love fishing, so we can definitely help with that,' Karly said, shooting me a wink.

She was very right; I loved fishing, along with Dan. Any excuse to go out deep sea, especially due to a zombie apocalypse, we were down for. 'Yeah, count us in, Steve,' I said, nodding at him. 'Before I split you guys up and assign duties, can you tell us what it is like over at the mainland?' Sam asked. 'Yeah, it's terrible. There are thousands of those things everywhere you go. We survived in Donnybrook for a fair while but got overrun due to some Unwanted's turning up,' I said. 'Unwanted's?' Sam asked curiously.

'Oh, it's our name for people that are still alive and looking for trouble,' Karly said. 'I like that you've named them,' Sam replied with a smirk. 'We encountered a few different types of zombies too, especially when leaving Sharon's that night,' Dan said. 'Go on,' Sam said. 'An absorber, I think from memory on the news over the past years, had whips with arrowhead-like ends and healed itself after we downed it,' Dan said. 'Then the normal Glazzers and Zoggo's, oh, and a few Shreiker's, the fast ones that make a tremendous amount of noise,' he continued.

'Seems like a moderate amount encountered then,' Sam said, looking at Steve and Michelle. 'What do you mean, there's more?' I said, surprised. 'Oh yeah, there's a few more. There's Crawlers and parasitic Oozers also. Crawlers are like large cockroaches in appearance. They bite the host, which causes a massive, irreversible infection resulting in cardiac arrest and subsequent reanimation. Oozers are very slow, and they release spores into the air, which also causes infection. They're highly infectious, so stay away if you see one. You'll know one when you see it, get bitten, and you're a goner. The crawlers seem to associate themselves with the Oozers so if you see one, an Oozer is probably nearby. Both are just bad news. The spores that the Oozers release into the air seem to cause infection through particle transmission. Nasty bastards. Lost a few friends to them. There are reports of other zombies, with one reported to be the size of a car, but we think that was an Absorber, eaten too many of his mates and grown very large and strong, but slow,' Sam said.

'So surely we're pretty safe on the island then, they can't swim, hey?' Sharon asked. 'Correct. As far as we know, they can't, but little is known about their strengths and weaknesses,' Sam replied. 'Because it's Friday, we will get you all to go to different areas to see where you can help. Steve will go out in the morning for a fish for whoever wants to assist him,' Sam said. Four hands shot up immediately.

'Excellent, so some quick rules. Don't take anything that isn't yours, drinking night is on Saturdays and lastly, the western part of this island is forbidden and off limits. I am not at liberty to discuss why, though there may be military assets there, so stay away,' Sam said. Michelle smiled, looking at everyone happily, 'Well if you'd like to all come with me, we can go for a walk, and I can show you where everything is.' We all got up from the table. Sam quickly grabbed my arm and pulled me back, 'not you.' 'I'll be ok,' I said to Karly as she looked at me, concerned. The others walked off out of sight with Michelle.

Sam sat out at the table with me. 'Tell me about yourself, Nathan. I know your girlfriend has briefly, but I want to know what you're like,' Sam said. 'Nothing special to report, really. I'm 31 and was working in mining as a Paramedic and Emergency Services Officer,' I replied. 'So dual qualified then. That could be really handy. Tell me, how much medical experience do you have?' Sam enquired.

'Decent amount, I can handle myself if I have the right equipment. I'm quite familiar with emergency pharmacology and trauma management, including medical conditions, but not a total whiz on everything, as you could appreciate.' 'Excellent, better than what we have now, which is nothing,' Sam said as he gazed out over the ocean. 'Can I trust you, Nathan?' Sam asked sharply, briefly looking in my direction. 'I need to show you something, as another opinion wouldn't hurt, but it is highly classified information.' 'Not if it's going to get me killed, but yes, I have integrity if you need me to give my opinion,' I replied. 'Come with me, and you would expect this goes no further than you or me, got it?!' Sam asked. 'Yes sir, my lips are sealed,' I said. Whatever I was about to see must be decent. Sam seemed pretty sketchy about it.

We walked behind the building where a WA Police cruiser was parked. 'Nice ride,' I said. I pulled the passenger-side door open and got in. 'Never been in front of one of these,' I smiled, looking at Sam. He pulled the police car onto the narrow bitumen road and drove towards the Kingston Barracks, pulling up outside a chalet.

A yellow-walled, tinned roof building stood before me, with red bricks around the entrance. 'So, you are about to see a long-kept secret of the island. You may also not have heard of them before. Hence why I was sceptical about showing you, but you look like you can be trusted, or you better be.'

I thought to myself, did he just threaten me? Was it worth seeing if it painted a target on my back? What if it was important? All these thoughts raced through my head as we approached the Chalet. This one looked slightly different from the others along the roadway; the number was smaller and read "Chalet 153" across the top of the door. Sam pulled a large key from beneath his shirt over his head. He glanced behind us quickly and slid the key into the locking mechanism. A mechanical sound was heard as the door popped open.

We entered the chalet. Nothing was unusual; the walls all appeared the same as the other chalets, and the smooth concrete flooring glared up at me. Sam walked to the centre of the dining room, bent over, and pushed the large table to the side, revealing a trap door. Holy crap, I thought to myself, the caves! We'd always heard about a mysterious cave system at Rottnest Island, but no one had ever managed to find it, so we wrote it off as folklore. 'This isn't what I think it is?' I asked Sam inquisitively. 'It sure is the infamous Rottnest cave system. You know why you couldn't find it previously?'.

Sam paused and stared towards the trap door. 'It's a military asset; we agreed with aboriginal elders to allow us to utilise the area.' I looked back at him in disbelief. 'Chance and I came here once looking for these caves. We walked past this chalet at least five times. I'm pretty sure Chance even made a joke about it being buried under a chalet,' I said, thinking back to the day. 'Well, here it is,' he replied. Sam pulled out a swipe card, and the trap door slid silently open. He proceeded to climb down metal stairs into the darkness. I quickly followed him down the ladder.

The rocky roof had little lamps bolted to it, providing just enough light for us to see our way. As we descended further and further into the underground base, I couldn't help but feel a sense of awe. I had heard rumours about these tunnels, but I never would have thought I'd have the opportunity to see them in person. It was like a miniature city hidden away beneath the surface of the island. I was impressed with the level of sophistication of the base.

It was clear that much thought and resources had gone into its design and construction. 'HMAS Brisbane lies just off the island's coast to the west,' Sam said as I gazed at the many screens. 'We saw faint flashes off the coast when the bridges were levelled in Perth,' I replied, still scanning the room. 'A necessary evil, unfortunately, to try and stem the flow from the metropolitan region,' Sam replied. He walked over to a large black filing cabinet and pulled it open, removing a folder from within.

Sam threw it down on the table. "TOP SECRET" was written in red across it. I quickly grabbed it and riffled through the documents. 'Dare I ask, but what has the military done to attempt containment, you know, more than the obvious things?' I asked curiously. Sam sighed, running a hand through his short-cropped hair. 'It's been tough,' he admitted. 'We've tried everything from quarantine measures to mass vaccinations, but nothing seems to be slowing down the spread of the virus. It can be transmitted through bites or scratches, making it especially difficult to contain. The virus seems to mutate too quickly for us to get ahead of it,' he replied.

I sighed, understanding the gravity of the situation. I knew that there were no easy answers to the zombie outbreak. All we could do was keep fighting and hope that someone could find a way to stop the spread of the virus before it was too late. 'There are classified reports from Chile and Sudan of zombies being captured and trials conducted on them in secret underground facilities, but the results of these trials have never been made public,' Sam said.

'I assume there was no good outcome from that?' I asked. 'No comment,' Sam replied, quickly grabbing the folder from me and stuffing it back into the black locker. 'The Infected Persons Research Centre and

HOPE were working on something before all hell broke loose. I'm still unsure of what that was, as we lost contact,' Sam said.

'Everything you have seen here today is highly confidential and sensitive to the nation, including this place. Furthermore, we are receiving an SOS signal from atop the BHP tower in the city. The message also says that they have something of interest that may turn the tide on the war against the zombies, claiming they worked in the Hostile Pathogens unit,' Sam said.

'We're not sure what it might be, but I don't want to sit around and miss an opportunity like this. It's likely there are survivors on that rooftop also,' Sam said as he held an arm forward, indicating I should begin moving out back toward the ladder. I turned around and walked back down the tunnel, my mind racing with the implications of the mission ahead.

Sam climbed the cold ladder first to open the security door, and I followed close behind. The ladder's rungs leading up to the security door were slick with condensation.

As we emerged from the underground base and returned to the waiting vehicle, I couldn't help but feel a sense of excitement and anticipation. This could be our chance to finally end the zombie outbreak and save countless lives. I just hoped that we were ready for whatever lay ahead. Sam grabbed my shoulder as we exited the villa.

'Remember, nothing to be repeated until I give a mission brief in the next few days,' Sam said, his voice low and serious. 'I'd like to stay in front of whatever this is, for not too many people to know, not with what's at stake.'

OUR ISLAND SAFE HAVEN

The cruiser pulled up at Thompson's Hotel, and I saw the rest of the group sitting around the outside table, talking. Karly jumped up and came over as I got out of the vehicle. 'Where have you been, Nath?' Karly asked me, curious for information. Sam exchanged a brief look at me as if to remind me of the secrecy of the base and our agreement. 'Ah, I went for a drive around the island. Sam discussed the responsibilities and the likes. Nothing too exciting,' I said nervously as Sam glanced back at me.

'What about you guys? How was the tour?' I asked. 'Oh, we've done heaps; we went and saw the water treatment system and vegetable gardens. They're quite impressive,' Karly said as we returned to the table. 'They have a really good setup here, so hopefully there's no weirdos to wreck it,' she replied. 'Hey man!' Dan yelled. 'Michelle, the caretaker, said we can go chill out for a while and that there will be a barbeque around five thirty this afternoon,' Dan said. 'Yeah? No arguments here. A barbeque?! I love barbeques!' I replied.

We grabbed our things and headed back up the path towards the chalets. 'Oh my god, oh my god, I didn't even think of it,' Sophie blurted out suddenly, 'There's power here! Power equals hot water!' she giggled excitedly while laughing. 'Oh yeah! Yay!' Karly squealed back. 'I call shotgun on first shower,' Sharon said as she ran up the sandy path. I laughed with Chance as the rest took off running. It had been a long time since we had access to hot water, and the simple luxury of a warm shower felt like a godsend.

When we reached the chalets, the girls were rummaging through their bags for clean clothes and toiletries. I couldn't wait to wash off the sweat and grime from our journey, and the thought of hot water running over my tired muscles was too good to resist. 'Righto, ladies, first, we will chill out and play some cards,' I told the group. No arguments were heard. I sat down with Dan and Chance and played a few blackjack games with them. Around twenty minutes later, Karly emerged from the bathroom. 'I feel damn amazing,' she said with a big smile on her face.

'My turn,' I said, pushing past her. I turned the tap on and undressed, stepping into the shower as the warm water ran through my hair and over my body. I couldn't help but feel grateful for this moment of normalcy. In a world overrun by zombies, the little things, like hot showers, kept us going and gave us hope for the future. I knew that we still had a long road ahead of us, but for now, I was just happy to be able to enjoy this simple pleasure.

We walked back down towards Thompson's. Halfway there, the smell hit us all at once. 'Holy lord, they have an actual barbeque! With actual meat cooking!' I said very excitedly. There's nothing quite like an Australian barbeque on a warm day. The smell of sizzling meat filled the air, tempting my taste buds and making my mouth water.

Sam and Michelle stood in front of a large barbeque out the front of the glass panels of the pub. 'Where did you get meat from?' Dan asked curiously. 'Son, we are on an island with a very large freezer at the back of the pub. The thing was chock-full of meat and still is. This is not every night; just a little welcome treat to settle you all in,' Sam replied.

The heat of the barbeque warmed my skin, and the smells filled my nose. It's a sensual experience that's hard to resist; all I could think about was sinking my teeth into a perfectly cooked sausage or steak. The aroma of sizzling onions and peppers added to the mouth-watering experience, making my stomach growl loudly.

We gathered around the table as the sun sank lower in the sky. Each person carrying a loaded plate. There was a sense of camaraderie and joy as we shared stories and laughed together, with the warmth of the evening and the good food bringing us all together. 'Geez, that was good,' Dan said, taking his last mouthful of sausage on bread.

'Oh man, nothing beats it; savour the flavour. I suppose it will probably be a while before we get another feed like that,' Chance replied from across the table.

The sun was beginning to sink over the horizon, casting a beautiful orange glow; the sky was painted with streaks of pink and purple, and a gentle breeze rustled the leaves of the trees. It was the perfect evening for a barbeque. 'So, you can all have a rest day tomorrow. I'm sure you're still very tired from the mainland,' Sam said.

We all nodded gratefully in silence. The group slowly retreated back to the chalet with full bellies and fell gratefully into bed. Karly and I discussed what our wedding would've looked like and came up with some pretty crazy ideas. We could hear Dan and Sophie in the next room laughing at something. We fell asleep pretty early.

I woke up to an empty bed, the sun pouring through the window and the sound of laughter from outside. I pulled my shorts on and walked out the back door to a slightly overcast morning. 'Here he is, Mr. Sleepy Head!' Sharon yelled. I smiled, still half asleep. Dan and Sophie lay in a hammock, strung between two shady trees. Chance and Sharon sat in chairs, and Karly lay in another hammock nearby. I climbed in with her, nearly tipping us both out. 'What's the plan for the day then for our day off?' I asked.

'We were thinking about hanging around here for a while, then going for a spin on the bicycles around part of the island,' Dan replied. 'That sounds great,' I said, feeling excited at the prospect of exploring the outdoors. 'Count me in,' I replied. 'Awesome,' Sophie said, smiling. 'We'll pack some lunch and some water and set off in about an hour. That gives everyone time to get ready and have some breakfast; there's some fruit on the table inside.' We lay around and soaked in the island's calm for a while longer.

'Want to go throw the frisbee?' Karly asked me. 'Yeah, for sure!' I replied, quickly eating an apple as we walked towards the sandy beach. Karly and I threw the frisbee back and forth for a while. The sand was brilliantly white as it ran between my toes. 'Yo! Let's go!' Dan yelled from up at the villa. I laughed with Karly at his demand as we walked back up along the beach. 'I vote we head in a northern direction, around to the west, and circle back,' I said. 'That sounds awesome; I'm pretty sure The Basin, Longreach Bay, and Geordie Bay are that way,' Karly replied.

We all walked side by side down to the bike rental shop. Using bikes was a fast alternative to walking around the island and allowed us to see more beautiful scenery. I grabbed a bike and headed out. Karly followed behind me, throwing me a helmet. 'Safety first, big boy,' Karly said sarcastically to me. I grinned back at her. 'Yeah, you're right,' I replied. We all jumped on the bikes and pushed off, heading for the basin. The fresh sea air filled my lungs and invigorated my senses. The sun was shining and the sky was a bright, clear blue as we rode through the picturesque landscape of Rottnest Island. It was around a fifteen-minute ride on bike to The Basin, including navigating some very challenging hills. We laid the bikes down quickly, tore our clothes off, and ran towards the water. I noticed an old "Snorkel Hire" stand to my left.

I grabbed a bunch of snorkels, goggles, and flippers, jogging them down to the beach. 'Holy crap, it is cold in here,' Dan squealed, dancing in the water, pulling at his shorts. It can be quite deceiving in Australian waters, especially coming from the Indian Ocean.

The sun can be glaring hot, and the water's still cold. 'Just throw yourself in and be done with it,' Karly suggested. I handed out the equipment, pulling a pair of goggles around my neck. I dove into the ocean, the water's cold refreshing as it enveloped my body. I swam down towards the seabed, the goggles allowing me to see the colourful fish and coral surrounding me. There was something very peaceful and calming about being underwater, though I also enjoyed being able to breathe, so I resurfaced to catch my breath.

'It's so nice down there,' I said, wiping the salt water from my face.

'Suppose we should play our normal game, so let's see who can dive down and grab a handful of sand. The first one to the surface wins,' Karly said quickly, diving beneath the surface.

I quickly put my goggles back on and dove down, kicking hard and propelling myself towards the sandy bottom. Karly was well in front, her long hair gliding in gold ripples through the water. I hit the bottom and grabbed a quick scoop of sand, pushing back off the ocean floor.

As I broke the surface, I saw that Karly had already held her hand triumphantly in the air, sand oozing from it. 'Ha! I win!' she said proudly. 'I'm impressed,' I replied. We swam around for a while longer, either down to check out the marine environment or floating around lazily on the calm surface.

As I stared across the shimmering water, Dan yelled, 'Look! A boat!'. I looked towards him as he pointed to the east. It was hard to see at first, but a small boat glided across the surface before disappearing around the side of the island towards Thompson's hotel. 'Wonder who that was?' Karly called. 'Let's go find out!' Chance replied. We swam to the shore and grabbed our clothes, pulling them on quickly.

We got on our bikes and began pedalling back from The Basin. On a downhill run, Karly slowly glided past me, pointing inland without saying a word. The sun bounced off Herschel and Government House Lake, a few kilometres away.

Then I saw it—the military warship off the coast. Its grey colour and dangerous look were an eyesore on the otherwise beautiful ocean view. The vessel appeared heavily armed, with several large gun turrets visible on its deck. The ship's radar arrays and communications equipment were visible on its superstructure, indicating advanced technology and capabilities. 'Jesus, look at that thing,' I called back to the others, pointing towards the ship.

We parked the bikes quickly out front of Thompsons. Sam stood with a young female, and he signalled for us to come over. 'Team, this is Lieutenant Baker, first name Lauren. She was assigned to this unit a few years ago,' Sam said. Lauren nodded at us quickly. She was in her mid-twenties with dark black hair and brown eyes.

She stood firmly in her military attire, a browning pistol on her waist and a rifle slung around her back. 'Everyone, grab a seat; we need to talk,' Sam said urgently. Karly looked at me briefly before sitting beside me. 'Ok, so hold questions until the end. We need to deploy a rescue team to the city. Lives are at stake, and help must be sent. Lauren has been busy sourcing a vehicle within the confines of the city.'

Chance suddenly interrupted, his eyes widening. 'You've been in the city by yourself!?' he blurted towards Lauren. She went to respond, though Sam raised a finger, 'question: time can wait until the end. So, as I was saying, Lauren has secured a ute loaded with explosives, and it's currently parked up at Elizabeth Quay.' Everyone's eyes widened as we looked at one another.

'I have information that personnel are trapped in a tower with information that could greatly assist humanity. The plan will be for Lauren and one other to head to Perth via boat at dusk. From what we understand, zombies are most active then. That ute is to go to the WACA Cricket Ground, from where a distraction has already been planned. When enough zombies are drawn into the stadium, a bomb will be detonated. The blast should only impact the stadium, though not its structural integrity if this gives you an idea of how far you should be when you detonate. From the stadium, you need to drive along Riverside Drive. We will be waiting in a boat, and from there, we will head for the tower. Now, who would want to...' 'Chance's arm shot up into the air so fast that, in fact, I thought he may have dislocated his shoulder. Lauren grinned at him. 'Well then, that was easy,' Sam said. 'Lauren and Chance will create diversion and distraction. The rest of you will remain with me. Sharon, you get lucky on this one; there are not enough seats on the boat over. If you could stay and help Michelle around the island, that would be great,' Sam said.

'No worries at all. You look after my kids,' she replied sternly. 'I'll get them all back in one piece,' he promised, shooting me a quick look. 'Each of us will have radios capable of communicating with each other within the confines of the city; Chance and Lauren, you two won't be able to contact us while setting the distraction,' Sam said. 'Roger that,' Lauren replied.

'Now, HMAS Brisbane reports a low-pressure system just off the north coast that may turn nasty overnight,' Sam said. 'Cyclone party!' Karly cheered. I remember she always talked about the cyclone parties they had in Darwin. I was excited to have one. I shot Chance a smirk.

'Anyways, as I was saying, let's complete our island duties today. I know you were off soaking up island life, but let's finish these tasks now. Tomorrow morning, we get up and do island checks around the main parts and the chalets. We need to secure loose items for the potentially damaging weather conditions, so they don't turn into projectiles,' Sam said.

'Karly and Sophie, if you don't mind going with Steve, sort out the boat and help secure it. Dan and Chance, please go with Michelle to help with netting on the crops to protect our food supplies. Sharon and Nathan, please head to the medical centre and ensure the ambulance is stocked with medical supplies in case we need them,' Sam directed us. 'Love that the guys have to do the food, and we get to play around with a boat,' Sophie squealed excitedly as she laughed with Karly.

'Come on, Nath, I'll give you a hand with the medical stuff. How exciting,' Sharon said excitedly. We left Thompson's and walked towards the medical centre. An ambulance was parked beside it. 'Standard WA ambulance, though this one probably has nothing in it,' I said, sliding the side door open. Surprisingly, it was stocked with everything you'd expect, including bandages, tourniquets, oxygen, and resuscitation equipment.

I opened the medical centre door and was immediately hit by the smell of antiseptic and disinfectant. The shelves had rows of medicine, bandages, and medical supplies. 'Damn, at least the place is clean,' I said. 'How do you know what to use and what everything does?' Sharon asked. 'Time, lots of practice, and plenty of learning. It's been an interesting career,' I replied. 'All these medications here can get us through a lot. We have pain management, injectable and oral, antibiotics, and tonnes more.

I'd be comfortable working out of here when the world is normal once more,' I said. We spent the next hour stocking up on medical supplies in an easier-to-use fashion and ensuring equipment was in working order. The ambulance was full of diesel, and supplies were stored securely in the back.

I was wiping down a bench when Karly and Sophie came in and said, 'Wow, Nath, imagine working here back in normal times!' Karly said. 'Yeah, I was just saying that. It's a nice island paradise with decent supplies,' I replied. I looked around the medical centre to ensure the windows were secured.

We decided to head back down to the main area. Chance came over with a look of disappointment on his face. 'Baked beans on bread tonight,' he said, rolling his eyes. I grinned and said, 'Oh man, that sucks!' 'Oh well, hearty meal it is,' Sharon said.

We all sat watching the waves crash against the shoreline. 'I miss travelling,' Sophie said wistfully. 'Me too,' Karly agreed. 'I miss seeing my family whenever I want,' Chance said. 'Yeah, and just being able to hang out with friends without worrying about getting sick,' Sharon added. We all nodded in agreement, silently hoping that someday soon, life would return to some resemblance of normalcy.

Around 2 p.m., the winds started picking up sand from the shore and whipping it relentlessly in our eyes. The low was meant to impact around 7 p.m. The palm trees began to lean in the wind, the fronds flicking violently. The wind whipped at my hair and made me feel colder. The clouds above the blustery weather started to look precariously close to merging into one. In the distance, a huge wall of clouds was heading towards the island. It was amazing to see but frightening at the same time.

I walked down to the jetty and noticed Karly sitting on the side of the boat, resting her chin on the metal bar, glaring out at the angry thunderstorm. Flashes of lightning were coming even closer together. 'What are you thinking about? Are you okay?' I spoke softly. 'The world... I don't know. I just feel like something is missing,' she said. I crouched down beside her and said, 'At least we have each other and some family and friends. It's going to be fine,' I said, trying to push her thoughts in a better direction.

'The world was fine when we were kids. Do you remember how free we were, just bumming around, no worries or cares in the world, just having fun?' she said. I grinned and looked at the boat floor before looking back at her. I know, babe, but we just have to keep continuing.' 'Sorry, I had a couple of shots of Tequila and thought I'd come down here before the madness started,' she said with a grin. I laughed. 'Classic, come on, let's head back to the pub before it starts raining,' I replied. Very dark, ominous clouds lay on the horizon, the ocean surface becoming choppy. The winds had picked up considerably. Indoors seemed like a good option, so we strolled the sandy pathway flanked by palm trees, heading back to the pub. I had my arm around Karly, sheltering her from the winds.

When we walked inside the pub, it was very warm and cosy, thanks to the large fireplace. Dan, Sophie, and Chance sat with Sam and Michelle at the bar. 'Ah, here they are, here's to you,' Sam called, raising a shot glass of a clear liquid. He gazed at me for a second longer and grinned, downing the drink. 'Where's mum?' Karly asked the group. Sharon emerged from the toilets almost on cue. 'Oh, hi guys!' she said with a huge smile, waving at us. Karly ran over and hugged her tightly. 'You ok, hun?' Sharon asked Karly.

'Yeah, I just had a mini-heart attack because you weren't here,' she replied with a happy look on her face. 'Gosh, I was just in the lady's room. Haha, come on, let's get a drink'. Small droplets of rain began to hit the large glass panels on the front wall of the pub.

Sam motioned to me to make more shots of tequila. I jumped the bar and grabbed the bottle, pouring the shots roughly. 'None for me tonight; I'm on medical duty to make sure we get through this storm in one piece, though I could be persuaded for one nice drink,' I said.

Sam raised his hand towards the liquor bottles and said, "The world is your oyster, my friend.' Dan raised his glass, looked at me, shrugged his shoulders, and recited our favourite saying, 'Peace, Love, and Zombie Attacks.' I chuckled. We all downed the shots together. Sam was on the counter as soon as everyone put their glasses on it, quickly refilling them.

The ceiling was retracting and folding backwards, and the lighting turned to a deep orange glow. It almost seemed like we were underwater, with the sunlight going in and out through the dark clouds. It was a beautiful sight—the waves smacking against the jetty and the sand blowing in the wind.

Over the next hour, the rain outside began bouncing off the street, splintering the yellow solar lights. Cold and wet outside, nice and cosy in here, I thought to myself. The large room was relatively empty, with only the six of us up at the bar. Sharon spoke intently with Michelle in the corner near a cracked window, both smoking. Dan approached me, 'How are you holding up, man?' he asked as my eyes finished slowly scanning the room. 'Good man, good. I need to tell you something, though,' I said, lowering my voice. I signalled for Karly to lean in and listen as well.

Dan's eyes lit up. 'What is it?' he asked. 'They have a decent military operation happening here; there's even a cave system. This is super-secret information and must not be repeated,' I said, looking backwards and forwards to both of them. 'When I went with Sam today, he took me to Chalet 153. That's where the entrance is to the cave system,' I said quietly. 'I bloody knew it!' Karly said, half whispering, half laughing.

'Well! Don't keep us waiting; what's in there?!' Karly said as her eyes widened with anxiety. 'Shhh, don't make what we're talking about obvious,' I said. 'Sam put a gun to my head today and threatened lead poisoning if I repeated what I saw.' Karly and Dan's eyes widened in fear. The wind pounded against the glass as the rain fell from the skies outside. The rain had calmed slightly, but the winds were still ferocious. Glowing blue lightning flashed in the distance, firing across the blackened, wild sky.

'Sam's pretty drunk. Let's slip off and check it out,' Karly dared us. 'Do you have a plan?' Dan asked. 'I do; come on, let's go now. Mum is at the bar, so I'll tell her to keep entertaining everyone,' Karly replied. I did a quick sweep of the room. Sam sat on a bar stool with his eyes almost closed, and Michelle rested her head on the bar. 'There's one last problem. Sam has the swipe card in his back pocket,' I said. 'So what?' 'It's a key card and key to the bunker,' Karly replied, reaching into her back pocket.

'You mean this key card?' she said, holding a white and silver keys towards us. 'Fell out of his pocket earlier, so naturally, I picked it up,' Karly winked. 'Let's sneak out the back door,' I said, slowly standing up. Karly approached Sharon and said, 'Mum, if Sam wakes up, feed him more shots.' 'Why honey?' Sharon asked. 'Never mind, just do it!' Karly shot back at her. 'We will be back.' Without hesitation, we slipped out the pub's back door and into the pouring rain, quickly grabbing our push bikes from the rack.

The heavy raindrops made it difficult to see, and we struggled against the wind as we rode through the deserted streets towards Chalet 153. The rain drowned out any other noise, leaving only the whirr of our bike tyres against the pavement. The puddles on the road splashed against us as we rode, drenching us to the bone. Raindrops poured from my hair into my eyes. Despite the treacherous weather, we knew that time was of the essence, so we pushed ourselves to ride faster, desperate to reach the chalet and uncover the hidden secrets.

We huddled together when we reached Chalet 153, dripping wet and breathing heavily. With shaking hands, Karly inserted the key into the door. 'Didn't you guys used to think there was a tunnel system on Rottnest?' Dan asked. 'Yep, and here it is,' I replied, pushing the door open. Inside, the chalet was dimly lit, and the air was thick with a musty scent. I grabbed Karly's key card and swiped it against the sensor. The door on the floor slid open. 'What exactly are we looking for?' Dan asked as we descended the ladder. 'Don't know, more information. I was briefly shown a top-secret document about trials, but there has to be more, so check as much as we can in five minutes and let's get out.'

We entered the screen-filled room. 'Holy crap, what a setup,' Dan exclaimed. 'Look in that cabinet there. I'll check this one. Grab anything that has top secret written on it,' I said. I riffled through the files in the black cabinet. Karly suddenly called, 'this one, Nath! It has "HOPE: Top Secret" written on it!' 'Did anyone bring a phone?' I asked. Karly pulled hers out and gave it to me. 'Open the document and slowly turn the pages, and I'll video record it so we can get out of here and read it later,' I said.

Karly slowly turned the pages as I recorded. We continued to pour through the files as fast as we could. 'Right, let's get out of here,' I said. Karly returned the file, and we left the base.

The rain was only a light sprinkle as we pushed back towards Thompsons. 'When we get back, put the stuff back in Sam's pocket, and we will retire to the chalets,' I said as we tore towards the building. As we walked inside, I saw Sam passed out on the couch on his stomach.

Karly swiftly returned the key card and key while Michelle wasn't looking. 'Well, I'm just about ready for bed,' I announced, shooting Chance and Sharon a quick look. 'Off so soon, dears?' Michelle asked. 'Yeah, big day,' I said back to her quickly. I gathered our things, and a few minutes later, we left the pub and headed towards the chalets. 'What have you kids been up to?' Sharon enquired.

'We've hit the bloody jackpot,' Karly said, waving her phone. 'We need to get back to our chalet, get into dry clothes, and read this report,' I said.

We changed into warm, dry clothes as the rain fell heavily outside again. We all gathered quickly around the table as Karly unlocked her phone. The video began playing when I noticed something. 'Hey, pause it and go back ever so slightly, I thought that I saw something,' I said. Karly pulled the slider back gently, revealing another folder under the one we looked through.

The top page only revealed a few sentences. "Reanimation of dead tissue and the potential impacts", "Ethics of using live human subjects in trials", "Behavioural patterns of zombies", and "The potential for using'. 'Shit!' I yelled, looking up at the roof. 'We totally missed that folder!' 'Oh well, let's focus on what this one says,' Karly replied.

The document revealed that units in Hostile Pathogens were noticing strange behaviour from zombies within the vast facility. The Infected Persons Research Centre acted like a zoo with huge pens. One page read, "Recent reconnaissance has yielded concerning information regarding the behaviour of zombies. Romeo unit reports that they have identified signs of coordinated zombie activity, suggesting that the creatures may develop higher-level cognitive function.

During a recent zombie retrieval effort for further studies, the Romeo unit observed a group of zombies exhibiting behaviour consistent with this hypothesis. The group was located in a cavernous area, and as the unit approached, zombies ceased individual attacks and appeared to regroup in preparation for a coordinated assault. This level of organization and tactical planning has never been observed in zombies before and raises significant concerns about the evolution of the zombie threat.

It is now clear that we cannot simply assume that zombies will remain slow, lumbering creatures with no higher brain function. Instead, we must be prepared for the possibility that they could become increasingly intelligent and sophisticated in their tactics. Further intelligence gathering and analysis is ongoing to assess the full extent of this new threat. 'Now they're smarter than you, Nathan,' Chance said. I laughed briefly, refocusing on the phone.

The next page was also insightful. "Our team has successfully restored a human from the zombie form, marking a major milestone in our efforts to combat the zombie apocalypse.

However, we must remain vigilant, as the success of our research has caught the attention of those who seek to impede our progress. A significant sabotage attempt has occurred in our laboratory, with two rogue agents absconding with critical data related to the above information. The theft of this data is a serious blow to our efforts and has significantly hindered our progress towards finding a cure for this devastating virus. We must act quickly to apprehend these individuals and recover the stolen data before they fall into the wrong hands."

We all sat there in stunned silence for a minute. 'Well then, that makes sense as to why we need to go on this rescue mission. Maybe the people in the tower have this data,' Karly said. I raised my eyebrows and nodded my head, staring at the table. 'That makes complete sense. Why risk a suicide mission into the city? That's why.' We discussed many crazy things for the next hour, and the room was excited about finding a cure. We all said goodnight and turned in for the night.

SMOKE AND MIRRORS

We all woke quite early. I suspected the excitable nature of the information we came across last night was the cause. 'We need to act as normally as possible around Sam and the others,' Sophie said. We threw some things in our backpacks and lay around for the morning, coming up with plans for what we would do when everything was back to normal or as normal as possible. It was around 330 p.m. when Chance and Lauren left for Barrack Street Jetty in the city.

The sun was still relatively high in the sky, piercing through the Perth skyline as the boat drew closer to the city. The whole place had a very surreal look about it. The boat skimmed across the water, and small waves provided little resistance against the powerful engine.

As Lauren cut the engine, ownerless boats bobbed against the jetty, drifting slowly towards the structure. Chance jumped out and tied the boat up, carefully scanning the area. The place was dead quiet, as far as he could tell.

It felt like he and Lauren were the only people alive in this city. The boat was secured, and they slung their backpacks over their shoulders. The pair moved quietly and quickly down the wooden jetty towards the vehicle's location. 'Geez, that bell tower is so creepy,' Chance said.

'I loved this area of Perth. Have you ever stayed at The Ritz before?' Lauren asked. 'No, though I've been up the bell tower and had dinner in the Riverside Bar and Restaurant,' Chance replied, pointing to his right. 'This has to be up there with the worst ideas ever. "Yeah, you'll be okay, Chance. Just distract thousands, if not tens of thousands, of zombies. It will be fun, they said,' he said sarcastically to himself. 'Zip it. Keep your mind on the task at hand,' Lauren replied.

The Ritz stood front row on the skyline, hiding a portion of Perth City Centre behind it. The city loomed in the background, the silence deafening. The sun reflected off the building's windows. 'There it is,' Lauren said, pointing towards a car. Lauren slipped the cover off of it. 'Excellent, as I left it,' Lauren said.

'Right, come around here and look at this map,' she said. 'When we drive, take the right turn out of here and just follow it the entire length down Riverside Drive. As we enter the city, continue straight onto Hay Street. When you get to Braithwaite Street, continue straight, and then take a left at Nelson Avenue,' Lauren instructed, pointing to the map.

'The place will probably be locked, so I've brought keys,' she said, grinning at Chance as she revealed a large pair of bolt cutters from within her bag. 'Nice, this vehicle is going to be damn noisy, though. Listen to the silence, would you,' Chance replied. 'Yeah, that's ok. We just do what we must do quickly and as effectively as possible,' Lauren replied.

'You're driving,' Lauren said to Chance. He got into the car and turned over the engine. It spluttered and coughed, then died. Chance looked at Lauren with a brief concern across her face. He fired the engine up again, revved heavily, then gave it a short burst. It roared and roared, then settled into a relatively quiet purr. 'Could you have found a shitter car?' Chance said sarcastically. Chance pulled forward and out onto Riverside Drive, the BHP tower disappearing in the rearview. It was one of the tallest buildings in the Perth Central Business District.

Lauren looked out her window at the city as it rolled by. The Supreme Court Gardens and Langley Park were dwarfed by hotels, towers, and residential buildings such as the Exchange Tower, Pan Pacific, Crowne Plaza, and Hyatt. As they came around the bend onto Hay Street, the Crown Towers could be seen standing dormant across the Swan River.

Chance turned left onto Nelson Avenue. 'We haven't seen a single zombie yet. Don't you think that's weird?' Chance asked.

'Yeah, sort of, but we know they're not as active during the day. It's worked out well for us,' Lauren replied. Gate 2, Stratton Entrance, was written in large letters, one of the entrances into the Western Australian Cricket Association or WACA, as most West Australians referred to it. 'Here, pull up, and I'll open the gates,' Lauren said, jumping from the vehicle and cautiously jogging to the gate. She raised the bolt cutters and quickly snapped the lock on the gate. It hit the floor with a metallic thud.

Chance drove the car through the compound. The staff car park came into sight as they passed the main building. Lauren pointed through the windscreen, 'Head over that way. That should give us access to the playing field,' Lauren instructed Chance. The vehicle pulled up, and Chance and Lauren hopped out. 'Weapons hot!' Lauren said in a raised whisper. Chance pulled out his firearm as Lauren raised her silenced assault rifle towards the looming light towers. 'Intimidating is the word that comes to mind,' Chance replied, nodding at the huge towers.

'Right, on me, we need to find the backup generators,' Lauren said. Chance nodded in agreement. They moved along to the edge of the cricket oval, taking cover behind the building. Lauren spun around the edge of the building to get a look down the corridor. Three rounds silently rang out from her muzzle. She reappeared a moment later, pushing her back against the wall. 'One nil, she said with a cheeky smile. They both entered the corridor past the recently dispatched zombie and headed around the concrete bend.

The main control room stood along the outer ring of the cricket oval. It was as grand and imposing as a missile bunker. Two doors flanked a line of neat and orderly tables. The massive panels had an array of gauges, monitors, buttons, and lights. The panels controlled the whole process of game management. 'Okay, sure, it couldn't be just one button,' Chance said. 'No shit! We need to turn the generators on. I believe they will be outside of this room, but on the other side, external to the venue,' Lauren said.

Chance flicked the main switch on, but nothing happened. 'Like I said, Sherlock, let's go look outside.' Lauren quickly pushed the backdoor open. Sunlight streamed into the room. 'It's 4:20 p.m., so let's pick the pace up a bit,' Lauren said, looking at her watch. Large generators stood dormant as Chance checked the fuel. 'Sweet, these look good to go. Let's fire them up,' he said, flicking the switch. The machine fired up as smoke billowed from the exhaust. 'Ok, sweet, they work. Let's set the explosives up and ensure everything is in place,' Lauren said to Chance.

They left the cricket centre and ran across the field toward where their makeshift bombs waited in the back of the ute. A good old ammonium nitrate explosion ought to sort them out, Chance thought to himself. They unloaded the nitrate onto the ground for the next thirty minutes. 'We need to plant the remote detonators here and here,' Chance said, pointing to the two corners. The explosives were finally set around 530 p.m. 'What are you like with being at heights? Lauren asked Chance. 'Yeah, not bad. I used to be in the emergency response team in mining, so I have a good idea,' he replied.

'Great, we've previously set a rappel line up over on that tower, so we can turn the lights on and head up. When enough zombies are here, we rappel down, get in the car, and then head back to the rendezvous point at Perth Underground,' Lauren said. 'Why are we waiting around with them!? Wouldn't it be smarter to crank the music and bail?' Chance asked. 'No, I need to be sure we take enough of them out to be worth it. Are you scared?' Lauren replied. Chance sternly replied, 'No, I just think it's a silly plan.'

Their ute was moved into position just below the most eastern light tower. They both separated and worked their way around the stadium, breaking locks and pulling open the large, slightly rusted steel gates. Once this was done, they met back at the tower. 'You ready?' Chance asked through breathlessness as Lauren nodded. The pair began the climb, reaching the top. 'Here, take this harness and put it on. Make sure it's on securely. Your mummy's not here to help now,' Lauren said, thrusting a harness towards Chance's chest.

He began the process of tying himself onto the rope after putting the harness on. Lauren grabbed her radio. 'Copy Sam. We're in position and set to go.' Sam replied, the radio crackling with a very weak signal. They knew someone was responding but couldn't make out what was said. Chance and Lauren waited and talked for the next hour.

Chance was quite interested in Lauren's military experience. The sun began to fade over the ocean. Lauren handed Chance a pair of ear plugs, saying, 'You're going to need these.' 'What for?' he asked curiously. 'Watch and learn, my man; watch and learn.' She flicked the switch, activating the ground's lights, and out of nowhere, ACDC's Back in Black began to boom loudly. Chance laughed, 'I am impressed. This will work a treat,' he yelled at Lauren over the music. The lights came on, illuminating the stadium. The last glimmer of sunlight sank over the horizon.

The first zombie appeared quickly. More started turning up fast after that, entering from all over the ground. 'Look at these bloody things. They're feral,' Lauren yelled to Chance over the music. Zombies were congregating around the venue from the west, mainly, but more were still pouring in through the gates. It was an impressive and frightening sight. 'Look at those two over there! They're literally eating one another!' Chance exclaimed. They could see for blocks from their vantage point above the WACA. The city streets were filled with the undead as they staggered toward the stadium, like a steady stream of water snaking its way toward a drain.

A torrent of blood thirsty meat sacks, chasing one thing only—fresh blood. Lauren raised her radio. 'Copy Sam. We're going to make a move soon. The stadium is pretty full now.' 'Roger that,' he replied through crackles, indicating they were close to Perth. As Lauren turned towards Chance, a single noticeable roar could be heard even over the music from somewhere below in the streets. Their eyes widened in fear as they spun around back towards the edge, laying themselves flat to get a better look. The sea of zombies below was horrible to see.

Chance abruptly pointed to one of the eastern entrances, 'What is it?'

Lauren yelled. And then she saw it. A larger zombie was piercing its way through the undead crowd, shoving past other zombies. She raised her assault rifle and peered through the scope. The zombie in question had smoother skin and appeared to be wearing armour. 'It has huge muscles!' Lauren gasped. 'Give me a look!' Chance replied, taking the rifle from Lauren. As he looked through the scope at the beast, another massive, distinct roar at a terrifying pitch could be heard.

The armour-clad zombie raised an arm and smashed an already injured zombie, completely splitting it in half, sending the two halves of its head face first into the concrete. 'Well, this is a bit of a pickle, then. I didn't expect something of that magnitude to show up. Reckon that can get up here, because if it can, we're sitting ducks,' Chance said, staring down at the zombies as he handed the rifle back to Lauren. 'Let's not find out,' she replied, taking aim at the beast.

She squeezed the trigger twice, the metal slugs striking the foul creature in the neck and through its metal shoulder pad. It roared as it was knocked over. It immediately rolled over and got up, peering up towards the tower. 'Shit, shit, time to go,' they both said, jumping to their feet. Lauren slung the rifle around her back and flicked the rope.

They connected themselves to the rope and jumped from the platform. It was a quick trip to the bottom, most likely aided by the fear Chance thought to himself as his feet hit the ground. 'Quick,' he said to Lauren, disconnecting her from the rope.

They ran to the car, zombies turning in their direction, arms reaching out for their warm bodies. Chance quickly started the vehicle and looked at Lauren. 'I'm not going to lie; I'm going to drive like I stole it.' Lauren laughed as she threw her pack into the back and jumped into the front. Chance gunned the engine, and they sped off through the horde of zombies at the eastern entrance, causing a great many of them to be knocked over and then shredded by the wheels. The vehicle turned sharply onto Nelson Avenue. 'There's so many of them!' Lauren yelled in a frantic tone.

They raced on, the road filling with zombies. Chance stepped hard on the pedal as they approached Braithwaite Street, slipping hard into the dirt and skidding towards the fence to avoid a zombie. He pressed the brake hard, causing the tyres to lock up momentarily. He pulled the vehicle back onto the street. 'I can't believe how many of them there are! We're going to need to swim back, otherwise we will just draw them all back to where the group is!' Lauren said in a worried voice. The car hit another zombie, and it disappeared under the bonnet.

'As we come around onto Riverside Drive, you hit the detonator just before we hit the water, and I'll drive into the Swan River. We can swim back. They won't be able to see us in the dark water, and the explosion will make them head in that direction,' Chance said. The car zoomed around the bend and headed straight for the grassy edge. The tyres made a loud thudding pop as they collided with the gutter.

Rubber flicked up past the doors as they careered towards the water. Chance peered into the rear-view mirror, seeing the bright flood lights of the cricket stadium one final time. 'Hit it!' he yelled. Lauren squeezed the detonator. The ground shook as the stadium detonated. As the vehicle approached the edge of the Swan River, it was hit by an unexpected shock wave, blasting it towards the water.

The car hit the water with a massive splash; icy cold water immediately seeped through the windows, numbing their bodies. Water surged in rapidly, turning the car into a sinking coffin. The frigid temperature made their muscles stiffen, and every movement felt slow and cumbersome. Chance and Lauren struggled against the rising water, which seemed to push them back with every effort to escape.

The doors were impossible to open; the pressure from the water was too great. Desperation fuelled Chance as he kicked at the back window, finally creating an escape route. They clawed their way through the narrow opening, gasping as the cold water engulfed them completely.

They both emerged from the water, spluttering. 'It's bloody cold!' Lauren squealed as she breathed quickly through pursed lips. They looked back towards where the stadium once proudly stood. A wall of dirt rose into the sky. The explosion seemed to be a signal to all the zombies that weren't immediately killed, as they all turned towards the stadium ruins and began to lurch towards it. They swam for around fifteen minutes until the boat could be seen. 'You two okay?' Sam's voice boomed. It was a welcome sound.

Chance and Lauren were pulled into the boat, looking like drowned rats. 'That was pretty damn impressive from what we saw from the boat back here, guys,' I said to the group with a grin on my face. 'Oh mate! The zombie fest going on within the cricket grounds was next level. There were bloody thousands of them,' Chance shouted as the wind whipped against his face. The boat cruised parallel to the city, back towards Elizabeth Quay. 'What the hell, Sam? So much for the explosives only impacting the stadium. It nearly levelled a whole city block!' Lauren yelled.

Sam didn't respond. It was now pitch black with no moonlight; the moon smothered by clouds. Lauren turned to us, saying, 'There would've been tens of thousands of zombies back there, I reckon. Oh, and just before we left, there was a different type of -' Sam abruptly interrupted Lauren. 'Quiet, we're getting close,' Sam ordered as he killed the engines.

There was no more talking. The boat drifted and gently bumped into the dock out front of a restaurant called The Revelry. It was dwarfed by the Ritz Carlton tower. I helped Karly off the boat, and then Chance and Lauren. Sam followed us off as Dan began throwing us our bags. 'Don't throw that one,' Sam said abruptly as Dan went to throw his large black duffel onto the dock. Sam reefed it from Dan. 'Jesus, OK, mate,' Dan said mockingly.

We pulled the bags over our backs and checked our weapons, ensuring there was enough ammo and that safeties were off. I glanced up at the city skyline, draped in darkness and eerily silent, as though it had been sent to bed and pulled the blanket over itself.

LET DARKNESS COME

We began walking along the concrete walkway. The government had done a really nice job of making this area beautiful. Different-coloured bricks created patterns. The calm river water gently lapped against the concrete edge as boats bobbed across the inlet. We walked towards the Oyster Bar restaurant. 'I'm scared; I really am. This is terrifying,' Karly whispered to me as she grabbed my hand. 'I know, this actually stinks,' I replied. 'We will be OK,' I reassured her. 'I'm just not good around zombies,' she replied with a deep breath.

I squeezed her hand in reassurance, and she smiled back at me. 'Scaredy cat', Chance whispered loudly from behind us as we approached the end of the docks. Sam stopped and knelt down, gesturing for us to kneel with him. 'We need to follow Geoffrey Bolton Avenue for another hundred metres or so, then we will be at the train line,' he said. 'What if there are zombies down there? I'm not going down there!' Dan asked, a slight crack in his voice. 'There should be a lot fewer zombies. They're normally drawn to noise, hence the stadium distraction. If we can stay quiet, we should be fine,' Sam said.

Large jacaranda trees lined the pathway to the road, and finally, at the train station, the dull moonlight cast shadows across the cobblestone road. 'See the glass panels over there?' Sam said, pointing towards the train station.

'We zip over there to where they end and take a U-turn. An escalator there will take us to the station,' he said. 'Let's get it done,' I said. We all limbered up, using our pistols to sweep along the path. 'Easy does it, guys,' Dan said nervously as we crept across the road. We were really exposed at the moment, should we be seen.

Zombie lollipops, I thought to myself. The group got to the end of the glass panels, and we quietly walked down the escalator in single file. I noticed I was taking in only small amounts of air. It was as if I breathed too loudly, zombies would hear us. I stepped onto the platform as Sam and Dan turned on their torches. It was pitch black and dead silent. I found a wall off to the side and peered around it. Silence. I could feel my heart thudding hard in my chest, almost like breathlessness was washing over me. Talk about a little bit of anxiety!

'Lauren, Karly, Nathan, come gather round,' Sam whispered loudly. 'We need to head just one stop away. It's about three hundred meters. When we get there, we get onto the platform, head up the escalator, and cross the street to the tower. Torches off. We can use our night vision on the rifles. Hold the person's shirt back so we can all stay together. Quiet and fast goes the pace, I think. Any objections?' he asked sternly, quickly glancing around at each of us. 'No? Good, let's go,' he said, standing up and turning around.

We headed towards the platform's edge, where "Mind the Gap" was written in yellow near the edge. I jumped down and turned around to help the others down. We proceeded forward into the train tunnel; any light was now completely gone.

The darkness enveloped us, a suffocating blanket that amplified every sound. 'Shit! Stop!' Sam said abruptly, his voice echoing off the cold, damp walls. 'Torches on!' The beams of our flashlights cut through the blackness, casting terrible shadows that danced with every movement.

A low, guttural moaning echoed from up ahead, sending chills down my spine. I peered around the group, my heart pounding again in my chest. A single train car stood silent on the track, its windows fogged and cracked. Inside, the twisted silhouettes of three zombies shambled aimlessly.

Their vacant eyes reflected the torchlight, adding to the growing sense of dread. We edged forward, weapons raised, the tension palpable. The smell of decay grew stronger, an acrid reminder of the danger that lay ahead. 'We have to go through it!' Sam whispered, his voice barely audible over the sound of our own breathing. Lauren and Sam crept towards the car, their movements slow and deliberate. Lauren pressed her back against one side, her eyes wide with fear and determination.

She raised her hand to the door, pausing to look at Sam. He nodded, and she quickly yanked the door open. In an instant, four silencer rounds rang out, each shot echoing like a death knell. The zombies crumpled to the floor, their lifeless bodies twitching.

Blood and brain matter sprayed the windows, painting a grotesque tableau. The smell of iron and rot filled the air, making my stomach churn. For a moment, silence reigned, broken only by the distant, echoing moans of the undead somewhere deeper in the tunnel.

A truly terrifying scream rang through the tunnel, rich and full of death. If death had a sound, this was it. The beam of Dan's flashlight shone on a head appearing from the top of the train car. 'SHREIKER!!!' Lauren screamed, unloading rounds in its direction. It quickly pulled back to cover and screamed again. 'Move!' Sam yelled, grabbing Karly and pushing her into the train car. We all jumped in quickly, scared for our lives.

More zombies appeared from nowhere in the direction we'd just come from, smacking into the car. Sam pulled the rear train door shut. 'We need to go!' Karly screamed from the other side of the train car. A zombie knelt on the other side of the metal door, its head and face covered, its arm reaching through the door towards the others. Lauren pushed past us, dropping down from the other end of the train, weapon poised and ready.

Chance was out next, followed by Karly and then me. A zombie fell from the roof of the train carriage, knocking Lauren to the floor. Sam unloaded a round into the back of its head and helped pull it off Lauren.

We ran through the tunnel and appeared on the next platform, pulling ourselves up. Adrenaline raced through my veins, my heart bounding.

We sprinted up the escalator towards the street level. 'Move!' Sam yelled, egging us to continue towards the BHP tower. We raced through Queen Street Mall towards the glass door of the looming tower. I stopped and turned around to see everyone quickly press themselves against the glass panels. I bent forward, panting, trying to catch my breath. I could feel every hard beat of my heart. The cool night air rushed in and out of my mouth. 'Holy crap, that was scary! Let's get off the street,' Karly said, looking up and down the group. No zombies followed us from the underground train platform. Sam pulled the door open, and we all filed in and stopped suddenly.

The foyer was not what it used to be, with a large hole now in the centre of the ground floor. 'Shhh,' Lauren gestured, raising her finger to her lips. Sam's flashlight beamed down into the hole. 'It's a nest,' he whispered. 'One big ass hive that needs to be taken care of,' he said. We all crouched down to look. 'You guys will have to climb to the tower's roof to locate the signal. I've got some business to take care of down here,' Sam whispered loudly to us.

A bloodcurdling scream rang from deep in the hole. Yep, I wanted to be as far away from this thing as possible, I thought. No arguments here. 'What are you going to do?' Chance asked. 'No time for questions now. You guys get a move on. I won't be far behind, Sam replied. The group crept towards the stairwell door. The door creaked lightly as Dan pulled it open and peered in. 'It's clear; let's go,' he said. 'I'll go first; I have a silencer on my rifle,' Lauren said.

This was going to be a long walk. Steps, my favourite, I thought to myself. 'Did anyone think about trying the elevator?' Chance said smartly. 'Shut up, Chance; keep your mouth shut. We don't want to draw any more attention to ourselves,' Lauren said clipped. He looked offended. We climbed the stairs slowly, ensuring we didn't accidentally trip or make unwanted noise.

This was going to take forever. Around every corner, I was filled with a sense of dread as sweat began to stand out on my skin. 'I feel claustrophobic,' Karly said before I had a chance to. 'Same here,' I replied as I began to feel the burn in my thighs. A round silently rang out from Lauren's rifle, dropping a zombie on the next flight. The rotting smell hit my nostrils instantly, causing me to dry reach. Karly did the same, pushing her arm into her face to cover the smell.

We stepped over the zombie and continued upwards. 'Let's pick the pace up,' Lauren said, turning back to look at us as she wiped the sweat from her forehead. I stepped over another zombie that lay halfway through the doorway and the stairwell. 'We must be close. That surely has to be the doors,' Karly said as we slowly made it to the next flight of stairs. In front of us were two massive doors with a green exit sign above them.

Lauren gently opened the door, peering out at the night sky. She gasped and closed it quietly, looking back at us. 'There's about seven zombies out there. We're going to have to take them out.' We all nodded as she stared back at the door. Our weapons were poised and ready to slay the undead. 'Three, two, one,' she whispered quickly, opening the door and aiming her rifle.

Two zombies were dispatched from silent rounds as I went for the closest one, grabbing the back of its shirt and driving my knife deep into its soft skull. I wasn't quite the zombie killer I thought I was. I was just very lucky.

Another zombie spotted me as I pulled my knife out and leapt towards me. Chance's knife stopped it in its tracks, straight through its dirty eye into its brain. The zombie fell to the floor. From the far corner of the building came a thundering scream that filled the night sky. 'Shoot it, Lauren!' Karly yelled as she raised her rifle. She squeezed the trigger, and the gun clicked, 'shit! I'm out of ammo; I need to reload!' she screamed.

That was my moment! I took off, sprinting towards the creature as it let out another roar into the air. It was almost like it was trying to cry for help. As I approached the zombie, I slowed and kicked it clean in the chest from the edge of the building. The beast had the wind knocked out of it as it sailed from the top of the tower. 'Holy crap!' Chance said as he raced over to help me up. 'That's a long way to go. Reckon, when it hit the pavement, it just continued straight to hell?' he laughed.

I let out an uneasy laugh. We made our way to the edge of the building, looking down to the empty street below. Chance and I slumped down against the railings. 'That's really something, this city,' I said aloud, taking it in. The others joined us. 'Phew. That was a bit crazy. Did you hear that thing scream? What a set of lungs,' Dan said. 'Yeah, until Nathan ended its solo performance with a fly kick,' Sophie said, laughing with Karly.

I always wanted to come to the rooftop of this tower; you could see for miles. You'd easily be able to see Rottnest Island if it wasn't dark. Smoke rose from the direction of the WACA. 'Time to look around to see what this signal was,' Karly said, holstering her knife. 'Where's Sam, I wonder?' I said quietly to Chance and Dan, raising my eyebrows briefly.

We looked around for a couple of minutes until Dan yelled out. 'Over here, come quick!' he said excitedly. We were greeted by a young, deceased couple lying on the ground beside one another; both had a single bullet wound to the head. 'Oh my god, they must have been stuck up here and run out of food and water,' Sophie said, tears welling in her eyes.

A transmitter lay next to the two of them. The corner of a piece of paper hung from the male's shirt pocket. Karly reached down and grabbed it, unfolding it quickly. 'What's it say?' Dan asked. 'Darkness cannot hide the undead; it only amplifies their fearsome presence. But we are not afraid. We stand together, our torches burning brightly, ready to face the terrors that lurk in the shadows. For in the face of fear, we are the light that will guide humanity towards survival. Remember us in good faith. Michael and Cathy'.

I reached down and felt the vial in Cathy's pants, pulling it out. The vial was small and humble, yet it held my gaze like a magnet. The glass was cold against my fingers, and the liquid inside was a deep, swirling blue that seemed to glow faintly in the dim light. I couldn't tear my eyes away from it—the way the liquid moved hypnotically, as if it were alive.

For a moment, everything else faded away—the moans of the undead, the cold wind biting at my skin, the weight of the world pressing down on us. All that existed was this vial and the mysteries it contained. What was it? A cure? A poison? Or something far more dangerous? 'They were so young, poor things,' Lauren shook her head. 'They probably couldn't think clearly anymore; I hear it can happen. Especially with no food, no hope, and no society to keep you strong,' she said. The wind blew through my hair; it was freezing up here. 'Medical professional, what do you make of this?' Chance said. 'Mate, I'm not sure, but we need to investigate this vial.' I placed the vial safely in my pocket.

'Team!' Sam yelled across the rooftop as he suddenly emerged from the dark doorway, dropping his black backpack. 'We're compromised. They know we're here!' he yelled desperately as he panted from running up the stairs. As if on cue, screams could be heard from the stairwell. 'The door!' I yelled, running as fast as I could towards the double doors left gaping wide open. I slammed them shut as Karly and Dan began to barricade it.

I turned to see Sam kneeling, rummaging through his bag. 'Lauren, pop this,' Sam said quickly, lobbing a flare at her. She ripped the tip off, instantly setting off the flare. A bright light lit the rooftop as green smoke poured from it. Lauren cast the flare aside and assisted the others with barricading the doorway. 'We need to hold them off for T minus ten minutes; Chopper is on the way,' Sam yelled, still catching his breath. 'Why didn't we just fly here if you had a helicopter?' I shouted at Sam. 'I knew you wouldn't come if I said there was a nest here, so mind your own business.' Sam snapped.

The door was firmly barricaded, yet no zombie could be heard banging against it. 'I have to tell you guys something. I wasn't completely honest with you. The real show is about to begin,' Sam said, bent over with his hands on his thighs. 'I've set C4 charges up in critical points up the stairwell. That hive needs to go if we want to have any chance of survival.'

We all stared at him. 'What?! It was the best chance to get them all together in a large group. They've been set on a remote timer for fifteen minutes. 'What the hell, man, not cool!' Karly said in an angry tone. I put my hands on my head and sighed, typical, I thought. I walked over to the tower's edge and carefully peered. Like a river of dead, thousands of zombies poured towards the tower. 'They're coming! There's absolutely thousands down there,' I yelled towards the group.

Suddenly, the two large doors splintered open as a huge zombie crashed through them. The force of the door hit Karly heavily, knocking her out of view. Sophie screamed as she stood in horror in front of the wretched beast. It darted forward, quickly grabbing her. The creature held her arm tightly, reared its head back, and then bent forward, sinking its teeth deep into her. She screamed loudly as it pulled backwards, tearing a chunk of flesh from her arm. Blood streamed onto the concrete floor. Lauren raised her rifle and fired three shots at the beast, striking it all three times, one of the bullets grazing Sophie's side. I'm not sure what the others were doing, but I ran towards the beast as it dropped Sophie. I raised my pistol and aimed for the beast's head, discharging a round at it. It ran with surprising speed at Dan and me. We continued squeezing the triggers on our weapons.

The beast spun around as bullets passed through its head and out the other side. It staggered momentarily, stumbled backwards, and finally toppled over. 'Chance! Get the door!' I yelled frantically as a zombie appeared through it. The zombie hit the ground after a round from somewhere behind me struck it in the face, spraying blood onto my shirt. Chance raced over, slammed the doors shut, and sat there as zombies hungrily banged against the doors. I shot around to look for Karly. She lay in a crumpled heap around ten metres away from where the beast had emerged.

She didn't look good. 'Karly!' I called desperately as I ran and sank to my knees, rolling her over. A large splinter, around 12 cm long, protruded from her chest near the right shoulder blade. 'Shit! I need help!' I yelled, not looking back. Karly opened her eyes slightly and smiled. 'I stuffed up, didn't I?' she asked. 'No, no, I think you've hit your head, and you've got a nasty splinter, but you're going to be ok,' I said reassuringly. 'I'll help you up,' I said, passing my arm around her back.

Karly groaned as she got up. 'Leave the splinter in there; we can take it out when we return. Can you take a deep breath? Make sure your lungs are okay,' I asked her. Karly took a deep breath. 'Yeah, that's all good; it just really hurts,' she said through winces.

'Nathan! Karly!' Chance yelled, pointing towards the rest of the group. We looked over. Sam held a pistol tightly, aiming down to where Sophie lay. Her arm reached up towards it, shielding her head from the gaze of the barrel. We limped over. Sam drew the weapon's gaze towards Karly and me. 'Not a step further,' he commanded. He aimed back at Sophie. 'Don't shoot me, please; I can explain,' Sophie sobbed. 'Drop it,' Lauren screamed at Sam as she emerged from behind a vent, her rifle poised, lining him up in her sights. Sam glanced at Lauren briefly, and a smirk ran across his face.

He looked back down at Sophie. 'You've been bitten; I'm sorry, but this is how it goes,' Sam snarled back at her. Tears streamed down her cheeks. 'I'm infected and have been for weeks. I got bitten weeks ago, back in the apartment, by that blasted dog. I hid it, hoping to spend my last hours on earth with my friends. And then I just didn't turn. I got pretty sick in Donnybrook and thought that was it, but then I felt better and didn't want to tell anyone' She sobbed at Sam. Sam gave a chuckle and then began to drop the trigger. 'This ends now. You and those undead creatures. This was meant to be a one-way trip for you guys anyway,' he shouted, suddenly swinging his gun towards Lauren. 'This is where your story ends.'

I'm not really sure what happened at this point; the air was filled with gunfire as shots rang through the night sky in a hail of bullets. I gazed around slowly as if in a dream. Sam was nowhere to be seen. Lauren stumbled a few feet across the rooftop before falling to her knees, both hands clutching around her neck as blood spilt down her front. Sam lay motionless on the rooftop, a hole in his forehead and shoulder as blood pooled around him. His lifeless eyes stared up at the dark night sky. 'Nathan! Help me!' Karly called urgently as she moved across to Lauren.

I ran over to help as Karly gently laid Lauren on her back. Lauren coughed and gasped through gurgles of blood as she struggled for air. 'What do we do? What do we do?' Karly sobbed in desperation. My heart broke at the sound of it, knowing that we could do nothing to save Lauren. 'We comfort her. I can't do anything for her,' I said quietly, holding Lauren's hand tightly. The faint whirr of helicopter rotors could be heard, echoing off the surrounding skyscrapers.

Lauren coughed as a stream of blood ran from the corner of her mouth. Her desperate gasps continued, slowed, and finally stopped. Her pupils dilated, and we knew that was it. 'Be at peace,' I whispered, running my hand over her face to close her eyelids.

The large black bird rose over the top of the building, circling the tower before steadily approaching the rooftop. The rotor blades whipped up dust and debris from the roof as they touched down. Zombies still pushed against the door. Chance still had his back to it, his heels digging into the floor. 'Hey, guys! We need to get out of here really quick,' Chance yelled. 'I can't hold them for much longer!'. The helicopter pilot yelled, 'I can't take everyone.' I turned my gun towards him. 'You will, or you'll wind up like your buddy over there on the deck,' I yelled at him.

Dan and Karly helped Sophie into the helicopter, but Karly's face was painted with pain. I ran over and picked up Lauren's rifle, and then ran towards the helicopter, stopping quickly and looking at Chance. 'Get in the chopper, and I'll run for it,' he called back. I squeezed in beside Karly. 'Mate, lift the chopper off the roof a little and be ready to move,' I told the pilot. 'It's going to be too heavy,' he said, looking back in fear. 'Just do it!' Karly screamed at him.

The pilot hesitated momentarily, then slowly lifted the chopper off the roof, turning it sideways so I could get clear shots. I raised the rifle to my chin, peering through the scope. Chance sat briefly for a moment as if in slow motion; wood splintered from the doors as the bullets passed through them. 'Now Chance! Run!' Dan yelled.

Chance rolled forward and ran towards us as fast as he could. Zombies poured from the double doors as I shot at what I could. The sound of the rifle echoed through the air, deafening us all. I could see the fear in Chance's eyes as he ran towards the chopper, his legs pumping hard. He quickly grabbed Lauren's duffel and threw it over his back as he ran.

The zombies were closing in on him fast, but I refused to let them get any closer. I aimed my rifle carefully, taking out one zombie after another. Finally, Chance reached the chopper and leapt for the bear paws of the helicopter. 'Fly!' I ordered. The chopper motor sounded strained with our weight, and the rotors worked hard to keep up.

The helicopter cleared the building and jolted to the right. 'I need to drop him off at another building. I can't hold it,' the pilot yelled. The black machine flew fifty metres to the right and slowly descended, jerking violently as it did. Chance let go when he was close enough to the roof, landing on his side and rolling.

HOPE

Alarms started blaring on the chopper's panel. Over the deafening noise, the pilot yelled, 'I have to put her down. She's too hot!'. 'We can't stay here. Sam has rigged that building to explode,' I yelled, pointing towards the dark tower with zombies flowing onto its roof. The pilot fought with the controls, desperately trying to steady the chopper. 'Hold on!' he called as the chopper lurched violently.

He managed to set it down with a bone-jarring thud. We scrambled out of the helicopter, the alarms still blaring in our ears. The night air was filled with the low growls of the undead from the tower across from us. 'We have to move now!' Chance urged, his eyes wide with urgency. This building was only two-thirds the height of the other building. Suddenly, the ground beneath the tower trembled, and a blinding flash illuminated the night as the building erupted in a massive explosion.

The force of the blast sent debris and shrapnel flying in all directions. We dove for cover, but the helicopter pilot, who was still inside the cockpit, was struck by a large piece of metal. His agonised cry was cut short as the chopper was peppered with lethal fragments. 'Pilot's down!' I yelled, but there was no time to mourn. The building's collapse sent shockwaves through the ground. We were on the roof of a building that now felt impossibly fragile in the face of such destruction. The night was torn apart by the roar of the explosion, the acrid smell of burning, and the deafening noise of collapsing concrete and shattering glass.

I looked up just in time to see the BHP building crumpling towards us, its massive structure folding in on itself like a house of cards. The sight was simultaneously awe-inspiring and terrifying—a monolithic giant brought to its knees. 'Move! Move!' Chance shouted, pulling us towards the far end of the roof. The ground beneath our feet vibrated with the force of the collapsing tower, and the air was filled with a thick cloud of dust and debris. Chunks of concrete and twisted metal rained down around us, the remnants of the building cascading into a deadly waterfall.

The noise was overwhelming—a cacophony of destruction that made it hard to think and breathe. We stumbled over the uneven surface of the rooftop, our movements frantic and uncoordinated in the chaos. The tower's collapse seemed to happen in slow motion, yet too fast for us to fully process.

I glanced over my shoulder and saw the tower's remains lurching towards our building, massive slabs of concrete breaking away and plummeting towards the earth. A particularly large piece of debris smashed into the side of our building, sending a tremor through the structure.

The building groaned under the impact, and for a heart-stopping moment, I feared it might collapse as well. But it held, and we clung to each other, gasping for breath in the choking dust. The air was thick and suffocating, filled with the acrid smell of burning and the deafening noise of collapsing concrete.

As the dust began to settle, the eerie silence that followed was broken only by our laboured breathing and the distant groans of the undead. My heart pounded in my chest as I strained to hear any sign of life. 'Is everyone okay?' I asked, peering through the dust that coated my eyes and everything around me. 'Yeah, I think so,' Karly replied, coughing into her hand. 'Right then, that was not ideal,' Chance said. 'Now what? If we head back down this tower, we'll be a buffet downstairs at street level,' I said. And then, faintly at first, the unmistakable sound of whirring blades could just be heard. 'Do you hear that?' I asked enquiringly, looking at the group.

'Yes,' Chance said, narrowing his eyes and scanning the skies. 'That's a chopper.' A spotlight cut through the haze, sweeping across the roof and bathing us in a blinding white light. The helicopter circled overhead, emblazoned with the emblem of HOPE, a welcome sight, to say the least. 'Over here!' I shouted, waving my arms and flashlight to catch the pilot's attention. The helicopter hovered with a voice booming out at us from the megaphone: 'Drop your weapons and keep your hands in the air.' We complied, putting our weapons near the wall.

The helicopter descended, the downdraft from its rotor blades kicking up another whirlwind of dust and debris. A rope ladder dropped from the side, and a team of HOPE soldiers, clad in tactical gear, swiftly descended onto the rooftop. Their leader, a tall figure with a stern expression, approached us with purpose. 'We need to leave now.' Relief washed over me, but it was tempered with caution. As we were led towards the helicopter, the leader, who introduced himself as Captain Reynolds, began to speak about the mission of HOPE. His tone was grave, hinting at the weight of his information.

'There's a lot I can't tell you right now,' Reynolds said, his eyes flickering with something unspoken. 'But you need to know that not everything is as it seems. Some complexities and operations go beyond what you've seen or heard That's why HOPE was formed—to fight against this corruption and find a real solution.'

The words left me with more questions than answers, but his voice had an undeniable urgency. 'What do you mean?' I asked, my voice barely above a whisper. Reynolds shook his head. 'I'm not at liberty to discuss details here. Just know that there are forces at play that complicate our mission. Our priority is your safety and everyone we can save,' he replied. I felt a glimmer of hope tempered with trepidation. Perhaps there was a chance to set things right and find a way to end this nightmare.

We climbed into the chopper, the roar of the blades deafening. Suddenly, I felt a sharp sting in my neck. My hand flew up to the spot and came away with a tranquilliser dart. 'What the—' I started to say, but my words slurred, and my vision blurred. I looked around, seeing my friends slumped over, the same darts protruding from their necks.

'We're sorry,' Captain Reynolds' voice sounded distant, almost remorseful. 'But we can't risk you knowing too much just yet, and we need to protect ourselves. You'll be safe. We promise.' The sedative was fast-acting, and the world around me started to fade. I looked out the window at the city below, a broken world spinning into darkness. My thoughts drifted to the vial in my pocket—the hope it represented, the danger it posed. As the darkness closed in, I held onto one thought: We would find a way. We had to. And then, nothing.

To Be Continued..